The Bay of Lost Souls

KILTIE JACKSON

ISBN-13: 978 – 1999866662

DEDICATION

This book is dedicated to YOU!
Yes, you – the person holding this book and reading it.
Every reader should have a book dedicated to them for
they are the reason we authors write them.
This one is yours.

Also by Kiltie Jackson

A Rock 'n' Roll Lovestyle
An Artisan Lovestyle
An Incidental Lovestyle
A Timeless Lovestyle

Waiting Since Forever

Radio Ha Ha!

A Snowflake in December

ACKNOWLEDGMENTS

A finished book is rarely the product of one individual and I would like to give my deepest thanks to the team who help me to get these missives out into the world.

John Hudspith is my ever-patient editor who takes my meagre offering and tidies it up into something worth reading. Despite his best efforts, my grammatical errors continue to be my undoing. Berni Stevens is the amazing lady who takes my waffle on board and produces stunning covers that always leave me breathless. Mark Fearn is my beta-reader extraordinaire who drops everything when I send over my manuscripts for his perusal. His honest feedback is much treasured. Zoé-Lee O'Farrell is the magnificent blog tour organiser who puts blood, sweat and tears into providing the best blog tours I've ever had. She is tireless in making sure the word gets out there and I am eternally grateful to her for all that she does. Also, while I'm on the subject, a big shout-out to all the wonderful bloggers who take the time to read, write up their reviews and share on their blogs – all your efforts are greatly appreciated.

My best friend since the beginning of time is Kym Wood who always has my back and "bigs me up" when I lack the confidence to do it myself.

Stuart James Dunne, my BFF and marketing guru – thank you a million times over for taking the time to train me up and for sharing your secrets.

To the members of my FB group, Kiltie Jackson's Speakeasy – thank you for all the encouragement you give, for sharing my books to the world and for helping me to laugh on the dark days.

An extremely massive and huge thank you to my wonderful Facebook groups – The Fiction Café,

Chick-Lit & Prosecco, Heidi Swain and Friends, TBC –
Reviewer Group and Jenny Colgan and More Great
Books. These groups share, promote and support all of us
authors in these ventures and this one appreciates them
greatly.

I can't forget my family who continue to read
everything and tell me to keep at it on a regular basis.

A special mention for the Moggy Posse who are just
the best bunch of furry feline friends and bringing up the
rear, because he's always there for me, my darling Mr
Mogs – love you, to the end of eternity… and a day!

Till the next time…

Kiltie

xx

ONE

Perrie Lacey stood reading the board in the car park and felt the dismay rapidly rise all the way up from her boots. How on earth could they justify having a car-free town and insist that all vehicles be left in the car park? She turned around and looked at her Range Rover which was practically bulging at the seams. It was going to take forever to walk this lot down to what was going to be her new home for the next six months. In fact, she'd have probably just finished emptying the car when it would be time to pack it all up again!

She returned to her stuffed vehicle, opened the back door and tried to figure out the best place to start. She could see the handle of the larger suitcase sticking out from beneath the bags of cat litter and decided she'd begin with that – it was on wheels and would be, by far, the easiest item to transport to the cottage first even if getting it out of the car was going to be a ball-ache. It was one thing buying forty-litre bags of cat litter when they only had to be carried from the doorstep to the under stairs cupboard; it was quite another when they had to be carted goodness-only-knows-how-far from a cliff-top car park.

With a few huffs and several puffs, she managed to extricate the suitcase and balanced it at the side of the car while she set about sorting out George and Timothy. There was no way she'd be able to carry two cat baskets, even without the suitcase, because both of her boys were hefty little sods and each weighed in at almost nine kilos. If there was ever a time to be glad she'd trained them to walk on a harness, it was now!

A few minutes later, as she pushed and fumbled two cats through the kissing gate and a suitcase over the top of the wall, she saw the sign which proclaimed, "Welcome to Broatiescombe Bay".

'Hrmph,' she muttered, 'Welcome, my arse!'

The cats pulled her along the small tarmac path and she pulled the suitcase. The boys were happy to be out and stretching their legs as the journey from London had been a long one and they weren't used to being cooped up in their cages for that length of time. When the threesome turned the corner and caught their first view of the little seaside town, they all ground to a halt. The cats stuck their noses in the air and Perrie did the same as they all drew in a deep lungful of the tangy sea air. She could hear the soft whisper of the sea in the distance but as darkness was rapidly falling, her actual view was restricted to the cobbled street in front of her. The old-fashioned street lamps were just coming on and their brightening efforts were further enhanced by the light spilling out of the shop windows on either side.

To her left, Perrie spotted a small hotel which was named "The Top O' The Hill". A large brass bell hung outside and swayed in the wind. She moved forward, giving George and Timothy a gentle nudge with her foot and passed a handful of shops which consisted of a fishing shop, a newsagent and a florist. Their street boards and postcard display-stands appeared to be secured with chains to hooks sunk into the wooden shop fronts and Perrie assumed this was to prevent them falling over in the wind or worse, being blown away altogether. They also had brass bells just like the one outside the hotel. The cobbled road twisted gently downwards and she walked past a second inn called "The Halfway House" – she made a calculated assumption that this was because it was either halfway up, or halfway down, depending on your viewpoint. She was, however, much happier to see the bakery as this was where she needed to go to collect the keys for the cottage although it did present the small problem of what to do with the cats. As the sign on the door proclaimed no dogs were allowed, she very much doubted cats would be permitted either, especially as her boys were bigger than some of your smaller dog breeds.

She looked around for somewhere to tie them up and breathed a small sigh of relief to see some hooks underneath the bakery window specifically for that purpose. Well, she assumed they were, given there was a metal dog bowl nearby with water in it. When she was satisfied that the boys were securely tethered, Perrie waited until the customers in the bakery had been served before heading inside. The first thing which hit her was the delightful smell that came from a good, old-fashioned, bakery shop – something which the chain bakers were sadly lacking – and the second thing was the rumbling of her stomach as it reminded her that she hadn't eaten since before seven that morning and it was now after three-thirty in the afternoon.

She was just about to tap the little bell on the counter when a vision in emerald-green walked through from the kitchen.

'Hi there, how may I help you?'

Perrie tried not to let her amazement show as she took in the small woman standing in front of her with her short, bright-green spiky hair, stunning green eyes, vivid green eyeshadow, green dungarees and accompanying green nails.

'Oh, hi, I'm looking for Sue…'

'I'm Sue and I'm guessing you must be Perrie?'

'That's right.'

Sue walked round from the other side of the counter and stuck out her hand.

'Lovely to meet you.'

Perrie returned the greeting as her hand received a firm, no-nonsense shake. The emerald eyes which looked her up and down were clear and intelligent. Sue might resemble a small leprechaun but Perrie was sure that nothing escaped her sharp gaze. She also exuded a warmth that Perrie felt herself responding to.

'Now, I won't keep you talking as I'm sure you just want to get yourself in and settled, so here you go.' Sue leaned behind the counter and picked up an envelope which she passed over.

'In there you will find the door keys and some additional information which might be useful to you. It's the first time there's been a new resident in the cottage for over fifteen years and it suddenly dawned on me last night that I should have put together an information pack for you.'

'Fifteen years?'

'Yes, old Mr. Rogers moved out in November. He was a school teacher and moved down here when he retired. Unfortunately, being on his own all became too much for him and he decided to go into an assisted living village a few miles up the road. I apologise if there is still a smell of paint – as you can imagine, after all that time, the cottage was in need of updating and freshening up. I hope it's to your liking.'

'Well, it looked lovely in the photographs I saw, especially the garden.'

'Ah yes, the garden… I'm afraid we haven't had the time to do anything about that yet. Mr. Rogers was keen on birds and built an aviary out there – we do intend to remove it in the next couple of months.'

'Erm, actually, the aviary was the reason I chose your cottage. I have two cats – you did say on the spec that pets were allowed – and I was going to let them use it as a cat run. I need to check it out but I think, with a couple of small alterations, it'll be perfect for them.'

'Oh! Well, in that case, we'll leave it be. My partner, Alex, will be pleased as he'd have been the one dismantling it.' Sue gave her a big smile. 'Instead, just let me know what alterations you require, and we'll get them sorted for you. Now, you'll also need this…' Sue handed her a large torch.

'Erm, why?'

'When you go out the door here, turn right, walk down to the sign for "Hettie's Hairdressers" and turn up that street. The streetlights stretch up to the top of the hill but stop at the last house; the path to the cottage, which is a further five-minute walk, is unlit, hence the torch. The outside lights are on timers, however, so you'll be able to see the cottage from the path. We don't want you walking past it and ending up going over the cliff into the sea.'

Perrie gulped at the unexpected prospect of meeting a sudden cold and watery demise.

'Err, no, I'd rather avoid that if I can.' She grabbed the torch and squeezed it into her pocket. 'Right, well, I'd better get on. Lots to do…'

Her hand was already on the door handle when Sue said, 'Oh, I forgot to mention, I've popped some bits and pieces in the fridge and cupboards for you. You know, milk, bread, butter, cheese… I also put a beef stew in there as I took a punt on you not feeling up to cooking after travelling. I then thought there was a chance you may be vegetarian so I also left you some homemade macaroni cheese.'

'I'm not vegetarian and the beef stew sounds perfect. Thank you, that was extremely kind.'

'No problem at all. Oh, and here, you may as well have a couple of these…' Sue picked up a paper bag and slipped in some doughnuts with vivid green icing on the top. 'St Patrick's Day is almost over for my business and they'll only go to waste. Now off you trot – go and get yourself settled in.'

As she untied the cats, Perrie reflected on how friendly Sue had been and came to the conclusion that the green get-up was her giving a nod to the Irish national day. She couldn't help but wonder though if Sue would still be as friendly if she knew the real reason for her new tenant being here.

TWO

'Hi, Morgan, sorry I'm late, the bus got stuck behind a tractor on the way home. I've just legged it all the way here.'

Morgan Daniels stuck his head out of the office door and took in the sight of Ruth bent double in the shop as she tried to catch her breath. When she looked up, her face was bright red and her hair was sticking out all around her face. Her school tie was askew and he could see her shirt tails had parted company with her trousers and were hanging down beneath the hem of her jacket. He didn't have the heart to reprimand her as she'd clearly done an Olympic sprint to get here.

'Don't worry about it, you're only a few minutes late.'

Ruth glanced at the clock above his head which read four-fifteen. 'Morgan, I'm thirty minutes late, which means you'll incur the wrath of Mrs. Feldman at the day-care centre. Quick, off you go before she actually does turn into the dragon she so well represents.'

'Ruth, you really shouldn't say such things about

your elders...' Morgan, however, was already pulling on his jacket and heading towards the door, for Ruth spoke the truth about the day-care manager and he already knew he was going to get an earful.

He let the door slam closed behind him and ran up the hill towards the small town-hall which doubled-up as the day-care centre. His daughter, Daisy, was in her last year of pre-school and would be joining the pupils of the primary school in six months' time. He was dreading it; she, on the other hand, couldn't wait!

He skidded and grabbed the cast-iron gate which stood open at the foot of the gravelled path that led up to the front door of the rather regal looking building. The action of grabbing the gate spun him around and he continued to leg it up the path at speed before sliding to a halt.

'Really, Mr. Daniels, your tardiness is quite unacceptable.'

Damn! Mrs. Feldman was standing on the doorstep and Morgan could tell from the set of her face that she was building up to launch quite the tirade upon his head.

'I'm very sorry, Mrs. Feldman, the school bus was delayed due to traffic which meant Ruth was late in getting to the shop to cover me.'

'Then you should have closed the shop, Mr. Daniels.'

'You know I can't just do that, Mrs. Feldman, it wouldn't be fair on my customers.'

'But you think it's fair for Daisy to have to wait for you to eventually turn up?'

He looked down and saw the blonde head of his daughter peeping round from behind Mrs. Feldman's legs. He immediately crouched down and opened his arms for her to run into.

'Hey there, my baby Astro, how *you* doing? Sorry

I'm late.'

'It's okay, Daddy, I knew you'd come. Mrs. Feldman is just being silly.'

Morgan had to quickly turn his burst of laughter into a cough. His daughter had a wonderful way of saying things exactly as she saw them, landing him in bother more than once. This was yet another of those occasions. He stood and swung her up onto his hip whereby she handed him her little schoolbag and then threw her arms around his neck, nuzzling her head under his chin.

'As I've already said, Mrs. Feldman, I'm very sorry for being late and quite understand if you wish to charge me for the extra time. Goodnight.'

He turned and walked back down the path, ignoring the blustering which was still coming from the mouth of the harridan on the doorstep. He could understand her being annoyed if his arriving late was a regular thing but it was only the second time it had happened in two years so he didn't feel her bad attitude was merited.

'What are we having for tea, Daddy?'

Morgan placed a kiss on Daisy's head.

'Fish fingers, baked beans, and baby potatoes.'

'No green stuff…'

'Not tonight, poppet.'

'Yay!'

He grinned at her reply. Most kids disliked the "green stuff" and Daisy was no exception. What she didn't know was that the Bolognese sauce she enjoyed so much had chopped Brussels sprouts mixed in or that the "baked beans" she hoovered up also had mashed cauliflower added to them. This way she got the goodness and he didn't get the tantrums!

'Right, this is where you get down and walk.' He let her slide down his leg until her feet landed on the cobbles of the main street. Directly across the way was the sign for her grandmother's shop, Hettie's Hairdressers, and Daisy loved to give it a little push every night to make it swing. She ran over to it now, pushed it, and then ran back to take his hand as they began the climb up the hill to their little terraced house at the top.

'I'm going to take big steps, Daddy, just like the mens on the moon, to get my legs all strong.'

'Okay, but hold my hand tight in case you slip. You don't want to fall and hurt yourself.'

'Daddy, what would have happened to the moon men if they had fallen?'

When her mother, and his darling wife, Harriet, had died two years before, Morgan's mother had told Daisy her mummy was now a star in the sky, coming out every night to watch over her as she slept. Since then, Daisy had become obsessed with the stars and the moon and already knew several of the constellations. One day, he'd shown her the videos of the moon landings on the computer, and that was when she'd decided she was going to be an astronaut when she grew up and making her legs "strong" so she could walk on the moon was her latest thing.

He'd just taken a breath, about to answer her question, when he heard a strange bumping noise. He looked up and saw a person-shape silhouette ahead of them on the hill. It had just drawn level with their house, the last one before the cobbles turned to rough path and the street lights came to an end, when the air was suddenly filled with the most horrific shriek.

'OH, FOR FUCK'S SAKE, YOU STUPID, USELESS PIECE OF FUCKING JUNK!'
Daisy stopped mid-big step, looked up at him with wide-open eyes and said, 'Daddy, that lady just said a bad word… two times!'

THREE

Perrie had followed Sue's directions and found the cottage exactly where she'd said it would be – at the top of the hill, five minutes away from her nearest neighbour. What Sue hadn't told her was that the bloody hill started off as a gentle slope but when you followed it around the bend, it turned into an almost vertical gradient! Honestly, bloody Everest had nothing on that damn thing! Getting the cats up it had been no problem but she'd almost pulled her arm out of its socket from dragging the case behind her.

Thankfully, the outside lights of the cottage had been on and she'd had a good look at it as she made her way towards it. On the website, it had reminded her of the cute little cottage in her favourite Christmas movie, "The Holiday" and here in the flesh, that hadn't changed. It looked just like a child's painting of a house – a door in the middle with windows on either side, upstairs and down. It had a chimney at either end, a large dormer window in the roof directly in line with the front door, a brick wall running around the perimeter of the garden and a pretty white picket gate in the centre which opened onto a path to the door that had small flowerbeds on either side where daffodils had broken through to welcome her and despite feeling utterly knackered and deflated, she smiled at the sight of them.

She parked the suitcase to the side of the little porch, hooked the cat leads over her wrist, switched off the torch and fished the door-keys out of the envelope in her pocket. She looked at the lock, looked at the keys and selected the big cast-iron one as being the one most likely to grant her access. She stuck it in the lock, where it fitted perfectly but the lock didn't budge when she tried to turn it.

'Damn it!'

She took her fingers out of her gloves and gave them a shake, trying to get the blood flowing back into them after they'd gone numb from hauling the suitcase along. As she bent and flexed her frozen digits, she felt the movement come back into them and at her second attempt, she managed to turn the key and felt the door give as the lock opened with a hearty clunk. With a twist of the handle, she stepped into the brightly lit and beautifully warm hallway. It would seem that it was not just the outside lights which were on timers.

Thanks to the floor plan on the estate agent's website, Perrie already knew the layout of the cottage. To her right was the lounge which ran the depth of the cottage and had French windows which opened out into the garden at the back.

To her left was the dining room which had been knocked through to incorporate it into the kitchen, making both rooms appear more spacious. She decided to put the cats in the kitchen for now while she sorted out what else she had to bring down from the car.

After taking off their harnesses, she checked out the

contents of the fridge and saw the meals Sue had left for her along with a big bottle of milk, some butter, cheese and, much to her delight, a bottle of white wine. *That* would definitely be getting cracked open later.

Perrie took out the milk and after a quick sortie through the cupboards, found a couple of saucers to pour a little into. Under normal circumstances, the boys would never be given milk because it could give them bad tummies but as it was going to be at least another half hour or so before she could feed them, then needs must because while Sue had kindly looked after her, a return trip to the car was needed to bring back what she required for the cats.

While dragging her way up the hill, she'd been mulling over how she was going to get a forty-litre bag of litter, two litter trays plus their food up to the cottage without making at least two trips and had decided to make use of the suitcase. She could empty its current contents onto the bed in the spare bedroom and take it back to the car park to be filled with the other essential items she needed for tonight. Everything else could stay packed up until tomorrow.

Pleased with her solution to the problem, she closed the curtain across the back door and pulled down the blinds at the window to ensure nothing spooked the cats while she was out. She made sure the door to the lounge was firmly closed and also the door to the small hallway when she stepped out to bring in the suitcase. It only took a couple of minutes to lug it up the stairs and tip everything out in the spare room. Perrie stopped for a moment to peep into the master bedroom, saw that the bed was fully made up and a glance around the bathroom door told her there were also towels in there. Both of these made her sigh with relief, knowing she wouldn't have to bring her own bedding and towels down from the

13

car tonight.

She bumped the empty suitcase back down the stairs and tried not to think of the big, squishy chair she had spotted when closing the lounge door. She knew that if she sat down now, she would never get back up again tonight and she had to get the stuff for her cats. Had she been here on her own, the boots would already be off and the wine opened but George and Timothy always came first and so, right now, they were the priority.

It didn't take too long to get back to the car park and she was delighted to see it was well lit up which made it considerably easier for her to gather what she needed. In no time at all, she had the litter, the litter trays – only the bases, the enclosed tops could wait till tomorrow – cat food and some toys packed into the suitcase. She closed it up, put it on its wheels, pulled out the handle and proceeded to make a move such as you would find in a comedy skit – namely, where she walked off but the suitcase stayed put!

A "Grrr" of annoyance was uttered as Perrie tilted the case against her leg and tried again. This time it moved but she needed both hands to get it going. When she reached the kissing gate, she had to lean the case up against the wall, bend down and use all of her bodily strength to shuffle it up onto the top of the stones. Unsurprisingly, it came down far easier on the other side, landing on her foot and causing her to yelp in pain. She limped along the path, pulling the suitcase, until she reached the bend where the town came into view and the tarmac pathway became the downward sloping cobble stones. At this juncture, a quick assessment was made and Perrie decided it would be easier to let the case go in front and allow its weight to pull it down the hill rather than trying to stop it mowing her down from behind.

She soon reached the little crossroads where she

needed to turn right and begin making her way back up the hill again. Common sense told Perrie that there had to be a pathway somewhere across the top which would cut out this seemingly unnecessary upward and downward route. She really wished the bakery hadn't been closed when she'd passed it on the way back to the car so she could have asked Sue the question. She hadn't felt confident enough to enquire in any of the other shops which were still open.

Now, as she tugged the heavy case behind her, Perrie's breaths were going in and out in short gasps. She walked around the bend and felt like crying when she saw the steep incline ahead. She was tired, hungry, aching from head-to-toe and beginning to wonder if she would have the energy to get herself, never mind the suitcase, up to the cottage. She stood still for a moment and tried to muster up the determination which had, until now, seen her through so much in her life – was she really going to let the matter of a not-so-small, steep hill be her undoing?

She clenched her teeth, let out a groan and with her head and body bent forwards and both hands behind her on the handle, she began to drag the suitcase up the hill. To her left, she could just about hear the roar of the sea above the noise of the wind that had picked up as she'd walked back from the car park.

Inch by sorry inch, she slowly made her way up the slope and felt like letting out a whoop of joy as she drew level with the last house on the right for this was where she reached the brow of the hill. She was just thinking how it would be easier from here on when, suddenly, she was yanked backwards once again, in a replay of the car park comedy sketch.

'What the hell?'

She tugged at the suitcase but it was refusing to move. Pulling the torch from her pocket, she switched it on, pointed it towards the bottom of the case and saw that one of the wheels had become jammed in between two cobbles.

Perrie pushed, pulled and jiggled the case but the wheel was stuck fast. She moved to the front of the case and bent down, using her body weight against it but to no avail. In a fit of temper, she released a hefty kick at the now inanimate object and heard a loud, ominous crack before the suitcase flew up across the cobbles, landed on its side where it balanced for a mere second before tumbling onto its front and started slowly sliding back down the slope towards her.

Unable to help herself, an expletive-filled shriek flew out of her mouth and the torch fell from her hand as she dived to the ground in an attempt to grab the handle as the suitcase began gathering speed. Unfortunately, the weight of the kitty litter was too great to prevent the downward momentum and Perrie felt herself being pushed backwards down the hill. She was going to crash into the brick wall on the bend and there was nothing she could do to prevent it.

FOUR

Morgan looked over at the woman who had just rent the air with the words no four-year-old should hear and watched in horror as the heavy object she'd been venting her frustration upon began to slither back down the hill, taking her with it.

He quickly pushed Daisy into his neighbour's doorway, barked at her to, 'Stay there and DON'T move,' before throwing himself, head first, over the cobbles. He landed with a bruising thud but his fingers had grazed along the length of the metal handle and he was able to wrap them around the top. Ignoring the painful jerk in his shoulder, he pushed his other hand down in between the cobbles and using it as a brake, managed to bring the runaway case to a halt. He watched the woman slide a few more inches until she too, came to a standstill.

He lay prone for a few seconds, catching his breath, and then stood up, making sure he kept a firm grip on the suitcase as he did so. He stepped around it and held out his hand to help the woman who was now pushing herself up onto her knees.

'Here, let me help you.'

'Thank you.'

The hand which fell into his grasped it tightly and he stood firm as she pulled herself up.

'Are you okay?'

'I'm alive, which I fear I may not have been had you not been so heroic. I think the wall down on the bend would have taken me off to meet my maker.'

'Well, if it hadn't, Mrs. Monaghan, whose garden is on the other side, most certainly would have! She would not appreciate you landing in the middle of her prize begonias or whatever flowers she's currently got growing.'

'Then I need to thank you twice – for saving me firstly from the wall and secondly, from the wrath of Mrs. Monaghan!'

'Trust me when I say that the latter would have been the more painful death.'

In the soft glow of the streetlight, Morgan saw a wide smile cross the woman's face. It was about all he could see as her bobble-hat had fallen down almost over her eyes and she had bent down to inspect the damage to the suitcase.

'Bugger! One of the wheels has come off.'

He leant forward and whispered quietly, 'May I ask you to curb your language, please. I have a four-year-old daughter just over there who learns new words faster than I can blink. I really don't want her going to her playgroup tomorrow sounding like a sailor's parrot.'

The woman's head spun round to find Daisy standing where he'd left her.

'Oh, I am SO sorry. I didn't see her there.'

'I don't want to sound like a prude—'

'No, I understand. I have nephews!'

She smiled again and then held out her hand. He

took it in his and shook it firmly.

'Morgan Daniels. Nice to meet you.'

'Oh! Err… Hi! Perrie Lacey, nice to meet you too although… I was actually just trying to reclaim the suitcase.'

Morgan felt his cheeks warm up and hoped it was dark enough to hide the accompanying flush.

'Where are you going with this thing, which, if you don't mind me saying, weighs a blooming ton? Are you heading up to the cliff to push a dead body over into the sea?'

'Oh, darn! You've sussed me out! Now what am I going to do?'

'Excuse me?'

Morgan felt the breath catch in his throat. His comment had been in jest but now… He looked closer and saw the corners of her mouth were tilted upwards.

'You're messing with me, aren't you?'

A small giggle accompanied her affirmation.

'I'm sorry, I couldn't resist. The truth is that I moved into Seaview Cottage this afternoon.'

'And you're bringing a dead body with you because…'

'I thought it would be a great way to meet the neighbours!'

Before Morgan could answer, Daisy's voice came over the cobbles.

'Daddy, how much longer do I need to stand here? It's cold.'

Perrie put her hand on the handle of the suitcase. 'You need to go. Thank you once again for helping and I hope you're not in too much pain.'

'Look, let me help you with this to the cottage. With only one wheel, you're going to struggle and I really don't want to see you sliding down past my window when I go to close the curtains.'

'Oh, I can't put you out any further…'

'It's not a problem, honestly. And I don't want to face Mrs. Monaghan if she finds out that I could have prevented her prize begonias from being squashed. I'm actually being quite selfish, if you think about it.'

'Well, if you really don't mind…'

'Not at all. If you could just take Daisy's hand for me, please.'

'Of course.'

He called Daisy over and once Perrie had picked up the little Buzz Lightyear schoolbag from where he'd dropped it, the three of them made their way along the path to the cottage.

FIVE

'Just in here, please. Thank you.'

Perrie pointed towards the corner in the kitchen. As soon as Morgan put the suitcase down, she opened it, took out the litter trays, grappled with the hefty bag of litter and filled the trays before placing them in the opposite corner. Almost immediately, George and Timothy came running out from under the dining table and jumped in. She could actually see the relief on their faces.

'Cat litter? You had cat litter in there?'

'Hey, a cat has to do what a cat has to do!'

She saw Morgan staring behind her.

'They're not cats, they're long-haired lions!'

'Norwegian Forests to be precise.'

She hunkered down to look at Daisy who was half hiding behind her daddy's legs.

'Do you like cats, Daisy?'

The little girl gave a small nod, her blonde curls bouncing around her face.

'Would you like to meet George and Timothy and

help me feed them? They might be big but they're very gentle and I'm sure they'd love to meet you.'

The little girl looked up at her dad. 'Can I help, Daddy?'

Morgan gave her a smile before saying, 'How about another time, Poppet? We need to get you home and fed.'

'Oh!'

Her little face fell and Perrie felt a small tug in her heart.

'Look, why don't you both stay for dinner – as a thank you for helping—'

As soon as the words left her mouth, Perrie halted. What was she thinking? She couldn't just ask some strange bloke and his daughter to dinner – his wife must already be wondering where the hell they were!

'Can we, Daddy? Can we stay?'

'Erm, you can call your wife…umm… partner to come and join us too…'

'Mummy's a star in the sky and I'm going to be a nastro-nut when I grow up so I can visit her.'

'Oh, I see.'

She looked at Morgan for clarification of Daisy's statement.

'My wife died and is now a star in the sky watching over us. Daisy is going to be an astronaut so she can meet her when she's older.'

There wasn't much Perrie could say to that so instead she offered up the only two meal options she had.

'Macroni, macroni, macroni…' Daisy chanted.

'Then that's what we'll have. Now, let me just pop the dish in the oven – which I had the foresight to turn on earlier – and then we'll get the boys fed. Once they've eaten, Daisy, I will introduce you to them.'

Perrie quickly shoved the large bowl of pasta in the oven, grateful that Sue seemed to think she'd need enough to feed a large family, and then, with Daisy's help, spooned out food for the cats.

'Well, now they're sorted and we've established that you guys are staying for dinner, I'd better take your coats and hang them up. We'd look a bit silly sitting at the table with our outside clothes on, don't you think, Daisy?'

The little girl gave a giggle and quickly wriggled out of her bright pink coat. Morgan also handed over his overcoat and she noticed the dirt on it where he'd slid down the cobbles with her.

'When that's dry, I'll find a brush to clean it off.'

'Oh, don't worry about it.'

Perrie smiled. A typical bloke but one who, now they were inside and under proper lighting, was more than easy on the eye. He was tall, she reckoned just over six-foot, with thick blond hair that was cut in an old-fashioned "short-back-and-sides" style which he suited and enhanced the square-cut of his jaw. He had big blue eyes which really stood out and commanded your attention – Perrie had to forcibly stop herself from gazing into them – and a nice, generous, mouth that seemed to always be smiling. The body, underneath the coat, wasn't too shabby either although if he was walking up that damn hill every day, he would be pretty buff!

'I'll… erm…' she gave a small cough, 'just go and put these out in the hall.'

As she placed the coats on the hooks by the door, she caught a whiff of a light, lemon scent. She put her nose closer to Morgan's coat and breathed in a lovely smell of lemon with a slight hint of vanilla. It wasn't too strong but it made her feel a tiny bit giddy.

Perrie Lacey, she admonished herself, *pull yourself together. The last thing you need right now is to be fancying the local widower. In fact, for someone who's supposed to be keeping a low profile, you've made a pretty, shitty start!*

As the reason for her presence in Broatiescombe Bay slammed back into her brain, she let out a deep sigh. Love, romance, or even friendship just wasn't on the cards for her.

Not now, not later and possibly, not ever.

.

SIX

'Here, let me get the door.' Perrie carefully took the keys which Morgan had had the foresight to put in his hand before lifting a sleeping Daisy off the sofa in Perrie's lounge where she'd been cuddled up between two vast balls of purring fur.

He was grateful for Perrie's offer to walk home with him as he couldn't have carried Daisy, her schoolbag and a torch along the path. She opened the door and stood back, letting him walk into his hallway first.

'Come in, I'll make us a coffee,' he whispered.

'Erm, if you don't mind, I won't,' she whispered back. 'It's been a long day and if I were to sit down now, I suspect you'd be carrying me back home, also sound asleep.'

He looked round at her in surprise and saw a small apologetic smile on her lips.

'Of course, I'm sorry. Another time?'

'We'll see…'

'Will you be okay getting back on your own?'

'I think that, without the encumbrance of a dead

body in a wonky-wheeled suitcase, my journey back to the cottage will be considerably easier this time around.'

'Well, please, take my card. My mobile number is on there – send me a text when you get home.'

'I'm sure I'll be fine, Morgan.'

'I have no doubt you will be but if my mother found out I'd let a lady walk home alone in the dark, she'd skin me alive!'

'I like the sound of your mother!'

'Hmm, you might change your mind when you meet her! Just text me, please.'

'Okay, I will. Goodnight.'

She closed the door quietly behind her and after looking at it for a few seconds, Morgan turned and carried Daisy up the stairs to bed. As he carefully swapped her jeans and jumper for her pyjamas, he thought back on the unexpected turn his evening had taken…

'MERIDA!'

Daisy's screech filled every corner of the kitchen-diner when Perrie walked back in from hanging up their coats.

Morgan looked up from the cat toys he and Daisy had been playing with to see Perrie walking towards them, a look of total confusion on her face as Daisy ran over and stood staring up at her in total awe.

'I'm sorry… what?'

He quickly got to his feet and explained.

'Merida is the princess in the Disney film, "Brave".'

Now that Perrie had removed her own coat and hat, it was easy to see why Daisy was so enthralled for, with her long, vibrant-red, curly locks and eyes the shade of aquamarine – a colour of paint he sold a load of in the shop – she was the human embodiment of one of Daisy's favourite princesses. If she managed to dredge up a Scottish accent, then he suspected Daisy would be packing her Buzz Lightyear bag and moving in!

'Is that so?'

He watched in amazement as Perrie sat on the floor, in front of Daisy, and said, 'So, tell me more about this princess?'

'Well, she's very brave and nothing frightens her and she speaks with a funny voice—'

'She's Scottish,' he'd interjected for Perrie's benefit.

'—and she has long, red hair, just like yours and she doesn't like boys. Well, not much. I don't like boys either.'

'*Och, she's Scottish, is she noo? Dis she sound like this when she talks, wee gurl? Is this whit yoo call a "funny voice" eh?*'

Morgan let out a groan as Daisy danced on the spot, thrilled to hear the accent just like Merida's fall from Perrie's lips.

'That's it,' he said, 'you've done it now! You have just become her new best friend and you can expect the offer of play dates and sleepovers to arrive very soon!'

'And I will look forward to receiving them,' had been the reply which had made Daisy's face light up even more.

'However, I think we need to check out the pasta as it must be nearly ready by now.'

When she walked past him, Morgan realised how tall Perrie was. He hadn't noticed it before, probably because they'd been standing on the hill, but now it was not only the glorious mane of hair that he could see but also her height and delicious curves which her jeans and baggy jumper could not hide.

'Five-foot, nine-inches.'

27

He jumped at her voice.

'How did…?'

'It's been that way since I was eleven when I suddenly shot up and stood way above my classmates. I was very popular when it came to being on the netball team but not so much for anything else. People are immediately aware of my height, it's a bit difficult to hide it after all, and it's usually one of the first questions I'm asked. And, if not asked, I know folks are thinking about it so I provide the information meaning the conversation can move along to more interesting topics.'

'Was it a big problem at school? Were you bullied?'

Bullying was something Morgan had read up on as he was worried about Daisy having problems when she went to school. Kids could be cruel and with her mum being dead…

Perrie gave a small shrug before turning back to the worktop where she began slicing up a loaf of crusty bread. 'Sometimes it hurt when I'd get snide comments about the weather up here and stuff like that. A couple of times some kids tried to get nasty with me but when I asked them if they *really* wanted to go down that road while towering over them, they quickly changed their minds and backed off.'

'But you're beautiful now – you could be a super-model!'

Morgan clamped his mouth shut as he heard the words fall out of it. Shit! Had he really just said that? Okay, they were totally true – she was beautiful. Her hair, her eyes, her oval face with, what his mother would describe as "a determined tilt to her chin", and her perfect bow-shaped lips in soft, ruby-red, she was a vision to behold even if she had a sailor's mouth on her when she was annoyed.

'Thank you, you're very kind. I did get stopped

once, while out shopping with my dad, and asked if I wanted to become a model – let's just say the bloke was given short-shrift from my dad and quickly did a runner. Well, most people do when a stroppy Glaswegian bloke confronts them. The matter was never spoken of again.'

'Your family's Scottish? That's how you could do the accent.'

'My dad is. Mum is from Birmingham and that's where I grew up.'

'You don't sound Brummie?'

'No, Mum was adamant that none of her kids would have a strong regional accent. She felt it could possibly hold us back in the future. I'm sure she had one of us lined up to be a news broadcaster on the BBC.'

'One of you? How many of you are there?'

'Three. Two of me and one brother and, no, none of us work for the BBC or any other media outlet—' She stopped suddenly and the smile on her face disappeared.

'Perrie? Are you okay?'

Morgan saw her physically give herself a shake.

'Yes, I'm fine. Anyway, less about me. I feel I'm doing all the talking here. Tell me something about you, please. Oh, hang on… Daisy, would you like to set the table for me, please? Do you know how to do that?'

Daisy walked over with an indignant look on her face.

'I'm not a baby, I know what to do with the table. I'm nearly five which is very growed up!'

'It is indeed. Five is quite the young lady. How long until your birthday?'

'It's more sleeps than my fingers but less than my fingers AND toes.'

'Which makes it two weeks or fourteen days,' he supplied on Daisy's behalf.

'My, that's very soon.'

'I'm having a rabbit and a party.'

'You're getting a rabbit for your birthday? That's a wonderful gift.'

'Nooooo,' Daisy giggled, 'my birthday cake is going to look like a rabbit. Will you come to my party?'

'Oh, well... I will need to check my diary but thank you for the invite – you're very kind.'

She caught his eye over Daisy's head and the smile on her face caused something inside him to unlock...

Morgan let out a sigh as he pulled the quilt up over Daisy's shoulders. He didn't want to get involved with anyone. After the pain of Harriet, he had no desire to allow anyone to get close to him again. Not only did he have Daisy to protect, but he couldn't face the pain that inevitably came with caring for someone. In the last year, once it was felt an acceptable period of mourning had passed, there had been plenty of offers – some subtle, some less so – from the single ladies in the town and several visiting tourists. All of the former had been gently refused although he'd accepted one or two from the latter. A quick fling holiday romance was just fine in his books but it now looked as though his new neighbour may have inadvertently found a crack in the brickwork around his heart.

SEVEN

Perrie pushed back her chair, took the toast-crumbed
scattered plate over to the sink and looked out of the
window for her first proper look at the garden. She dried
her hands and unlocked the back door which opened onto
a small patio. To her right was a table and chair set,
sitting outside the French doors of the lounge. Just off the
patio, to her left, was the aviary and directly in front, at
the end of the lawn, was the peak of the hill which she
estimated to be about thirty feet or so. Casting her eye
around the garden, Perrie saw the hill had been cut into in
order to create the garden and gabion baskets full of rocks
held the hillside back on two sides while a row of mature
trees ran along the bottom edge.

She looked over at the aviary and seeing the big, old-
fashioned, padlock, recalled the small bunch of keys
sitting in the cutlery drawer. She went to the drawer,
opened it and picked up the keyring. She inspected the
keys for a moment and saw a couple which looked like
the kind of keys that went with cast-iron locks. With a
small buzz of excitement in her stomach, she made her

way to the long wooden hut, all the while thinking of how sad an individual she must be if a potential playground for her cats could make her feel this way.

The second key she tried fitted the padlock and when she opened the door and stepped inside, Perrie found herself in an area which was more like a standard garden shed. It was larger than she'd realised from the online photographs with a storage cupboard behind the door and shelving around the walls. The cupboard contained a six-wheel trolley – the kind that could move heavy goods up and down stairs – but the shelves were empty. A door to her right led out into the aviary itself and the terracotta tiles set under her feet gave her cause to smile as these would be easy to keep clean and wash down. The height of the construction was several inches above her head so she put it to be roughly six-foot which was a nice height for the boys who enjoyed a good clamber up a tree trunk. Some of the old aviary fittings were still in place, such as tree branches strung horizontally across the space, and she tested these for strength. Some were too flimsy and would need to come down as they wouldn't support the weight of the cats but there were half-a-dozen which were more than strong enough and could stay. These, along with the two large cat trees currently boxed up in the Landy, would provide plenty of exercise and stimulation for George and Timothy. They were going to love it in here!

This thought prompted her to move. The heavy grey sky suggested rain wasn't far off and she wanted to try and retrieve more of her belongings from the car. After all, the sooner her stuff was in the cottage, the sooner she could begin to relax and unwind.

As she was closing up the padlock, she looked towards the trees and saw a dark green gate hidden behind them. The path under her feet led right to it. Her curiosity was piqued but the gate was locked when she tried the handle. The keyring in her hand, however, provided the solution and when she pulled the gate open, she found herself looking along a small tunnel which had been carved through the hill. Daylight spilled through a wrought-iron gate at the other end and, sure enough, she had a key for that too.

When she stepped through, Perrie let out a small gasp. She was standing at the top of a winding pathway that appeared to lead down to a small parking area below. Well, she assumed that's what it was from the few cars she could see there.

At that moment, a snippet of the previous nights' conversation came back to her – Morgan had mentioned something about a car park but before he'd had a chance to expand on his comment, Daisy had interrupted with a question and the conversation had moved on.

Perrie rushed back to the cottage and found Sue's welcome envelope. She quickly scanned the information within and there they were, the details informing her of the parking space which came with the cottage and a small, printed map showing her how to get there. The details also advised that a small hut was located next to the parking space where the trolley she'd found in the aviary could be stored. She let out a little squeal of delight at this titbit – getting those cat-trees up to the cottage would now be considerably easier.

Half-an-hour later, Perrie was ready to go and claim her parking spot. She'd taken the trolley down the path which, thanks to its winding demeanour, wasn't too steep although the last bit was stepped which explained why the trolley was a specialist one. It was now stashed in the little hut provided, waiting for her imminent return.

With a skip in her step, and the broken-wheeled suitcase in her hand, Perrie locked the front door of the cottage and headed off to collect her car.

Ninety minutes later, the kitchen door was slammed closed and Perrie heaved a sigh of relief as big, fat, heavy drops of rain began to throw themselves at the kitchen window. She'd lost count of how many trips she'd made up and down the path and she knew she'd been chancing her luck on the last two as the sky above her had grown steadily darker and darker. All that remained in the car was one cat tree and some cat litter. Neither were urgent and could easily stay there for another day.

She looked at the big railway clock on the kitchen wall as her stomach let out a growl of hunger and saw that it was almost one o'clock.

Right then, she thought, shower first then a bite for lunch followed by an afternoon of some serious unpacking as she took in the pile of boxes in front of her which the cats hadn't wasted any time in sprawling themselves across.

'Make the most of them while you can, lads, they won't be around for long.'

She gave George and Timothy a quick scratch under their chins as she walked past on her way to the hallway and the nice warm shower she was looking forward to.

EIGHT

Morgan looked at his watch and then at the pile of boxes
in front of him. He turned to check he'd removed all the
St Patrick's Day greeting cards, going through the
displays on either side of the empty shelves to make sure
no stragglers had been misplaced. Satisfied he'd rounded
them all up, he sealed the box and moved it to the back of
the shop, ready to be returned to the stock room until next
year.

He pulled the box marked "Mother's Day" towards
him and began stacking them in the vacant space he'd
cleared. As he performed the mundane task of bend, lift,
sort and place, his mind crept back to the night before and
the unexpected meal he and Daisy had shared with Perrie.
What stood out foremost in his head was that, despite
sharing quite a bit of himself with her, Perrie had made
little mention of herself. After telling him about her
parents and siblings, she'd all but clammed up when the
conversation turned towards anything personal.

With hindsight, Morgan was surprised at how much
he had revealed. As a rule, he tended to shy away from

being the centre of the conversation but Perrie had somehow managed to draw him out. Was it her reticence to share personal information which had led to him filling in the gaps? Had that been the case, he wondered, with the ladies he'd been on dates with over the last year? Where he'd previously thought them self-centred because they seemed to speak only about themselves, he now pondered if they'd also been reacting to his own taciturnity.

Perrie had been most skillful, however, and it was only now that he saw the full extent of how the night had become about him. He'd shared how daunting it had been taking over the art shop after Harriet had died – that it had been a crash course in learning what felt like a whole new language even though his wife had very considerately left him with a rather detailed textbook which covered almost everything he would need to know. Unfortunately, it had only related to her art supplies shop and she'd been rather short-sighted by not including at least a couple of paragraphs on how he should cope without her.

The more Morgan recalled of the evening, the more he now began to worry that he'd come over as being a pathetic widower. He'd never told anyone, not even his own mother, the dark desolation he'd gone through in the weeks and months after Harriet had gone and yet, last night, he'd bared his soul to a woman he'd only known a few hours. She now had all the dirt on how, if it hadn't been for Daisy, he'd have taken the lethal combination of pills and booze that would have sent him into his own eternal sleep. Three times he'd been that close to the edge and three times his love for their daughter had saved him. Somehow though, Perrie had shown empathy and he certainly hadn't felt judged. Thankfully, Daisy had come back to the table at that moment – only a loo break had been able to tear her away from the cats – and the

36

conversation had moved away to more general chat about the town.

He kicked the empty card box to the side and moved over to rearrange the birthday card display, intent on clearing a section for some Easter cards. The full range of his stock would go out once Mother's Day had passed but some customers were organised early birds so it was worth having a few out on the shelves otherwise he'd be in and out of the stock room trying to fulfil their requests.

As he moved the cards around, he came across one with a large fluffy cat on the front. It immediately made him think of George and Timothy and he realised Perrie was still at the forefront of his mind. The woman intrigued him, there was no doubt about it. Even Daisy was taken with her – she'd talked about her "Merida" all through breakfast and couldn't wait to get to nursery so she could tell her best friend, Mandy, all about the new princess who now lived close by and was coming to her birthday party. Morgan's protests that Perrie hadn't received, nor accepted, an official invitation yet had fallen on little deaf ears. He was sure that Perrie would attend Daisy's party for she had indicated as much but he'd get Daisy to write out one of her spare invitation letters tonight. It was a convenient excuse to see her again although he didn't question himself too closely on why he wanted to.

The ping of the bell above the shop door announced the timely arrival of a customer and Morgan took the opportunity to push away the internal interrogation that he wasn't yet ready to face.

NINE

Perrie let out a long groan as she pushed the heavy desk in front of the window. She was up in the attic, the third bedroom in the cottage, and was doing some rearranging of the furniture. She guessed this was intended to be a teenager's bedroom given the work desk which had been placed against the far wall and the small, compact fridge where bottles of water or fizzy drinks could be stored.

For her, however, it was the perfect office space but staring at a blank wall whenever she looked up was not on and so she'd just heaved the surprisingly solid, wooden desk over to sit in front of the big dormer window. It fitted the space perfectly and the view was improved one-hundredfold. The single bed was pushed into the corner along the wall and had been decorated with a couple of throws she'd found in the airing cupboard and the cushions from the master bedroom. It was now a cosy place for her to sit when she needed to read through her notes. She'd also commandeered the small bookcase from the second bedroom and had placed some of her research material upon the shelves but the really rare books, which were on loan from Cambridge University, remained safely in the box they'd been transported in. Finally, she'd put a small table next to the fridge and placed her travel kettle on it along with a box of herbal teas. While walking down to the kitchen for refreshments was good exercise, there were times when she didn't want her train of thought interrupted and so liked to have the means of a hot drink close by.

Perrie stood in the middle of the room and gave a nod of satisfaction. The small changes felt good and she knew she'd be happy working in here. She walked over to the desk and threw open the windows, letting the salty sea breeze cool her skin after her exertions. She pottered about for a few minutes, arranging her pen pot, laptop and other bits of stationery in the drawer before letting out a sigh. Her office was now ready for her to work, unfortunately *she* wasn't yet ready to work. It was almost two weeks since she'd moved in and where her office should have been the first thing she'd sorted out, it had turned out to be the last.

'Monday!' she said aloud to the room. 'I'll knuckle down on Monday.'

She pulled the windows closed and made her way down to the kitchen. The cats were out in their new run and she wanted to check they were okay. As she passed the fridge, Perrie's eye was caught by the brightly coloured invitation she'd received from Daisy to attend her party in two days' time. After some lengthy deliberation – she didn't want to attend but wanted to upset Daisy even less – her acceptance had been posted through Morgan's letterbox and although the birthday gifts she'd purchased online – a space-themed craft set and a glow-in-the-dark T-shirt – had arrived, she still had to buy wrapping paper. She'd been putting off going down into the town since she'd arrived and had only briefly ventured outside the door twice. The first occasion had been to post her acceptance to Daisy's party and the second had been a late afternoon drive to the large supermarket ten miles away.

Perrie knew she had to summon up the courage to go outside, she couldn't stay holed up in the cottage for the whole six months she'd be here. It was another reason why she'd forced herself to accept Daisy's invitation but the thought of facing people terrified her. Yes, it may have been more than eight months since her face had been plastered over a number of daily newspapers and on most of the TV news channels for a few weeks but people had long memories and there was no guarantee someone wouldn't recognise her.

She stood chewing on a fingernail while watching George and Timothy bouncing around in the cat-run.

'At least you guys seem to be enjoying yourselves.'

She smiled through the fencing at their antics as they chased each other over and under the boughs of their trees.

'Okay, Perrie Lacey, get over yourself! You came here for a fresh start so it's time to get started!'

With a conscious effort, she pulled her shoulders back and lifted her head high. Unlocking the run, she called the cats indoors, put down some food for them and gathered up her coat and handbag. It was now or never.

As she stepped through the gate onto the cliff path, Perrie tugged her woolly hat down over her ears. The sharp wind was taking no prisoners and she was glad she'd tucked her curly locks up inside it otherwise they would be whipping painfully across her face.

She walked over the rough, semi-gravelled path and onto the grass which waved wildly about in front of a dry-stone wall. Perrie guessed there was probably about thirty feet from the foot of the wall to the edge of the path. Her view, when looking straight ahead, was one of endless sea and sky, coming together in a distant horizon. Upon reaching the wall however, and looking down to the left, her view changed to one of red tiled rooftops, short and tall chimneys and small walled gardens, some better kept than others. Cobble-stone pathways wound their way between the higgledy-piggledy houses and she marvelled at the ingenuity of the builders who, many centuries before, had hewn through the tough stone cliffs to create this little community. When she cast her gaze to what lay directly beyond the wall, she saw roughly six feet of grassland followed by a direct drop where some large rocks and boulders were just about visible and took a guess that many more of the same lay directly at the foot of the cliff.

She stood for a moment longer, allowing the sharp salty air to clear the cobwebs from her mind and soul. In years gone by, humans had put much faith in the restorative powers of the sea and it was easy to understand why. A mild sensation of feeling invigorated began to flow through her and Perrie gave a small nod of acceptance to the impulsive decision she'd made to come to Broatiescombe Bay – it had definitely been the right call.

Turning away from the wall and the view, Perrie found herself walking a little straighter and taller as she returned to the path. Her earlier worry had dissipated and she found herself now looking forward to exploring this gorgeous little town.

When she reached the bottom of the evil hill – it was

going to take some time before she could think of it as anything else – she turned right and began to slowly make her way down the main street.

She passed by the old cottages, with steps down to their brightly painted doors which matched the painted frames of the tiny windows, and was thankful she hadn't rented one of those for, with her height, she didn't fancy the chances of avoiding a few concussions. Shops were interspersed between the residential buildings and her attention was drawn to a small art gallery. When she looked in the window, some of the paintings and pastels on display carried a similar view to the one she'd admired only a short while before from outside her cottage. She wondered if there was a local artist who regularly produced drawings for the tourists to take home as mementos or if the influx of artists that Morgan had mentioned sold their work to the gallery. There was an eclectic mix of styles, from what she could see hanging on the walls near the window, so she suspected a number of artists brought their wares here in the hope the tourists would buy them.

Perrie continued to make her way down the hill, following the wide path as it turned this way and that and managed to avoid the temptation to follow some of the smaller alleys that led from it. She would save those for another time.

She stopped outside a pretty blue cottage with red window boxes to treat herself to a caramel slice – a pile of which were on a small table alongside some other delicious looking baked goodies – and dropped a pound in the honesty box next to it. She placed the cake carefully in her bag, knowing she'd enjoy it later this evening after her dinner.

She'd just turned to admire a bow-fronted shop window displaying old-fashioned sweet jars when the sound of shouting, accompanied by a ringing bell, filled her ears. She looked over her shoulder to see two strapping lads walking down the hill with a large wooden and wire crate on wheels being guided between them.

'Here, love, you might want to step inside a minute, out of the way. The wheels on those old crates could give any supermarket trolley a run for its money!'

Perrie glanced round to see a small, older lady beckoning her into the shop. There was a shout as the crate swivelled off course and she decided to take her rescuer up on her offer and stepped inside the shop just as the young men brought the crate to a halt, pulled a package out and knocked on the door of the cottage opposite.

She gave the woman who was now standing behind the solid wood counter, a look full of curiosity.

'They're the delivery boys,' she said, answering Perrie's unspoken question. 'Motorised vehicles can't come down here so deliveries are left at the delivery hut up top and the lads bring them down on the crates throughout the day. They also help the shopkeepers with their supplies so when I have to go to the cash-and-carry to replenish my stock, I leave it at the hut and they bring it to me.'

'Of course! I've heard about these. And now I've seen them in action.'

'Yes, it's a novelty the first few times but that bloody bell is a right bother when you're on the phone or trying to serve customers. Not so bad in the winter but when the door is open in the summer, I often feel like throwing the darn noisy thing off the cliff!'

'How often do they deliver, then?'

'It used to just be twice a day but now we've got the internet and folks doing more of this online shopping thing, it can easily be four or five times.'

'Hmm, I can see how that could become annoying.'

'Oh, I shouldn't complain, the internet has helped my business enormously and I send out plenty of original Devonshire fudge every week. The boys deliver on the way down and collect on the way back up. There's a small post office in the gift shop near the top – the boys take everything there, get it all franked and the like, then pass it to the post van each night. It saves my legs from having to walk up that hill and I don't have to close the shop.'

'So, every cloud has a silver lining?'

The woman smiled. 'I suppose it has, when you put it like that.'

Perrie moved away from the door to look around the sweet-filled interior. She'd seen shops like these when she'd visited the living-style museums which had become popular over the last decade or so – small towns which consisted of old houses and shops from bygone eras which served to remind or educate on how life was lived in years gone by. Most of them had a traditional sweetshop just like this although it was clear that this shop had always been in this location, in one guise or another.

'How long has this been a sweet shop?' she asked, as her eyes ran along the labels on the jars. There were so many childhood favourites looking back at her.

'It became a dedicated sweetshop in the early 1980s, before that it was a general grocers. My father was in charge then but when supermarkets began to make their mark, business started to drop off. He noticed that the sale of confectionery was still strong so he wound down the groceries and ramped up the sweets. He encouraged my mother to make more of her homemade fudge and it sold well. When he retired, I took over. My daughter now makes the fudge and I sell it. The tourists love it.'

The sweet, heady smells of chocolate and sugar were assaulting Perrie's senses and the old saying of feeling like a kid in a sweet shop was ringing true. There was no way she was leaving here without taking something diabetes-inducing with her.

'I think I need to try some of this famous fudge. I'll take a bag of that, please.'

'Coming right up. So, are you just visiting for the day?'

This was it! The moment Perrie had been dreading – people asking questions about her. Somehow, she had to find a way of being polite and friendly but without giving too much away. She had to find the balance of saying enough to satisfy curiosity without saying anything that would encourage further curiosity.

'No, I'm renting a cottage for six months.'

'Ah, would that be Seaview Cottage, by any chance?'

'Yes, it is.'

'Sue mentioned she'd rented it out. Welcome to Broatie, I hope we look after you while you're here. I'm Iris – feel free to pop in and say hello whenever you're passing.'

'Perrie!' She stuck her hand over the counter and a firm shake passed between them. 'Thank you for that, I'll be sure to do so.'

She was placing her second sweet purchase of the day next to the caramel slice in her bag when she spotted Morgan through the window. He was walking up the hill and appeared to be having a rather animated conversation on his mobile. She twisted round so there would be less chance of him seeing her should he happen to glance in her direction.

'Right, I'd better get going, Iris. I need to find wrapping paper before the shops close for the day.'

'Oh, you'll be wanting the card shop down on the seafront for that. They'll be closing in about half-an-hour.'

Perrie smiled her thanks. 'I'd better get a move on then! Thank you, Iris. I'll see you again soon.'

It was still light when she exited the shop but dusk was on its way. She walked quickly down the hill but was still taken by surprise when she turned a bend and saw the ocean laid out in front of her. She stepped out from between the buildings and found herself standing on a vast esplanade. The lights along the seafront were beginning to flicker on and reminded her that she didn't have much time left to complete her errand. She would have to continue her exploring another day.

She walked over to the far side of the esplanade, turned her back on the crashing waves and cast her eyes along the row of shops until she found what she was looking for – Harriet's Art and Card Shop.

She pulled her coat collar up against the wind and walked towards it while briefly looking in the other shop windows that she passed on the way.

Tomorrow, she thought. She had no plans for the following day so she'd come back down for a closer look and maybe even treat herself to lunch at one of the pretty tearooms and cafés.

A little bell pinged as she opened the door of the card shop, causing her to smile. A young girl turned and smiled back.

'Can I help you?'
'Yes please, I'm looking for some wrapping paper.'

TEN

Perrie stopped to catch her breath. Finding the various flights of stairs between the cottages may have been a shorter and quicker route back up the hill but they were also considerably steeper than the meandering cobbled main street. Something her lungs were now realising as they burned inside her. She'd always thought she was reasonably fit but the hills around here were doing their best to convince her otherwise. It looked like both she and her Fitbit would be getting a good workout over the next few months.

She was standing outside Hettie's Hairdressers, pretending to look at the opening times and price list while trying not to puff like an old steam train, when she heard the sound of a child crying. She turned round and came face-to-face with Morgan, carrying a clearly broken-hearted Daisy in his arms.

'Oh, my goodness, Daisy, what's the matter?'

She instinctively put her hand on the little girl's back and began to gently rub it while looking at Morgan for an answer to her question.

'Mrs. Campbell phoned me this afternoon to say she couldn't make Daisy's birthday cake. She'd planned to bake it tomorrow but her mother has fallen and broken her hip. She lives in Plymouth and Mrs Campbell needs to go there first thing tomorrow morning.'

'Oh, Daisy, that's too sad.'

Perrie looked at Morgan again. 'I'm guessing there's no one else who could do it?'

'No. My mum can't bake to save herself, and Hettie,' he inclined his head towards the hairdressers, 'is fully booked tomorrow. She had to move appointments to make sure she could attend the birthday party on Saturday.'

'Don't want no party now!'

Daisy blurted out her comment before turning her head away and burying it in her daddy's shoulder.

'Could Sue in the baker's shop help?'

'With more notice, she could have done something although celebration cakes are not her forte, but Friday and Saturday are her busiest days and she simply won't have the time. I even asked the mini-market but they only do special orders for pre-made birthday cakes. It looks like we're having a birthday party with no cake.'

'I'll do it for you!'

The words had tumbled from Perrie's lips before she'd had a chance to think them through and she hoped the shock she was feeling at having uttered them wasn't showing in her face.

'Do you bake?'

'It has been known...'

Usually when she was feeling stressed and wound up – it was a great way of taking some time away from your problems, but that was something Morgan didn't need to be aware of.

'Can you do a rabbit?'

Perrie smiled at Daisy's question. 'I can try. Last year I made a Humpty Dumpty cake for my nephew and it looked okay.'

'Would you do that for us?' Morgan's face held a hopeful expression.

'Well, it depends on Mrs. Campbell. Would she be prepared to let me borrow her tins and provide the ingredients? There are no baking tins at the cottage and I'd prefer not to waste time going shopping in the morning.'

'Here, if you can take Daisy, I'll phone her and ask. I've paid a deposit and she must already have the ingredients in…'

Perrie took the little girl in her arms and Morgan walked over to the side of the path, pulling his phone from his pocket as he went.

'Hey, don't cry, Daisy, we'll sort something out. Even if I can't bake a rabbit, we'll make sure you have a cake of some sort.'

'I've told everyone I'm having a rabbit. No one has had a rabbit cake before and they don't believe I'm having one. Nancy Wilson called me a liar!'

Perrie managed to hold in the sigh that almost escaped her. It seemed that no matter what age you were, there was always that one girl or woman who managed to make you feel about two inches tall.

Morgan put his phone back in his pocket and he was smiling as he walked back towards them.

'Mrs. Campbell has said she'd be more than happy to let you borrow her tins and have the ingredients. She said we need to go and collect them now and has asked for you to come along as she has a favour to ask.'

'A favour? What kind of favour?'

'She wouldn't say. Just asked me to bring you when I went to collect the stuff.'

'Very well. I suppose she doesn't want to lend her tins to just anyone.'

'Perhaps! Let me drop Daisy off here with Hettie and we'll go round. She only lives two streets away.'

Two hours later, Perrie stood in her kitchen and wondered what on earth had just happened. To say Mrs. Campbell had been a force to be reckoned with would be the year's biggest understatement! Morgan had explained on the way there that Mrs. Campbell had been a Home Economics teacher and then Head Teacher of the nearby senior school before she'd retired. Perrie could honestly say that, while the woman might be retired, her teaching demeanour was not. She'd grilled Perrie on a few of the basic baking techniques before subtly talking her into taking on three other cake orders which she'd had to cancel. Perrie was now making Daisy's birthday cake and an 18th birthday cake for this coming Saturday and was expected to do two further cakes for the following weekend – one for a Christening and the other, a fruit cake nonetheless, for an engagement party.

Mrs. Campbell had explained that while the cake-making was not an actual business, it was a nice little side-line which supplemented her pension. So, no pressure to ensure she didn't let anyone down then, thought Perrie.

She decided to have some cheese on toast while she studied the recipes for the two cakes required this week, after which she would weigh out all the ingredients for both in preparation for the morning. That way, she could just get up and get on, then, if there were any disasters, the big supermarket was only ten miles away...

Her head shot up!

'Oh, you stupid bint!' she blurted out to no one. 'That's what you get for speaking before thinking!' It had only just occurred to her that she could have simply offered to drive to the supermarket along the road and bring back something off the shelf. Sheesh! Talk about making life difficult for yourself!

ELEVEN

Morgan checked his watch again. It was now one-forty-
six pm. A whole minute had passed since he'd last
looked. He swept his gaze around the lounge. Balloons
with the number five were dotted all around, the sofa and
chairs had been pushed to the side to allow space for
party games, and in the dining room, the dining table,
along with the breakfast bar into the kitchen, was laden
with sandwiches, mini-scotch eggs, little sausage rolls,
iced-topped cupcakes and bowls of crisps. There was,
however, a large empty space in the middle where the
birthday cake should have been sitting.

When he'd dropped Perrie back at her cottage on
Thursday night, after helping with the baking equipment,
all she'd said was she would be in touch. It was now less
than fifteen minutes before the party was due to begin, the
guests would start arriving any minute now and they were
still minus the piece de resistance!

Daisy was standing by the window, watching the
path to the cliffs and waiting hopefully for a glimpse of
someone carrying a cake. Morgan had expected a phone

call to ask for assistance with transporting said cake and the lack of request now had him worried. Surely Perrie would have let him know if there was a problem. She didn't strike him as the kind of person who would let down a five-year-old child. But then, how well did he know her? They'd only spoken twice – the first time when he'd come to her rescue and the second when she'd come to his. Or he thought she had. Now he wasn't so sure.

'SHE'S HERE! DADDY, SHE'S HERE!'

Daisy was already dashing to the front door and had opened it by the time he got there.

'Merida! Have you brought my cake? Is it a rabbit? Can I see, please?'

'Daisy! Step back and let Perrie in. And stop calling her "Merida" – that's not her name.'

Perrie grinned at him as she stepped through the doorway.

'Oh, I don't mind, Morgan. Being called after a Disney princess is not so bad. Now, where can I put this?' She nodded at the large, upside-down, cardboard storage box she was holding in her hands.

'The kitchen would be best, I think. Can I take that for you?'

'No, it's fine. I've brought it this far; I think I can manage a few more feet.'

'Why didn't you call me? I would have come along and got it.'

He guided her through to the kitchen at the back of the house.

'I nearly did until I figured out how to package it up. With the wind out there, I was concerned for its safety.'

'Well, I must say, I'm impressed with your creativeness.'

'I hope you're saying the same in an hour's time when

we take it out the box.'

'Am I allowed a peek?'

'No, you're not. I want it to be a surprise for both you and Daisy.'

'Spoilsport!'

'Guilty as charged!'

Just then, the front door opened and his mum, Emily, walked in followed by Hettie. They quickly divested themselves of their coats and he introduced them to Perrie while taking her coat and putting it in the cupboard under the stairs.

'Would you like a drink?' he asked, while quickly rearranging the food on the table, filling the space he'd left for the cake. If Perrie wanted it to be a surprise, then so be it. He wasn't inclined to disagree.

'Yes, please.'

'Wine, beer, tea, or coffee?'

'Hmm, as there are children around, I suppose a coffee would be the sensible option.'

'Hah, you speak for yourself, Perrie,' his mum held up the wine she was pouring into some glasses, 'Hettie and I are on the hard stuff. We know exactly what it takes to cope with a room full of sugared-up kids and it's not coffee.'

Perrie smiled. 'Actually, I've just remembered my nephew's last birthday party and you're right. Please,' she looked at the bottle, 'count me in!'

Morgan felt his shoulders sag with relief. He didn't know why he'd been concerned about introducing Perrie to his mum and Hettie but concerned he had been. It wasn't like there was anything between them. This thought produced a small kick in his chest but he ignored it as Daisy yelled from the front room that her guests had arrived.

'Happy Birthday, dear Daisy, Happy Birthday to you!'

Perrie smiled at the wide-eyed awe on the faces of the little girls standing in a circle around Daisy as they sang to her. She wondered which one was Nancy Wilson – the one who'd made the nasty comment to Daisy about not having a rabbit cake. Well, she'd be eating her words now – quite literally – when she received her slice of the pink iced, bunny-shaped sponge.

She looked at the cake as Daisy's grandmothers placed it carefully on the now-cleared table and couldn't help feeling proud of her creation. Morgan had asked her if she'd like to do the honours but she'd declined – being the centre of attention was the last thing she needed or wanted. When she'd started baking the day before, she'd made the 18th birthday cake first as it was a straight-forward, multi-tiered, sponge cake and was a good one to practise on. It had turned out just fine and it hadn't taken long for her to relax and begin enjoying her unexpected tasks.

This enjoyment had led her to expand upon Daisy's request for a rabbit and her cake had been transformed into a bright pink rabbit sitting upon a green-iced lawn with a chocolate-covered tree-stump behind it which led down into its burrow. What Daisy didn't know, and no one else did either, was that when the "burrow" was cut into, loads of pink-coloured chocolate M&M's were going to spill out thanks to a phone call to her brother who worked near Piccadilly Circus where the big M&M shop was situated. He'd been tasked with procuring a large bag of the pink coloured sweets and getting them sent by special delivery to ensure she had them this morning when she had to assemble the cake. She now owed him an expensive meal the next time she was in town.

When Hettie and Sarah had been lighting the candles on the cake, ready to carry it through to the dining table, she'd given them a small wink as she told them where to cut it first but had said nothing more and she now had her phone trained firmly on Daisy's face as they prepared to take out the first slice.

The gasps, squeals and excited chatter that went up as the pink sweets tumbled down onto the large silver platter made Daisy's face light up like a beacon! She was glowing with joy and Perrie caught every second of her delighted surprise. She would forward the video to Morgan later. She also did a sweep of the party-guests and soon discovered who Nancy Wilson was – the perfectly-coiffed, Armani-wearing, little madam with the sulky face. She only knew it was an Armani dress because her sister had been drooling over it a few months before and lamenting the fact she had two boys and no girls to buy it for.

Perrie had just switched off the video and was putting the phone away in her pocket when a blonde-haired woman came to stand in front of her. A woman who had no concept of spatial awareness and stepped right into her personal space, an action Perrie abhorred passionately and which instantly got her back up whenever anyone did it to her. She took a step back and picked up a plate of sandwiches to ensure the blonde kept her distance.

'I understand you made the girl's birthday cake today.'

Perrie blinked in surprise at the woman's tone and apparent lack of awareness of whose party she was attending.

'Yes, that's correct. I made *Daisy*'s cake.'

'Well, I want you to make one for my Nancy. It's her birthday in four weeks. Give me your phone number and

I'll call you with the details.'

'Err, I think you need to speak to Mrs. Campbell. I believe she is the lady who makes the celebration cakes for the town.'

'I want you to make it. Mrs. Campbell could never come up with something like that.' A pink nail-tipped hand was waved in the direction of the dining table where several children were still admiring the surprise cake.

'Well, I only made this cake as a favour to Mrs. Campbell as she was indisposed. I'm not in a position to take on any future orders for her.'

'Look, I don't think you understand me. I want *you* to make my Nancy's birthday cake. Now give me your number so we can talk later in the week.'

Perrie straightened her shoulders and looked down at the woman. Even in her three-inch heels, she was no match for Perrie's height.

'I understand very well, it is *you* who doesn't understand that I will not be taking an order from you – of any kind – regarding the baking of a cake for your daughter's birthday. Now, if you'll excuse me…'

Perrie turned and with the greatest of effort, walked casually away towards the kitchen while counting in her head to prevent losing her temper. What an obnoxious woman. Suddenly she felt sorry for little Nancy if that was going to be her role-model in life.

'Hey, you did well there. Personally, I'd have decked her one!'

She looked to her side to see a woman wearing dungarees over an old woollen jumper and her dark-brown hair tied up in a messy bun with a cotton scarf wrapped around her head. Her chocolate brown eyes danced with mischief and a large smile was on her face.

'I didn't think a brawl would go down too well at a five-year-old's birthday party. Figured I might save it for the next time I'm at the pub.'

The woman laughed as she stuck out her hand. 'Babs Middleton. Lovely to meet you.'

'Perrie Lacey.'

'It's nice to see someone other than myself stand up to Cleo Wilson. Most of the yummy-mummies are too scared to do so because her mother is the local councillor. I don't know quite what she could do if anyone pissed off her daughter but few are prepared to find out.'

'I see.' Perrie didn't want to say much in reply as getting caught up in the local bitch-fest wasn't to her liking.

'Anyway, less about the not-so-lovely Cleo, I've got better things to be getting on with in my life. What brings you to Broatie? My mother was telling me you've rented Seaview Cottage for six months.'

'Your mother?'

'Iris, from the sweetshop.'

'Oh! You make the fudge!'

Babs grinned at her. 'Among other things.'

Just then, a little girl came running up to them.

'Mummy, Daisy's gran told me to give this to you to look after.'

Perrie looked down and would have known this was Bab's daughter anywhere – the dungarees, dark-brown pigtails and large brown eyes were a dead giveaway.

'Ah, the obligatory goodie-bag. Yes, darling, I'll keep a hold of this. Now, off you go, I think that's the last game before we go home. You don't want to miss it – it looks like Pass the Parcel.'

The little girl ran off and Babs rummaged in her pocket. She pulled out a battered business card and handed it over.

'Look, let's grab a glass of wine sometime where there are no screaming kids and we can hear ourselves

think. My number's on there. It would be nice to hang out.'
She squeezed Perrie's arm lightly before walking off to
watch the children play their game. Perrie looked down
and saw the name of the art gallery she'd been admiring on
Thursday. She stared at the card in her hand for several
seconds and then, checking no one was looking, discreetly
ripped it into small pieces which she tipped into a
discarded crisp packet and shoved deep into the bin thus
ensuring she wouldn't be tempted to give in and call at a
later date. It hurt her to do this for she'd liked Babs and
could see that she'd be fun to be around but Perrie knew
that friends were a luxury she could no longer afford.

TWELVE

It was Monday morning and Perrie let out a sigh as she
sat down at her desk in her new loft-space office. She'd
had a lovely chilled out Sunday, curled up on the big cosy
chair next to the log burner in the lounge, where she spent
half the day reading and the other half binge-watching a
new costume drama series. It had been quite peaceful and
it would be too easy to repeat it all again today but she'd
vowed to get back in the saddle this morning and so here
she was.

She'd already had a productive day having been up
early to do some baking and four small steak pies were
now cooling on the kitchen work-top – one for dinner
tonight and the other three destined for the freezer.
George and Timothy were out in the run and her phone
alarm was set to go off in two hours to check on them for
she was all too aware of her tendency to lose track of time
once she became immersed in her work. She cracked
open the window a notch and her gaze took in the sea
view outside. It was a dark, squally day with heavy grey
clouds racing across the sky and she could hear the large

white waves colliding noisily against the shore. Although the garden was reasonably protected from the wind, she was glad she'd pulled down the heavy plastic blinds in the cat run. Mr. Rodgers had put his all into creating a five-star aviary for his birds and her boys were now reaping the benefits. They would be sheltered from any wayward elements and she could lose herself in her work without the distraction of worrying about them.

She leant forward, switched on the angle-poise lamp on the desk, adjusting it slightly, wiped her hands thoroughly on a soft cloth to ensure they were clean and then took a tatty old book out of the box by the side of the desk. She placed it carefully down, opened her large notepad and positioned her free-standing magnifying glass.

Within five minutes she was fully absorbed in the minutely written words and oblivious to everything else around her.

'Huh! What? Eh?'

Perrie sat back, rubbed her eyes and wondered what had disturbed her. She picked up her phone and saw the time was almost five o'clock when there was a loud knocking on the front door. She made a calculated guess that there had been an earlier knock and it had been that which had brought her back into the here and now.

She pushed her chair back and ran down the stairs, calling out 'Coming!' as she hit the last flight. She tried not to appear too puffed as she opened the door.

'Merida!'

A pair of little arms wound their way around her

thighs and a small blonde head buried itself just below her stomach.

Perrie bent over to return the hug and used the opportunity to get some air back into her lungs. When she straightened up again, she was able to smile at Morgan rather than grimace painfully.

'Hey, guys, lovely to see you. Come on in.'

'I think someone has yet to learn the correct rules of etiquette on waiting to be asked in...' Morgan smiled as his eyes dipped down towards Daisy and then back up again.

Perrie gave a small laugh. 'I can think of worse ways for someone to invade your home.'

'Even so, she needs to understand that she can't just run into people's homes like that.'

'Daddy, Daddy, tell Merida we have presents for her.'

'Daisy, you can't keep calling Perrie "Merida" – it's not her name.'

The look of dismay on the little girl's face was too much for Perrie. She hunkered down until she was level with the pair of big cornflower-blue eyes.

'Daisy, I am more than happy to be your "Merida" if that is what you want to call me. I have no problem with it. However, if you think I'm *gauny walk aboot talkin' wie a Scoattish accent aw 'ra time, ye huv anither think comin', hen!*'

Daisy burst out laughing at Perrie's Scottish voice and the sound made her smile. As she straightened up, Morgan said, 'I think you're being a little indulgent with her.'

'Oh, what harm is it doing? If it makes her happy to think she has her own Disney princess, then I have no problem with playing along.'

Also, Perrie thought to herself, knowing that children

62

have a penchant for inane chatter, she would rather Daisy called her Merida as she had come to Broatiescombe to be anonymous and being called a different name entirely would help with that.

'Well, if you're quite sure.'

'I'm more than sure, Morgan. Now, won't you please come in out of the cold.'

'In a moment... Daisy?'

The little girl skipped out into the porch and picked up a box which she handed to Perrie. 'These are to say "Thank you" for my lovely rabbit birthday cake.'

Perrie looked down at the beautifully gift-wrapped box, complete with a label declaring that handmade fudge resided within.

'Oh, Daisy, that's very kind of you. I like fudge and I know I will enjoy this. Thank you.'

She bent down and placed a kiss on Daisy's cheek.

'And these are from me. Also, to say "Thank you" for an exceptionally lovely rabbit birthday cake.'

Perrie found herself face-to-face with an exquisite bouquet of soft, creamy-white roses and their sweet, heady scent wrapped itself around her.

'Wow, Morgan, these are glorious. Thank you. There really was no need.'

'There was every need, Perrie. You saved Daisy's birthday. Do not underestimate the competitiveness between five-year-old girls to have the best party. She already has a tough time with some people due to her circumstances; your cake ensured it didn't get worse and that means a lot to me.'

'I'm just happy I was able to help. Now, are you planning to stand there all night or come in because it's getting cold around here?'

Morgan finally crossed the threshold and Perrie closed the door behind him while discretely turning the thermostat on the wall up a few notches.

'I understand that roses are safe when it comes to cats? We checked on the internet first.'

'Yes, they are. Thank you for that, although I'll be sure to place them where the boys can't get at them.'

'Is it true that lilies are very dangerous?'

Perrie hung his jacket on the coat-stand and retrieved Daisy's duffle coat from the floor where she'd dropped it.

'Yes, they are. Their pollen can cause rapid kidney failure if ingested and, more often than not, the outcome is fatal.'

'Then I'm glad we checked and didn't get you those.'

Perrie smiled at him. 'Me too! I can't stand the smell of them.'

'Merida, where are George and Timothy?'

'They're out in the cat run, Daisy. Would you like to help me bring them inside and feed them their dinner?'

'Oh, yes, please!' Daisy's face lit up.

'Come on then.' She held out her hand. When the little girl took it, she smiled as she glanced back at Morgan. 'Looks like you've pulled the short straw of putting on the kettle and sorting out the drinks.'

Morgan had found the cafetière, retrieved the packet of coffee from the cupboard, was warming the milk in the microwave as he had seen Perrie do the last time they'd been here and was just mixing up a drink of blackcurrant squash for Daisy when the back door banged open and Daisy came running in.

'Daddy, look! George and Timothy walk on a lead

just like dogs do!'

He looked down to see her holding tightly onto a leash which was attached to the harness one of the cats was wearing. Perrie was right behind her with his brother.

'Well, I have never seen *that* before!'

Perrie grinned as she closed the door, locked it and then bent down to take the harnesses off the cats.

'It's not uncommon. Most cats will walk on a harness if their slaves take the time and have the patience to train them. With these guys being so big,' she gestured towards her boys, 'it's a blessing they like it as I can take them on walks to ensure they get the exercise they need. I took them out along the cliff path a couple of times last week and they loved it.'

'I bet that got you some strange looks.'

'At first, other walkers thought they were small dogs. It wasn't until they drew closer, and realised they were big cats, that the odd looks came. There were a couple of occasions where I wished I could have photographed their faces.'

'Can I come with you when you take them out again?'

Perrie looked down at Daisy. 'We'll need to discuss it with your daddy first but I don't mind. However, before we do that, would you like to put this bowl down for Timothy, please? I'll do George's because he can be a little boisterous and I don't want him to knock you over.'

Morgan watched his daughter carry the big silver bowl carefully over to the cats and place it on the floor. He didn't know which cat was which but she clearly did.

'Coffee is ready!'

He poured it into two cups and placed them on the worktop.

'Daisy, come and sit up at the breakfast bar to drink your juice. Let the cats eat their dinner in peace.'

'Would you both like to stay for your tea?'

'No, we can't impose on you again—'

'Yes, please!'

Morgan looked in despair at his daughter who was bouncing up and down on the bar stool.

Perrie smiled at them both.

'Morgan, you're not imposing. I made some steak pies this morning and as luck would have it, they've not yet gone into the freezer. You are more than welcome to stay.'

Oh, blimey! Why did it have to be homemade steak pie? One of his favourites and something he hadn't had for far too long. Morgan's mouth watered at the thought.

'Erm, would that be with mash, peas, and gravy?'

Perrie grinned widely at him. 'It could be...'

He swallowed. 'Then we would love to accept your kind offer.'

'YAY!'

They both laughed as Daisy waved her arms in the air above her head.

'I hope I haven't spoiled your own dinner plans?'

Morgan thought of his near-empty fridge which hadn't been replenished as usual on Saturday morning due to Daisy's party. Pasta and a jar of sauce had been on the cards for tonight – a make-do meal which wouldn't have been anywhere near as tasty as what Perrie was offering.

'No, you haven't at all. Tonight's tea will keep for another day.'

'Great! Well, in that case, you can peel the spuds, I will sort out the pies and the veg and, Daisy, you have the most important job of all – brushing the cats! Here, I'll show you what to do...'

THIRTEEN

'Daisy, please don't touch that, darling. There's a good girl.'

'But I'm bored, Daddy.'

Morgan tried not to sigh as he took the tube of vivid purple paint from his daughter's hands and placed it back on the shelf. He hated having to bring her to the shop when he was working but he'd had no choice. A burst pipe at the town hall had flooded several of the rooms including the one they used for the day-care group. The short notice meant he had no one to look after Daisy. Hettie was fully booked – Wednesday was one of her busiest days as that was when the older ladies of the town came in for their weekly do's – and his mum was on volunteer duty at the hospital near the big town. She'd already left by the time the call came through to tell him that the play group was cancelled for the rest of the week. So, Daisy was now stuck in the shop with him all day and it was a situation neither of them enjoyed. She got bored and he got distracted trying to keep an eye on her while also trying to assist his customers. Broatiescombe might be a little town but the combination of art supplies and a gift shop brought in a steady stream of custom and the days usually rushed by.

'I know you're bored, Daisy, but there's not a lot I can do about it. Why don't you sit in the office and read for a bit? You did bring your book, didn't you?'

'I've already read it twice.'

'Then why don't you draw a picture?'

'Because I've already done drawing, Daddy.'

Morgan looked at the clock. It wasn't even eleven yet. This was going to be one very long day.

The doorbell chimed behind him.

'Look, Daisy, I've got a customer. Please, just stay in here.'

A sulky look sat on her face but she nodded at his request.

'Good morning, how may I help you— Perrie? Hi!'

'Hey, Morgan. How are you today?'

Before he could reply, Morgan felt a bump against the back of his legs as Daisy rushed past him and threw herself at Perrie.

'Merida!'

Perrie immediately crouched down to Daisy's level. 'Hey, poppet, what are you doing here? Shouldn't you be at playgroup?'

'All the toys have been drowned!'

'Excuse me?'

Morgan rolled his eyes. 'What she means is there has been a burst pipe at the town hall and several rooms got flooded, including the one they use for the playgroup.'

'Ah, I see.'

'Can I come to your house and play with the cats? It's boring here!'

'Daisy! You can't keep inviting yourself into people's homes! Perrie, I am so sorry. Now, did you come in for something specific?'

She straightened up and walked over to the counter. Once again, he was struck by her height and her gorgeous red hair. On the last few occasions when they'd been in each other's company it had either been hidden under her hat or pulled up in a messy bun but today, it had been pulled into a long plait down her back. Several tendrils had been pulled free by the wind and they hung in soft curls around her face. She was so striking to behold and he had to force himself not to stare at her – something he found himself wanting to do quite often. Her aquamarine eyes twinkled with humour as she approached the counter.

'I was hoping you might stock highlighter pens. My green one has dried up and I don't have a spare. I use them to colour-code areas of my work.'

'Umm, yes, I do have those in stock. They're just over here.'

He walked out from around the high counter and found Daisy standing next to Perrie, holding tightly onto her hand.

'Daisy? Seriously? Can you please leave Perrie alone? She's not your toy!'

'But, Daddy…'

Her bottom lip began to quiver and Morgan drew in a deep breath in anticipation of the tears that were about to fall. It wasn't his fault she was stuck here in the shop so why did he have this overwhelming feeling of incompetence? He closed his eyes and waited for the wailing to begin.

'Daisy, do you know where the highlighter pens are? You do? Then would you mind getting two bright green ones for me, please. And don't run because you might fall so take your time, there's no need to rush.'

Morgan opened one eye to see Daisy walking over to

the pens and Perrie watching him in amusement.

'Having a bad day?' she asked.

'Well, it's not an ideal one.'

'Let me take Daisy back with me.'

'I can't ask you to do that.'

'You didn't, I offered. You know, you really need to learn to accept when someone is making you an offer you shouldn't refuse. Like sharing a dinner or helping out when you need a baby-sitter.'

'I don't want to interrupt your work.'

'You're not. I worked far later than I should have last night so I can take it easy today. I would love to share it with Daisy if you're okay with that. I understand that you don't know me all that well so you can say no if you'd be happier.'

'Perrie, I know Daisy is more than safe with you. Are you quite sure?'

'Yes, I am. I was thinking of an ice-cream treat when we leave here and then a walk on the cliffs with the cats – is that alright with you?'

'Ice-cream at eleven in the morning? Is that really a good thing?'

'Ice-cream at ANY time is a good thing!'

'Well, if you think you can cope with the sugar rush…'

'Hence the walk on the cliffs.' She winked at him. 'Plenty of exercise and fresh air – just what every five-year-old needs to burn off excess energy.'

'Here you are, two green pens. Would you like a bag for them?'

Perrie burst out laughing at Daisy's words.

'Daisy, Perrie has very kindly offered to look after you for the rest of the day, so go and get your coat and bag.'

Morgan turned back to Perrie. 'I really appreciate

this.'

'Hey, it's cool. Pick her up when you finish work. Now, how much do I owe you for the pens and I don't need a bag for them.'

'The pens are on the house – it's the least I can do.'

'Don't be daft – let me pay for them.'

'No, please.'

'Okay, fine.' She gave a small shrug as she dropped them into her handbag. 'Thank you.'

'Right, Titch, are you ready to go?'

He did up the buttons on Daisy's coat before walking her round the counter where she held out her hand for Perrie to hold.

After placing a kiss on her head, and telling her to be a good girl, he held the door open.

'You ladies have a good day.'

'We will, Daddy. Bye-bye!'

He watched through the window as Daisy waved to him and then turned away, clearly chattering to Perrie. He was still standing watching as they walked into the Ice-Cream Parlour a few doors down and long after the chime of the doorbell above his head had grown silent, he was still standing by the window, wondering why the shop, and his chest, now felt so empty.

FOURTEEN

'That's it, Daisy, pull the fork towards you. Don't push down too hard, do it gently.'

Perrie watched Daisy as she concentrated on scoring the lines in the potato topping on the cottage pie they'd made for dinner. Her little pink tongue peeped out from between her lips and her forehead was scrunched up. She looked incredibly cute and Perrie felt a little burst of pride at how well she was doing. All that was left now was to sprinkle some grated cheese over the top, pop it in the oven, and it should be ready to dish up when Morgan arrived.

He'd looked so stressed in the shop this morning, so she'd made the decision to cook dinner again tonight. They had talked on Monday night about how he tried not to rely too heavily on his family to help him out but Perrie knew that with the situation he was in, he needed to reach out to them more. He couldn't allow his pride to stand in the way of what was good for Daisy. Although it was clear that the town hall being flooded was out of his control and it was just one of those moments which couldn't be prepared for. She was glad she'd been in a position to help out.

'George and Timothy have finished eating, Merida, may I brush them now?'

'You most certainly can, Daisy, and I'll do the washing up before setting the table for dinner.'

'Would George and Timothy like me to read them a story? I have my book in my bag.'

'I think they would like that very much. When you've finished brushing them, we'll go into the lounge and you can all snuggle up on the sofa.'

When the knock came on the door a little while later, Daisy was half asleep with her head resting on Timothy, and Perrie was deeply engrossed in her novel.

'Hey, come on in,' she whispered to Morgan when she opened the door. 'Daisy's dozing on the sofa with the cats.'

'Ah, that explains the whispering,' he replied quietly and with a smile.

'Come through to the kitchen where we won't disturb her.'

'Oh my, that smells good.' Morgan's nose was up in the air like a Bisto kid advert.

'Homemade cottage pie.'

'I love cottage pie, it's one of my favourites.'

'Yes, Daisy said. We made it together.'

'Hi, Daddy, you're home.'

They looked round to see a sleepy Daisy standing in the doorway, rubbing her eyes.

Morgan crouched down and she ran into his open arms. Perrie smiled at the loving scene in front of her. She felt a lump form in her throat and turned away to fill the kettle, taking a little time to compose herself before she spoke again.

'Right then, Daisy, now that you're up and about,

let's get dinner sorted shall we.' Perrie gave her a grin as she drained the carrots and peas they'd prepared earlier and placed them on the hob, ready to receive the hot water once the kettle was boiled.

'Daisy, get your stuff together so we can get out of Perrie's hair and let her have her meal in peace.'

'Oh, no, Morgan, you guys are staying. We're eating together. After all, Daisy helped to make the pie, it's only fair she gets to eat it.'

'Perrie, that's far too kind of you but I can't accept. You can't keep feeding us like this – it's not fair on you.'

'It's not fair on Daisy to have made this and then be subjected to fish fingers!'

Morgan looked down at Daisy.

'You like fish fingers!'

Perrie felt her heart do a little flip as Daisy looked up at her father, opened her big blue eyes as wide as they could go and replied, 'I do like fish fingers, Daddy, I just like cottage pie more. And this one has cheese on the top too because you like that. I told Merida that was your absolute favourite so she put it on for you.'

Morgan's eyes swung back in her direction.

'There's cheese on the top?'

'Sure is.'

'Why didn't you say? That changes everything! There is, however, one condition.'

'Which is?'

'You join us for Sunday lunch this weekend, *our* treat.'

'Oooh, can we have chicken, Daddy?'

Holding her gaze, Morgan replied, 'If Perrie likes chicken, then that's what we'll have.'

'I like chicken very much.'

'So, that's settled then. You'll join us on Sunday?'

'I would be honoured to.'

74

'Yay! I can show you my dollies, Merida, the ones I told you about earlier.'

'I can't wait, Daisy. Now, go and wash your hands, dinner will be ready soon.'

Twenty minutes later, they were all sitting around the table and Morgan was making very appreciative noises over how tasty his pie was. Perrie was surprised at the warm feeling his praise had generated inside her.

'Thank you again, Perrie, for looking after Daisy today. I'm really grateful to you for doing so.'

'Honestly, Morgan, the pleasure was all mine. We had a lovely afternoon together.'

'I hope she wasn't any bother.'

'Not at all. We did some shopping – which we're now eating – and then we took the cats for a walk along the cliff path.'

'I showed Merida where Muggeler's Cove is.'

There was a clatter as Morgan's fork dropped onto his plate.

'Daisy, you have been told you must never go near the edge of the cliff. It is far too dangerous and you could be badly hurt—'

'Morgan,' Perrie put her hand over his, 'We didn't go near the edge, Daisy pointed to where it is from the pathway. She even explained that she's not allowed near the cliff edge because it's not safe. She was a very good girl.'

'Oh, I see. I'm sorry. I'm sorry, Daisy, I know you're a good girl. I shouldn't have snapped like that.'

'It's okay, Daddy,' she sighed, 'I know you just worry about me.'

Perrie caught Morgan's eye and they both struggled not to laugh at Daisy's reply.

'That's right, darling, I do worry about you. As your father, it's part of my job.' He gently caressed her blonde head before picking up his fork and resumed eating.

'Would I be right in thinking it is actually called Smuggler's Cove and that no Harry Potter muggles are involved?'

Morgan smiled. 'You would be correct. It's a small cove which was once used by the local smugglers many years back. It has a beautiful sandy beach which is inaccessible most of the time due to the tides. There's a cave halfway up the cliff wall which can only be reached by boat on certain tides. Legend has it that there was a secret entrance to the cave from the top of the cliff but no one knows where it is despite several attempts to locate it. If it existed, it has been buried over time.'

'Wow! That's an exciting bit of local folklore. How interesting. Have you ever been in the cave?'

'When I was a teenager, we occasionally went in but you need to be quite masterful with the rowing boat and it was a long haul to get there around the headland. There are steps cut into the stone which lead down to the beach on the rare times when the tide is low enough although they're now quite worn and can be treacherous.'

'It all sounds rather exciting though, to a boring old townie like me.'

'Well, let me check out the tides to see when it's next likely to be accessible and we can maybe go down for a picnic. If timed right, you can usually get a four-to-five-hour window when it's safe.'

'That would be awesome!'

'Would I be allowed to come, Daddy?'

'I'd have to check what state the stone steps are in, poppet. If they look very bad, then no one will be going down to the beach. It's been quite a few years since I've been down there, so I'm not making any promises to anyone.'

'We will leave it for you to decide, Morgan. Now, are we all finished because there's ice-cream in the freezer. Raspberry Ripple for Daisy and Mint-Choc Chip for the grown-ups.'

A two-voice chorus came back at her and Perrie smiled at the matched enthusiasm of father and daughter over their preferred choices of frozen, creamy delights. The smile stayed on her face as she cleared the table and realised how much happier she felt when Morgan and Daisy were around.

FIFTEEN

Perrie knocked on the door and stood back. Her stomach seemed to have become a butterfly reserve given the way it was flipping about. She had been looking forward to, and dreading, this meal in equal measure.

On Thursday morning, after the lovely meal with Morgan and Daisy the night before, she'd sat down with herself and had a darn good think on things. The whole point of coming to Broatiescombe Bay had been to hide away and get on with her work. She'd had no intention of becoming friends with the locals and the cottage had been chosen because it was set away from the centre of the town. She most certainly had not expected to fall – quite literally – into the arms of Broatie's most eligible bachelor. Well, that's what she had gleaned from the chatter around the room at Daisy's birthday party.

Part of the dilemma, as she saw it, was how to extract herself from the blossoming friendship without upsetting anyone's feelings and bringing unwanted attention to herself. The other part of the dilemma was that she wasn't sure she wanted to step back from Morgan and Daisy. She enjoyed their company; she enjoyed the warmth that filled her when she was with them, and she'd loved the afternoon she'd spent with the little girl. She was a delightful child and Perrie had found herself falling a little bit in love with her. Her sunny personality lit up everything around her.

'Merida! You're here!'

Before Perrie could reply, a voice floated down the hallway.

'Daisy, is that the correct manner in which to greet a guest?'

'No, Daddy. Sorry.'

Daisy looked back up at Perrie.

'Good afternoon, Merida, thank you for coming. Please come in.'

She stepped back, held the door open wide and gestured with her hand for Perrie to enter.

'Thank you, Daisy, and thank you for the beautiful welcome. As you are the lady of the house, I have brought you this small gift as a thank you for inviting me here today.'

She handed over a small bouquet of flower-designed lollipops, held together with a red ribbon, and was thrilled with Daisy's excited response.

'Wow! Thank you, Merida.'

She ran off, calling on her father to come and see what Merida had brought her. Perrie trailed along behind, feeling a little shy despite having been in the house before for Daisy's party.

Morgan stuck his head out the door. 'Hey, we're in the kitchen, come through.'

Perrie walked in and placed the bowl she was carrying on the worktop.

'I've brought a trifle as my contribution to the meal. I hope you guys like it.'

'Hmmm, yummy, yummy! Daddy was supposed to make a thing called Eton Mess for pudding but he forgot to buy the migrangs!'

'Thank you for that, Daisy!' Morgan raised his eyebrows at his daughter's lack of discretion.

'You should have called me – I could have baked some meringues for you.'

'Perrie, you're a guest, you're not supposed to come to the rescue of my failed pudding.'

'Well, it looks like I kind of did!' She gave him a grin and forced herself to ignore the little squeak which rose in her throat when he grinned back.

'Here…' she handed over the carrier bag which had been digging into the skin of her elbow, 'white wine to go with dinner. It only came out of the fridge ten minutes ago so it should still be chilled enough to drink now if you think a glass will help you to relax.'

'Ah, the tension on my face hasn't gone unnoticed then?'

'No. Why are you stressing?'

'We rarely have guests for dinner – family doesn't really count – and after the lovely meals you have fed us, I want this one to be perfect for you.'

'Oh, Morgan, there's no need to worry about that. I find great company to be far more important than the food. Now, why don't you carry on with whatever you were doing and I'll pour a couple of glasses of vino?'

She turned to the cupboard where she'd seen Hettie take the wine glasses from at Daisy's party and was taking two off the shelf when Daisy came running in.

'Merida, come and see my dollies. I've brought them downstairs for you to see.'

'Daisy, I hope you haven't brought down ALL of your dolls…'

'No, Daddy.'

She looked up at Perrie and gave her a little wink. 'Just most of them,' she whispered.

'I would love to see your dolls, Daisy, as long as Daddy doesn't need me for anything here.'

'No, you're good to go. I just need to baste the roasties and then I'll be through to join you.'

Daisy grabbed her hand and pulled her down the hallway to the lounge where she found the sofa filled with dolls of all shapes, colours and sizes. They had long hair, short hair, red hair, brown hair and blonde hair. Some were wearing traditional dolly dresses while others were in dungarees and T-shirts. Perrie couldn't recall the last time she'd seen so many dolls in one place that wasn't a toy shop.

'Can you guess which one is my favourite, Merida?'

'Well, let me see…'

Perrie knew immediately which doll it was but pretended to mull them all over.

'Hmmm, could it be the Victorian doll with her blonde ringlets…' she murmured just loud enough for Daisy to hear. 'No, I don't think so.'

She picked up a ragdoll, with a floor-mop hair-do, and pretended to give it a close inspection. She could see Daisy hopping from foot to foot out of the corner of her eye.

'Nope, it's not you either,' she said, as the ragdoll was set back down.

'I have to say, Daisy, it's very difficult to guess but I think I'm going to choose… that one!'

Daisy let out a squeal.

'It is! It is! How did you know that?'

'Honestly? The astronaut outfit was a bit of a giveaway!'

The little girl giggled with delight as she hugged her doll to her chest. Just then, Morgan walked into the room and let out a groan when he saw the sofa.

'Oh, Daisy, I said to bring down a few… Come now, take them back up. Dinner will be ready soon and if you want some trifle afterwards, the sofa needs to be cleared first.'

'Okay, Daddy, I'll do it now even though Merida guessed that Martha is my favourite dolly. Do you know why she's called Martha, Merida?'

'No, I don't know.'

'Because Mars is a planet in the Solar System and Martha begins with M-A-R which is nearly Mars.'

'Wow, that is very clever. I can tell that you are going to be a wonderful astronaut when you grow up.'

This caused Daisy to chortle again and they could still hear her giggling as she clambered back up the stairs with her arms full of dolls.

'And wash your hands for dinner while you're up there!' Morgan called after her.

'Yes, Daddy.'

'You have a lovely way with her,' Morgan said, 'Not everyone gets to meet Martha – you're quite honoured.'

'Oh! I'll take that as a compliment.'

'It's meant as one. Thank you for the time you give her, it's nice for her to have adult female company that's not a grandparent.'

'I enjoy being with her, she's quite special.'

'How come you have such a relaxed way with kids? You don't have any, do you?'

Something must have crossed her face because Morgan immediately said, 'Oh, Perrie, I'm so sorry, that was an insensitive comment. Please, don't feel you need to answer.'

She took a drink of her wine and used the moment to push down the twisted sensation that had risen up at his question.

'I have two nephews, not much older than Daisy. I've had plenty of practice on child-speak with them. It's nice to have another little one to share it with.'

Morgan opened his mouth to reply but the ding of the timer on the oven had him close it again.

'I think that's a classic case of "saved by the bell". I have a horrible feeling I was about to say something which would have found me digging an even bigger hole to bury myself in.' He gave her a little wry smile before rushing off to investigate the state of his roast potatoes.

Saved by the bell indeed, Perrie thought to herself. The subject of children, or lack of them, really was somewhere she had no intention of going.

To take her mind off the conversation, she wandered over to the bookcase in the corner. The bottom shelves were filled with various children's books and she was elated to see them. She set great store by children enjoying books from a young age; as an avid reader herself, she knew only too well the delights contained between the covers. She looked up at the higher shelves – shelves which were crammed with books – and noted a large number of historical thrillers lined up. She couldn't help the small smile that crept across her lips when she saw them as she was rather inclined towards this genre herself.

Ten minutes later, they were all sitting around the table. As Morgan and Daisy argued over who should have the biggest roasties, Perrie sat back, sipped her wine and simply enjoyed the feeling of not being alone.

'D-a-a-a-a-d!'

'Shh, Daisy.'

'D-A-A-A-D!'

'Daisy, I asked you to shush while we're talking. You know it's rude to interrupt.'

'But, Dad...'

Morgan held his breath so as not to sigh in exasperation. Daisy's stage whispers, accompanied with eye-rolls and head twitching in Perrie's direction, couldn't have been any less subtle if she'd tried.

Perrie's eyes were glinting with amusement as she raised her eyebrows.

'I said after pudding, Daisy.'

'Well, it's nearly after pudding. You and Merida have finished yours and I'm almost finished mine.'

'Oh, very well then!'

'Can I do it? Pleeeeeeease...'

'Okay.'

Daisy put down her spoon, sat up straighter in her chair and took in a big breath before saying, 'Merida, would you like to come with me and Daddy to visit the Wild Gnome and Flower Serve next Satdays?'

Perrie glanced at him for help.

'I think you mean "The Gnome Reserve and Wildflower Garden", Daisy. Wild gnomes might not be quite to Perrie's liking.'

'Oh, I don't know, I think wild gnomes could be very interesting. Perhaps, your daddy could tell me more.'

Perrie flashed him a smile and he was surprised again by the warm sensation it generated within him. He took a drink of his wine to calm himself.

'The gnome reserve is a little place a few miles from here. It's a haven for gnomes who no longer have a garden of their own. It's really a woodland walk with gnomes dotted around. Some of them are a bit old and knackered, if I'm being honest, but through the eyes of a child, they're magical. Daisy loves it.'

'It sounds delightful and certainly something worth seeing.'

'Yay!' Daisy waved her arms above her head in glee. 'Daddy, I'm finished now, please may I play in the garden?'

'Sure. Go and change first.'

Morgan looked at Perrie as Daisy slid off her chair. The soft, caring expression on her face as she watched his daughter run from the room made his insides flutter again. He quickly picked up his wine glass when she turned back to him.

'So, now that Daisy's left the room, what is this place really like?'

'Actually, I don't know. I found out a few weeks back that it has been relocated to a local garden centre. The family who owned the original reserve have sold up and the new owners weren't keen on keeping the gnomes. Luckily, the garden centre stepped forward, offered to take them on and have created a whole new space for them.'

'I see. But you haven't told Daisy?'

'She doesn't always cope well with change. The Gnome Reserve was one of the last places she visited with Harriet before she died. Although Daisy can't remember the actual day out, she knows she went there with her mum, so I don't know how it'll go when she finds out.'

'And, let me guess, you're hoping that my being with you might be enough of a distraction for Daisy not to get too upset?'

'I'll be honest, the thought had crossed my mind. It was Daisy's idea to visit and to ask you to come along – I simply didn't dissuade her when she asked because I could see the benefits. I hope you don't mind.'

After a small pause, Perrie replied. 'No, you're fine. I'm sure it'll be a lovely day out and I am partial to a garden centre.'

'Thank you.'

He turned around and pulled the wine bottle from the chiller.

'Top up?'

'Oh, why not. I don't have to drive anywhere.'

When the glasses had been refilled, Morgan picked his up and after checking Daisy was okay out in the garden, he said, 'Why don't we go through to the lounge.'

Perrie sat in the chair by the fireplace and Morgan took up his usual spot on the sofa. He looked at her for a second before saying, 'You know, for all the time we seem to have spent in each other's company over the last month or so, I don't know anything about you. You know almost all there is to know about me yet you remain a mystery. I can't work out if I've simply been rude by not asking or if you've purposely avoided sharing.'

'I'm not big on talking about myself. I'm actually rather boring, if I'm being totally honest.'

'I don't believe that for a moment. So, what brought you to our little bay?'

'A desire for peace and solitude.'

Morgan burst out laughing. 'Oh, yeah? And how's that working out for you?'

Perrie laughed with him. 'I may need to recheck the definition of solitude – I think I've got it wrong!'

'May I ask what you do to pass the time when my daughter and I aren't forcing ourselves upon you?'

She took a sip of wine and he could almost hear her mind whirring as she debated whether or not to share more of herself with him.

'I do a lot of reading.'

'Oh, me too. What do you like?'

'I like to mix it up and try to read a broad spectrum of genres although I am partial to some romance and thrillers.'

'Do you like historical thrillers?'

'I have been known to read them.'

'Well, if you haven't already, I highly recommend you read J.P. Lassiter – his books are so good. Fantastic historical detail. I have the whole series if you want to borrow them although they are all hefty hardbacks as I can never wait for the paperbacks.'

'Thank you, that's a kind offer. I'll keep it in mind.'

'You're welcome. So, what else do you do when you're not reading?'

'Erm... I write.'

'Write?'

A faint blush touched her cheeks as she nodded.

'What do you write? Not novels...?'

She nodded again.

'Wow! That's amazing. Now I'm in awe!'

'Oh, please, don't...'

'No, seriously, that's such a great gift to have. What genre do you write in? Maybe I've read some of your work.'

'I write historical thrillers and... I think you may have done...'

She gave a discrete nod towards the bookcase.

Morgan looked at the bookcase, then at Perrie and then back at the bookcase. It took a moment but the penny finally dropped.

'NO WAY!'

She smiled, gave a little shrug and sipped her wine, clearly waiting for him to get his head around this revelation.

'Seriously? Are you J.P. Lassiter?'

'Guilty as charged, I'm afraid.'

'But… you're famous!'

'I try not to be.'

'Why? Why would you keep it a secret?'

'I'm not interested in being famous. I don't want to be mobbed by people when I'm in the supermarket or sitting in a cathedral somewhere trying to do research.'

'I feel a right idiot now.'

'Why?'

'For banging on the way I did.'

'Please, don't. It's wonderful to hear that you enjoy my work so much. And recommending it? Biggest compliment you can give an author. So, thank you.'

Morgan let out a chuckle. 'I'm guessing you won't be wanting to borrow any then?'

'No point, I already know how they end!'

This caused more laughter but when it ceased, Perrie gave him a very direct look.

'I'd be grateful if you kept this information to yourself, especially around the town. I… I couldn't bear to have people pointing and whispering.'

'Your secret is totally safe. If anyone asks, I will give a very vague response that you do research or something.'

'Thank you.'

'No problem. Now, I do need to ask one question… when's the next book out and what happens to the young Prince that was rescued?'

SIXTEEN

'Damn! Shitting, shitting damn and shit!'

Perrie was pacing and limping up and down her kitchen. She'd only been pacing until she'd kicked the table leg in frustration. Her soft trainers had been no match for the solid wood and her bruised toes were now throbbing painfully.

She glanced at the mobile phone sitting on the kitchen worktop, the unread message staring back at her. She'd seen the first line and had already guessed what the rest of it said.

It was Morgan confirming the time to meet on Saturday.

Whilst bathed in the warm, rosy hue of a cosy family dinner and feeling relaxed after good food and nice wine, she'd given no thought to the consequences of her actions when she'd accepted Daisy's invitation to visit the gnomes.

In the cold light of day on the Monday morning, however, it had been a different story and she'd been mentally, along with verbally, berating herself since.

She let out a huge sigh, stopped pacing long enough to pick up the phone, look at the screen and chuck it back on the worktop again.

The pacing resumed as her thoughts ran in all directions around her head.

She'd come to Broatiescombe Bay to get away from everything around her. She'd wanted complete isolation but her older sister, Aggie, had been adamant that the dilapidated cottage on a remote Scottish island wasn't an option. Aggie hadn't wanted her to go anywhere, not after all that had happened, but Perrie was insistent. Seaview Cottage had been the compromise as they'd been to Broatiescombe Bay a couple of times when they were children on family holidays and the cottage was close enough to civilisation should anything go wrong but enough outside of the town to give her the privacy and solitude she craved.

Well, as Morgan had said, how was that working out?

In a nutshell, it hadn't!

Without any desire or intention, she'd somehow found herself becoming attached to the delightful Daisy and her father. Where some people were disagreeable enough to tell folks to bugger off without hesitation, Perrie wasn't like that. Her kind, generous nature had been both a blessing and her undoing. Maybe if she'd been a bit more hard-faced, her life wouldn't be in the mess it was now.

Her phone pinged again. She stopped pacing and saw it was a second message from Morgan. She knew he was confirming the time for their trip, two days from now. She knew one of the messages would be telling her how much Daisy was looking forward to it.

She also knew that no matter how she was feeling right now, she couldn't let Daisy down.

If she was being downright honest with herself, she'd loved the normality of the lunch on Sunday. She loved the normality that she felt whenever she was with Morgan and Daisy. Her life hadn't been normal in over a year – in fact, it was even longer now that she thought about it, and now she craved it. She wanted more and even though she knew it couldn't possibly last, she found herself sending a reply to Morgan, agreeing to the 10 a.m. start he'd proposed.

To hell with it, she thought. Her life was going to implode again in the not-too-distant future, she might as well grab the few days of happiness that she could get.

SEVENTEEN

'Daisy seems to have taken the news okay. What do you think?'

Morgan looked at the smile on his daughter's face as she skipped along the path, exclaiming with delight when she found another gnome.

'I think we've dodged a bullet there. I could tell from her face, when I told her the gnomes had moved location, that it had upset her. If you hadn't been there, I think we could have had a meltdown moment. Thank you.'

'I didn't really do anything.'

'Oh, but you did, by explaining that as humans often move house, sometimes with great regularity, then why shouldn't gnomes. Your story-telling skills, and the tale you created of the gnomes loading up their barrows in the middle of the night to sneak away to this new place, was ingenious and took her mind away in a different direction. I'll be honest, you had me enthralled with the adventures the gnomes got up to on their travels. I think you could do a side-line in children's stories – you'd be awesome. How do you do that?'

'Honestly? I just get pictures in my head, like a little film reel, and I put them into words. I had a vision of the gnomes performing a moonlight flit and I simply embellished it to keep Daisy amused.'

Before he could reply, Daisy let out a squeal and came running back towards them.

'Merida, Merida, come see. They have a gnome with hair like yours.'

Daisy grabbed Perrie's hand and dragged her along the path, leaving Morgan to amble along behind.

He took his time, strolling slowly along, watching Perrie as she interacted with his daughter. She was so sweet and kind to Daisy and he knew it was genuine. His involvement, which had been short-lived, with a woman late last year was his comparison. Elspeth had made out she liked Daisy, on the couple of occasions they'd met in the shop, but it had always felt forced to him. Seeing Perrie with her now proved that he'd been right.

A gust of wind blew across the path and caught Perrie's curls, dragging them across her face. Morgan was happy to admit that when he'd opened the door to her this morning, and set eyes on the explosion of loose, vibrant, red curls around her face and shoulders, his breath had caught in his throat. She so rarely wore her hair down like that and it was a sight worth seeing. Daisy had been ecstatic to have her own full-blown Merida for the day. The long, ankle-length floaty skirt had only added to the illusion.

An older couple came towards them on the path. Perrie and Daisy stepped to the side to let them pass. As they walked by him, the man smiled and said, in a lilting Irish accent, 'Sure, it's a lovely wee family ye have there, son. Cherish the moment; they grow up and are away far too soon.'

Morgan returned the smiles. 'Thank you, sir, I

already do.'

He turned back to see Perrie bending down, pointing something out to Daisy and they were both rocking with laughter. He quickly pulled his phone from his pocket and took a photograph, capturing the moment for ever.

He slipped the phone away as he hurried to catch them up, desperate to share their joy. Daisy was clearly enjoying Perrie becoming a part of their lives and if the feelings he experienced when she was around were anything to go by, she wasn't the only one.

'Merida, do you think Timothy would like the red ball or the yellow one?'

Daisy held up the two cat toys for her inspection.

'I think he'd like the yellow one and do you know why?'

Daisy shook her head.

'Well, scientists have found out that cats don't see as much colour as humans can but it's believed they can see shades of yellow and so they could be attracted to it.'

'But cats can see in the dark. I know because we read a story at playgroup and the cat could see when humans couldn't.'

'That's right. What they can't see in colours, they make up for in other ways.'

'I think I'll get the yellow ball for Timothy.'

'And I will get the red flashing one for George so he doesn't feel left out.'

Daisy took her hand as they walked over to the till.

'Merida, I do like George too but Timothy is my favourite because he lets me lie beside him. George doesn't do that.'

'I know what you mean. Even though they're brothers, they have very different personalities. George is a wild hairy whirlwind who only seems to stop for food and sleep whereas Timothy is gentler and more relaxed.'

'Do you think they'll like their new toys?'

'I'm sure they will.'

She smiled at the assistant as he passed Daisy her little paper carrier bag and she popped it on her arm, clearly feeling all important at being tasked to carry the toys.

'Come, let's go and find your daddy.'

They found Morgan by the jigsaw puzzles. Daisy ran over and he swung her up in his arms.

'Daddy, we got new toys for George and Timothy. See...' Daisy waved her bag in the air.

'That's nice. I'm sure they'll really like them.'

'Are we going home now, Daddy? I'm hungry.'

'If we're all done here?' Morgan turned to Perrie with a raised eyebrow.

She smiled. 'I'm done if everyone else is.'

'Then let's go.' He placed Daisy back on her feet and they made their way out to the car park.

Once on the road home, Perrie turned to Morgan and whispered quietly, 'I've a Bolognese sauce marinating in the fridge. Why don't you and Daisy come over for dinner?'

'Why are you whispering?' Morgan whispered back at her.

She smiled at him. 'Because I didn't want little ears to overhear and put you on the spot as we both know her answer would be in the affirmative!'

'Daisy, Perrie has invited us to dinner... again!' He threw her a bemused look before glancing in the rearview mirror to look at Daisy. 'It's pasta with Bolognese sauce

– would you like to go?'

'Oh, yes please! I love Bognese pasta.' Daisy bounced up and down in her child seat. She waved the paper bag she was still holding. 'I can give Timothy his new toy.'

They soon arrived back in Broatie and were making their way from the car when Morgan said, 'Perrie, are you okay to take Daisy straight to yours? I just want to pop home and pick up some wine as my contribution to the meal.'

'There's no need for that, I've got wine in.'

'I'd like to bring something. The ratio of meals provided is falling far too heavily on your side right now. Please.'

She looked at him, understanding the need he felt to be "doing his bit". She'd been there herself. She got it.

'That would be lovely. Thank you.'

'Red or white?'

'I really don't mind.'

She gave him a smile and held her hand out for Daisy.

'Here, Daisy, are you okay to come with me while your daddy pops home for a few minutes?'

When the little girl placed her hand within hers without any thought or hesitation, Perrie felt a stirring warmth flow through her. There was no doubt about it, she was totally falling in love with this little bundle of blonde delight.

She nodded to Morgan as he walked off in the opposite direction. How she felt about him, on the other hand, was something she hadn't yet fathomed.

EIGHTEEN

'Daisy, you've got a blob of sauce on your nose!'

Morgan and Perrie laughed as Daisy's tongue came out to try and lick away the offending item.

Morgan rolled his eyes as he replied, 'My daughter… classy to the last!'

He looked over at Perrie sitting opposite and was happy to see her eyes shining with laughter as she watched Daisy's antics. Quite often, when she was unaware that he was looking at her, he saw sadness in her eyes. It would leave as soon as she caught his eye but in unguarded moments, it seemed to him as though she was carrying some heavy burden. Her shoulders would sag and her face had a bleakness about it that twisted his insides.

He longed to ask what was troubling her so much but didn't want to intrude upon her privacy. From his own experiences after Harriet's death, he knew how frustrating and downright annoying it could be when people, thinking they were being kind, would constantly ask him how he was feeling, how he was doing and say if he ever wanted to talk… Oh, those last six words… how he'd hated them. And still did! The last thing he'd wanted to do was talk. The words that could even go halfway to explaining the depth of the cold, numb pain that had consumed his very being had not yet been invented. He'd always understood that Daisy had been the only thing to keep him sane. Harriet had been insistent that he must put her first after she'd left them both to walk the path of life without her. She'd known him well, sometimes too well, and the promise she'd extracted from him had been painfully given. It wasn't that he didn't want to care for their daughter, it was simply that without Harriet, he didn't want to live.

If he had ever said that aloud, in the weeks and months after she'd gone, to any of the well-wishers who'd said "if you ever want to talk", he'd most likely have been locked up and Daisy taken from him.

No, he understood all too well the need to keep your pain locked up inside but how he wished he could help. Perrie was lovely – it seemed so wrong that she should be suffering alone.

Just then, Daisy let out the biggest and noisiest of yawns. He looked at his watch – almost seven o'clock. No wonder she was tired; it had been a long day for her and all the fresh air was now taking its toll.

'I think it's time a little lady went home to her bed.' He gave her a gentle smile as he placed his napkin on the table and stood.

'Aww, Daddy, do I have to?'

'Yes, darling. It's nearly your bedtime and you've had a busy day.'

'What will you do once she's asleep?'

Morgan looked at Perrie in surprise. 'Err, probably tidy up a bit, watch some telly…'

'Why don't you go and get Daisy's jammies and

night-stuff and she can sleep in the spare room. She can have a sleepover and I'll bring her back to you in the morning. That way, you can stay a while longer.'

'Oh!'

Perrie gave him a smile. 'When my sister, Aggie, was a single mum with her eldest boy, the one thing she found the hardest was being alone after he went to bed. She used to say that Friday and Saturday nights were the worst, that was when the loneliness bit the hardest. So, I understand the "tidy up and watch some telly". I'm sure Daisy would love to sleep here with Timothy beside her and you get to be "Morgan" for a few hours rather than just "Daddy". We can chuck on a movie, open that other bottle of wine you brought over and just chill out. What do you say?'

Morgan stared at Perrie and learnt a valuable lesson – never underestimate the intuition of women.

'I say thank you so much. That sounds amazing.'

'Then off you pop – don't forget a change of clothing for Daisy in the morning. We'll go up and get the bedroom ready for her.'

Morgan grabbed his jacket and as he was heading out the door, he looked back to see Perrie gently wiping Daisy's face and explaining to her that she was staying the night. When Daisy threw her arms around Perrie's neck and hugged her close, a tight lump formed in his throat and he was wiping his eyes as he walked up the path.

'Oh, I needed that! I can't remember the last time I laughed so hard. My sides really are aching.'

Perrie looked over at Morgan, stretched out on the sofa, rubbing his side with one hand while discretely blowing his nose with the other. They'd found an old Norman Wisdom film about to start on one of the many TV channels and had spent the next hour and a half laughing furiously at the little man's antics.

'I'd forgotten just how funny he could be.'

'My dad is a massive fan. Watching a Norman Wisdom film in our house was always a big deal. Dad would rearrange the furniture to make it feel like we were at the movies. Beanbags were placed in front of the sofa and I sat there with Aggie and my brother Marcus. Mum and Dad sat behind us. We'd have glasses of fizzy juice with straws, hot dogs and popcorn.'

'Are your parents still alive?'

She smiled. 'Oh, yes, thankfully, although they now live in Spain meaning I don't see them as often as I would like. Dad developed arthritis and they decided to move to the warmer climate for the benefit of his health. They absolutely love it – they've thrown themselves right into the community and it is now very much their home.'

'You've never felt the desire to join them?'

'No, I haven't, although I wouldn't rule it out in the future. Mind you, they might not want me there. I think my presence might put a little downer on their partying.' She grinned at the thought.

'So, they're pretty outgoing folks?'

'Absolutely! We constantly had people visiting our house. The door was always open and anyone who happened to be around at meal times would find themselves being fed, regardless of their plans.'

'Well, that explains a lot.'

'What does?'

'Why you're always feeding Daisy and me – it's what you grew up with. Your mum sounds like one of life's nurturers and I suspect you are the same.'

'Hmm, maybe...'

'No, definitely. I've watched you with Daisy. You have nurturing tendencies running right through you. Have you ever wanted children?'

The question came at her like a bolt from the blue and hit her right in the chest. She sucked in a deep breath and tried to calm the sudden pounding of her heart.

'Uhm, erm...'

She couldn't speak. Hell, she could hardly breathe. Her chest felt tight, like she'd been winded. The twist in the conversation had been too sudden and she wasn't prepared. She gasped as she placed her hand on her chest bone and rubbed it, bending forward to try and ease the tightened muscles.

'Oh, my goodness, Perrie, are you okay?'

Morgan was by her side, his face twisted with concern.

'Back,' she managed to squeak, 'rub it...'

She felt his hand between her shoulder blades and it began to move in firm, but gentle, circles. Soon, the spasm passed and her breathing slowly began to return to normal. She sat up and gave him a watery smile.

'I'm so sorry about that—'

'No, Perrie, I'm sorry. I didn't think. I just jumped in and asked my question without any consideration.'

'It's... it's...' She shrugged.

'Look, you don't have to say a word. My question was clearly a painful one. I'm sorry.'

'I... can't...'

'Hush, say no more.' Morgan took her hand between his and clasped it to his chest. 'Perrie, I know you have things going on that you don't share, I've seen you when you think no one is looking, but my ears are yours should you ever need them.'

She looked at the kind man kneeling on the floor by her side. From nowhere, she began to giggle.

'What?'

His bemused look made her giggle even more.

'Perrie?'

By this time, the giggles had turned into full-blown laughter.

'Ears... four ears... look a bit stupid with... four ears...' she hiccupped, in between the tears running down her face and the snot sliding down her nose.

She saw it slowly dawn on Morgan what had set her off and he began to smile too.

'Well, you could put them under your chin, there's a bit of space there.'

This caused her laughter to bubble up again.

'Or on your forehead – they'd keep the rain out of your eyes.'

'You'd need to make sure they were the right way round otherwise they'd get full of water. I hate that sensation after you've been swimming.'

'Good point. What about the back of your head? Then you can hear people talking behind your back.'

This made her laughter die away.

'Hmm, I think I'd rather not know, to be honest.'

'Yeah, perhaps not.'

Morgan moved back over to the sofa and slipped his feet into the trainers he'd pulled off earlier.

'Are you okay now?'

She noticed the laughter had also left his voice and a serious tone had replaced it.

'Yes, I'm fine, thank you.'

'Are you sure?'

'Yes, honest.'

'Okay. Well, I'd better get myself home. I'll come and pick up Daisy in the morning, just text me when she's ready.'

'I can drop her back, it's no problem. You enjoy having a long lie in – I'm betting they're few and far between.'

He gave her a wry grin. 'You can say that again. If you're sure it's not too much trouble?'

'It really isn't.'

'Then I suggest you come for breakfast. I do a pretty mean fry-up...' His hopeful look was all she needed.

'Oh, you do, do you? In that case, how could I possibly refuse!'

Morgan stood and they made their way out to the hallway. As he was pulling on his jacket, he said, 'You know, we're going to my mums for dinner tomorrow, why don't you come with us? I know she'd love to meet you properly – Daisy talks about you rather a lot.'

Perrie glanced down at the floor before replying.

'Thank you for asking but I'm afraid I can't.'

'No problem but if you change your mind, you'd be very welcome.'

She gave him a small smile but didn't reply.

'Thank you again for dinner, for taking such good care of Daisy and for a lovely relaxing evening. I'm sorry I messed it up at the end.'

'Morgan,' she placed her hand lightly on his arm, 'you didn't mess anything up. I've enjoyed you being here and I hope you feel you've had a small break from being "Daddy".'

'I have.'

She watched as he shuffled awkwardly from foot to foot.

'Right, I'd better get going then.'

He leant forward and placed a soft kiss on her cheek.

'Thank you for everything today. I'll see you in the morning.'

'Goodnight, Morgan. Thank you for letting me be a part of your day.'

She stood in the porch until he shut the gate behind him. With a final wave, she closed the door and locked it. Her fingers found their way to the spot on her face where his lips had kissed her. The tingling sensation she'd experienced had lingered and she really didn't want to face what that could possibly mean.

NINETEEN

'Oh, bloody hell!'

Perrie looked down in dismay at the pool of milk rapidly growing around her feet. Sod's law meant the bottle had landed with the spout closest to the floor therefore giving a clear run for the contents to flow out.

'Why do they have to put the seal on so bloody tight?'

She bent down to grab the bottle, slipped and landed on her butt next to the now almost-empty plastic container.

In despair, she pulled her knees up to her chest and rested her forehead against them. The cold, wet liquid was seeping through her dressing gown and pyjamas but she didn't care. She was so tired and her body felt exhausted.

Since waving goodbye to Morgan on Saturday night, she'd been in complete turmoil. On Sunday, instead of staying for breakfast as had been planned, she'd dropped Daisy back home then made a speedy exit while making the excuse that she'd suddenly had a flash of inspiration and must get it written down immediately. Morgan had made noises of understanding as she'd legged it from his door.

Sadly, the truth was less inspiring – she'd woken up to the realisation that she *was* growing too close to Daisy and Morgan and she needed to step back. She was beginning to care far too deeply for them and she couldn't allow that to happen. In the long run, she'd end up hurting them and that was the last thing she wanted to do. Unfortunately, her heart wasn't taking on board the sense her head was advising. Where her heart was concerned, it was already too late – she could no more stop caring about Daisy and Morgan than she could stop breathing.

The inner fighting between head and heart had seen her tossing and turning for the last three nights and sleep had been near-on impossible. She'd buried herself in her work and had kept herself going by consuming vast amounts of coffee. The caffeine was most likely contributing to her inability to sleep which was why she'd decided to have a latte – the intention being minimal coffee and high on the "latte" element of the drink.

Perrie sat where she was for another moment before letting out a grunt and pulling herself up with the aid of the worktop.

'Crying over spilt milk, quite literally, ain't gonna get me anywhere!' she muttered, as she picked up the roll of kitchen towel and began laying it over the puddle which surrounded her. She then stripped off her nightclothes, chucked them in the washing machine and proceeded to wash the kitchen floor in nothing but her birthday suit, grateful again for the isolated location of the cottage.

She made it into the shower without any further incident, which was a surprise as she wouldn't have been at all shocked if the postman had arrived and knocked on her door. She was anticipating it turning into one of those days.

She showered and dressed and after checking the fridge to see if another bottle of milk was miraculously hiding in there, even though she knew there wasn't, Perrie picked up her handbag to go and buy some more. Maybe a walk down to the mini-mart on the seafront would help to clear her head. She'd been cooped up in the cottage since Sunday morning – a few blasts of sea air might give her weary body and soul a lift.

The sun was shining brightly as she made her way down the hill. June had arrived and the chilly wind had moved over to make way for a softer, warmer breeze. It lightly lifted the curls around her face as she arrived on the main street through the town although Perrie was so deep in her thoughts, she barely noticed. The arrival of summer was welcomed by most and normally she'd have been among them but this year, she was dreading it as her future grew bleaker with each passing day.

'OOMPH!'

Lost in her distracted thoughts, Perrie had barrelled right into someone and almost knocked them to the ground. A reflex action saw her grab an arm tightly and when she saw who she was gripping, she almost let out a moan. She'd been right to think this was going to be a crap day.

'Hey, hi there, Perrie, how are you doing?'

'Hi Babs, are you okay? Sorry I bumped into you – head in the clouds… wasn't paying attention.'

'I'm fine, I'm fine. I'm to blame too – standing out here right in the middle of the street, getting in everyone's way. I was checking how my window display looked from out here. What do you think of that beauty?'

Babs pointed to the art gallery window which now featured a gloriously vibrant picture of the sun setting across the sea. It was a large piece, taking up a big portion of the window space, and it screamed at you to come closer and let your mind be carried away by the magnificence of the view in front of you. The smaller pictures Babs had placed alongside it only served to complement it and it them.

'Wow! That is something else! It's breath-taking.'

'Isn't it just? I can't see it hanging around for long so make the most of it while you can.'

'Is it a local artist?'

'Yes, she is. Not Broatie born-and-bred, but she's a part of us now.'

'She's really talented.'

'She is. So, where are you off to while so deep in thought?'

'The mini-mart. I decided that today was the day I should throw two litres of milk all over the kitchen floor and then fall over and bathe in it for good measure.'

'Should I rename you Cleopatra?'

This caused Perrie to laugh. 'I believe she preferred donkey milk or something like that. I don't know if Bluebell the cow's would have the same effect.'

'Come in for a cuppa. I'm about to make one for myself, why not join me?'

'Oh, I wouldn't want to trouble you—'

'You're not. Like I said, I'm making one for myself. Lugging those paintings around is thirsty work. Besides, *Cleo*,' Babs nudged her side with a sharp elbow, 'I'm guessing you've not had a cuppa yet this morning since you threw your cow juice around the kitchen.'

Laughter flew out of Perrie again at Babs' words.

'You would be correct there. Okay, thank you, a cup of something hot would be nice.'

Ten minutes later, the two women were sitting on the small sofa in the little viewing room. Babs had dimmed the lighting, making it feel quite cosy and relaxing.

'You didn't call me after Daisy's party...'

Perrie took a sip of her green tea with lemon as she tried to think of what excuse she could give. Before she could reply, however, Babs carried on.

'It's okay, I'm not mad or upset or anything like that. I just picked up a vibe that made me think we'd probably get on quite well.'

'I'm sorry. I've been busy with work—'

Babs put her mug down on the coffee table in front of them and took Perrie's hand.

'Hey, I said it's okay. I... I...'

Suddenly, she took Perrie's mug from her, placed it on the table and grabbed both of her hands, holding them tightly within her own.

'What the hell—'

Perrie tried to pull her hands away but Babs was holding them too tightly.

'Oh, Perrie, the darkness around you... so dark, so very dark. Your pain... how do you cope? This is a heavy burden you carry but... I can see hope. The journey is coming to an end, soon you will be free. But wait, I can see a light in your darkness... golden light. The light of a child who gives your heart respite. She is a golden child. She will be your future happiness—'

'STOP! WHAT ARE YOU DOING?'

'Eh? Why... wha—'

Babs blinked rapidly, staring at Perrie as a look of shock came over her face.

'Perrie! I am *SO* sorry! I don't know how that happened. I can see... stuff, if you know what I mean. I would never give a reading without permission but when I touched your hand, everything you're dealing with right now flowed into me. I can feel the... the... torment, yes, that's the best word, torment you have inside you.'

Babs stared hard into her eyes. Perrie felt as though she was probing into the deepest part of her soul.

'THAT'S why you didn't phone me, you don't think you're good enough. Bad things have surrounded you and you keep away so as not to cause pain to others.'

Perrie yanked her hands from Babs' grasp.

'Enough! Say no more. Please…'

'Oh, Perrie, don't shut yourself off, let others help you.'

'No, it's not possible.'

'It is. If you let it.'

Perrie stood up, picked up her handbag and put it over her shoulder.

'Thank you for the tea.'

She walked over to the door and as she was opening it, Babs called over to her.

'Perrie, when you need me, I'll be here. When you're ready to talk.'

'I can't.'

'Yes, you can.'

'No, Babs, I really can't.'

With that, she slammed the door behind her and rushed off back up the hill. When she got home to the cottage, she saw the post had arrived. A heavy feeling of dread filled her heart upon seeing a corner of a brown envelope peeking out from between the junk mail which still arrived for the previous occupant.

She pulled it out to check the recipient's name before dropping everything else on the hall table and staggering into the lounge where she sat down heavily on the edge of the sofa. She stared at the envelope for an age before ripping it open, unfolding the letter within and reading what it had to say.

She read it three times, allowing the words to sink in, before letting it slip from her fingers and drift down to the floor.

Well, Perrie thought, Babs had almost got it right –
the journey was coming to an end although she'd never
be free from the darkness.

She pulled her mobile phone from her pocket and
sent a five-word text to her sister.

Court date has been set.

TWENTY

Morgan leant against the dry-stone wall which ran along the grassland opposite Seaview Cottage and looked over at the blank unseeing windows with the curtains drawn in every room. It had been ten days since Perrie had bailed on their Sunday breakfast and he hadn't seen or heard from her since. The presence of her Range Rover in the car park told him she was still in town.

He'd tried to call but each time it had gone straight through to her voicemail; his texts read undelivered. He kept replaying that last evening together, picking it apart to see what he'd said or done to make her pull away from him so suddenly. Okay, he acknowledged his comment over her desire to have children hadn't been his finest moment but he thought they'd moved past it and it had been resolved. Was he wrong? Had it hurt more deeply than he'd realised, causing Perrie to feel she had to put some distance between them? If so, he had to find a way to put it right but he could only do that if she would speak to him.

To make matters worse, he wasn't the only one to

notice her absence. Daisy was now asking on an almost daily basis where her Merida was and why hadn't she seen her for so many sleeps. His daughter had still to learn the finer points of time and so the passing of days was measured in how many nights of sleep she'd had.

Whether intended or not, Perrie had slipped quietly into their lives, had become a part of them and they were both feeling her absence keenly.

The wind rustled the plastic bag lying on the grass at his feet. He glanced down and hoped that its contents would provide him with the "good reason" he felt he needed to go knocking on her door. He could only hope...

He picked the bag up and walked towards the garden gate, his long legs clearing the distance with just a mere handful of steps. Morgan made sure the gate was firmly closed behind him – Perrie had previously mentioned that George occasionally liked to try and make an unexpected bid for freedom – and made his way to the front door. He hesitated for a few seconds before knocking, trying to hear any sounds from within but he was met with silence. He let the doorknocker fall gently and waited.

A minute later, he was still waiting. He put his ear to the door and listened but could hear nothing. He let the knocker fall again, a little more forcefully this time, but still no one answered.

By now, he was beginning to worry. Maybe Perrie had had an accident. Maybe she hadn't been avoiding him but was lying injured at the bottom of the stairs...

He bent down to look through the letterbox but couldn't see anything for the door curtain had been pulled across. He hammered the door again, calling out her name at the same time, and was beginning to consider calling Sue at the bakery to bring the spare key, when he heard a scraping noise which he quickly realised was the curtain on the other side of the door being pulled back. He waited while the bolts were pushed open and the key turned until, eventually, a small crack appeared and Perrie's aquamarine right eye was glaring at him.

'Morgan, how can I help you?'

Her voice was dry and raspy, sounding almost as though she hadn't used it for a while.

'May I come in?'

Morgan kept his voice gentle. He didn't know what had happened and wasn't sure what to do but he knew from past experiences with Daisy, when she was upset, that a gentle approach got him better results.

The blaze of aquamarine disappeared behind an eyelid. There was the sound of a small sigh before the door was eased open just enough for him to squeeze through. When it was closed again, Perrie turned to face him and Morgan had to work hard at not letting the shock of her appearance escape from his mouth.

Her beautiful red hair was hanging limply around her shoulders, looking unbrushed and unwashed. The shadows under her eyes were so dark they could be seen clearly in the muted light of the hallway and her cheekbones stuck out sharply, indicating that she'd lost weight, yet with her slim build, there hadn't been much for her to lose in the first place.

'Bloody hell, Perrie, you look awful!'

'Thanks, Morgan. When are you starting your new job in the Diplomacy Corp?'

'Shit! Sorry! I didn't mean it like that. Have you been ill?'

She didn't answer but instead turned and walked through into the kitchen. Morgan followed behind, mentally berating himself for his stupidity.

'Would you like a tea or a coffee?'

He walked over and took the kettle from her hands.

'*I'll* make the drinks – you go and sit down.'

The fact there was no argument over this told him how out of sorts she was.

He turned back to fill the kettle and discretely took in the debris around him. This was the first time he'd been in her kitchen when it wasn't immaculate. The breadboard lay to one side, covered in crumbs which had spilled over onto the worktop. Several butter-covered knives lay alongside the sink beside a small pile of side plates. When he opened the cupboard to get out some mugs, he found it empty and had to wash two from the number littered around the room. He gathered them all up and placed them in the dishwasher, adding the knives and the plates. He wiped down the worktop and when emptying the crumbs into the bin, took a quick look at the contents. The only items he could see were cat food tins. The lack of any ready-meal containers in there, or dirty pots by the sink, suggested that, unless Perrie had taken up eating cat food, the only thing she'd been consuming was toast.

No wonder she was skin and bone!

Even though he knew she wasn't keen, Morgan put some extra milk in her coffee. As he sniffed the contents of the long-life carton, he wondered just how long she'd been ill for if she'd resorted to using her emergency rations.

He placed the mug in front of her and sat down opposite.

'Right, young lady, would you like to explain what has been going on?'

He made sure he maintained a light tone, exactly like he did with Daisy.

'Oh, it's nothing, I've been poorly – I think maybe a dose of the flu or something. Believe it or not, I'm beginning to feel better. This is the first day I've been properly out of bed.'

'You should have called me.'

'I didn't want to bother you – you've got enough to deal with.'

'Not enough that I couldn't come to help a friend who was ill.'

Perrie didn't reply and just gave a small shrug.

'I've been trying to call you and have sent numerous text messages…'

'I don't know where my phone is and I guess by now the battery will have died so trying to call it will be a waste of time.'

'Well, that'll explain why I kept getting your voicemail.'

'I guess so.'

'What about the cats, do you need any help with them?'

Perrie let out a small, sharp, laugh. 'Morgan, I would need to be six feet under before I can't look after them. That's where I was when you arrived – bringing them in from the run.'

'So, you won't look after yourself but you'll do everything to look after them.'

'Pretty much.'

The fact she looked so sheepish as she said this was what stopped Morgan spewing forth a litany of expletives across the table.

'So, what do you need?'

'I'm sorry?'

'What do you need? You're out of proper milk, so I'll pop down to the mart and get you some. I'm guessing you'll want some more bread, what else?'

'No, I'm fine, Morgan, honestly. I can go down tomorrow.'

'Perrie, that hill out there is a killer when you're well

and healthy; there's no way you'll make it back up in your current state.'

'About that position with the Diplomacy Corps...'

Morgan grinned. This time, he wasn't about to apologise.

'I'm saying it as it is because you're being too damn stubborn about accepting my help. When was the last time you ate a proper meal?'

'I can't recall but I think perhaps the night you and Daisy were here.'

'Perrie! That's almost two weeks ago!' No wonder, he thought, she'd dropped so much weight if she'd been eating nothing but toast since then.

'I've not been hungry.'

'Right, well, you can't eat a proper meal straight away so it'll need to be something simple and light. When I was a kid, my mum always gave me tomato soup and cheese sandwiches as a first meal whenever I'd been poorly – how does that sound?'

'Actually,' she gave him a small grin, 'really rather nice.'

'Good. Well, you take yourself into the lounge, rest up on the sofa while I go and do a bit of shopping. I'll probably be about twenty minutes or so.'

'But, what about Daisy?'

'Don't you worry about her, she's with my mum.'

He picked up the mugs and took them over to the dishwasher. After placing them inside, he turned back to her.

'She's missed you, you know. We both have.'

When Perrie didn't reply, he squeezed her shoulder gently.

'Right, I won't be gone long. Are you okay with me leaving the door on the latch while I'm out?'

'Yes, that's fine.'

'See you shortly.'

As he hurried up the path and through the gate, Morgan felt the weight of his earlier worry drop away. He hadn't done anything wrong after all. Perrie had merely been ill and while *that* concerned him, along with the fact she hadn't felt she could ask him for help, whatever was developing between them was still there.

This thought made him smile and he quickened his steps, rushing to get her what she needed to begin her return to good health.

TWENTY-ONE

Perrie listened to the door close gently behind Morgan.
Her head bowed down, her chin rested on her chest, and
she closed her eyes tightly, trying to hold the tears at bay.
She'd thought she was all cried out by now but apparently
not. The kindness of this lovely man had tears threatening
to spill out again.

With a groan and a sigh, she heaved herself off the
kitchen chair and went over to the cupboard where the cat
food lived. The only lie she hadn't told Morgan was the
one regarding the welfare of the fur-boys. She spooned
their food into their bowls and put it down, leaving them
to scoff while she went into the lounge.

A solitary sunbeam had made its way through a
small chink in the curtains and she walked over to shut it
out. Between the lack of sleep and the crying, her eyes
were now sensitive and the bright sunlight outside was
too painful.

Perrie glanced around the lounge, making sure there
was nothing lying about which would give away the
cause of her distress. She knew the dreaded letter lay

upstairs on her bedside table and there was zero chance of Morgan seeing it but erring on the side of caution, she went up to put it away in a drawer.

She stood for a moment and read it again – she'd lost count now of how many times she'd taken in the words in front of her but they never changed, no matter how much she wished that they would.

The walk back downstairs brought the weight of her guilt upon her with every step. She'd lied to Morgan and hated herself for doing so.

She hadn't had the flu; she had stupidly made herself ill. Even though she'd known the letter would arrive one day, it was still a shock when it had. She hadn't been prepared for it. As the days passed by without news, she'd lulled herself into a false sense of security. Yes, she had tried to put some distance between herself and the little Daniels family but deep down inside, a part of her had hoped that maybe everything would just go away and she could begin a new life which had Morgan and Daisy at the centre of it.

The brown, C5, envelope had taken that hope away.

Once the text to Aggie had been sent, she'd broken down on the sofa, sobbing over all that had been lost and would be lost again.

After a time, she'd dragged herself through to the kitchen, fed the cats and then crawled upstairs to bed where she'd had yet another restless night. Most of it had been spent tossing and turning but on the few occasions where she did manage to nod off, her dreams had become nightmares and it was her crying out which woke her up.

This had become the pattern for the days and nights which had followed. She'd forced herself to eat but a slice of toast here and there wasn't enough although she had absolutely no appetite for even that.

The stress and panic of what was coming had

tormented her day and night, causing her to spiral ever downwards and it was only knowing her beloved cats needed her that had kept her going and prevented her doing something from which there would be no way back.

As she sat on the sofa, waiting for Morgan to return, a thought came to her. She still had several weeks of her life as it was now, so why not make the most of them. Why should she deprive herself of the temporary happiness they could give her? Everything was going to change soon enough, of that there was no question, but would it really be so bad to pack in some nice memories before it did?

A small feeling of peace sparked up inside her. People were going to be hurt if she walked away now or in six weeks' time so what did it matter? After all, what was that old saying…

"Might as well be hung for a sheep as a lamb!"

When Morgan walked back in the door a short while later, Perrie was sitting in the kitchen, towelling her hair dry. After coming to terms with the decision she'd made, she realised what a hideous state she was in and that included not having showered or bathed since goodness only knew when. This had resulted in her dragging herself up the stairs as fast as she was able and having a quick but thorough scrub down in the shower.

As she sat now, exhausted but in clean clothes and smelling fresh, Perrie understood again just how restorative a shower can be and the smile she flashed at Morgan as he placed two shopping bags on the table, was brighter and far more genuine than those she'd forced out earlier.

'Hey, you're looking a bit more chipper!'

'Thank you. I'd forgotten how great that first shower feels when you've been under the weather and not had one for a few days.'

'Well, once we get some food inside you, hopefully you'll feel even more human. Now, I took the liberty of picking up some extras for you as I noticed the fridge was a touch bare when I was getting the milk out.'

As he spoke, Morgan was emptying the shopping bags and she was thrilled to see that he'd bought a selection of cooked meats, a fresh crusty loaf, some salad items, milk and a couple of large bars of chocolate along with the cheese and soup he'd gone out for.

She pointed to the chocolate bars. 'Do these class as essential items?'

'Absolutely! Don't you know that sugar is a vital requirement in regaining your strength. I confess it was a toss-up between the chocolate or a few bottles of those fizzy, glucose drinks. Would you rather have had those?'

'Urgh! Hell no! Nasty stuff!' She wrinkled her nose in disgust. 'Your decision was the right one. Thank you.'

'It's no problem. Now, let me get this soup on to warm up while I make your cheese sandwiches.'

'I can do those—'

'No, you won't. Just sit down and let me pamper you a little.'

'Yes, boss!'

He grinned at her and Perrie felt herself melt inside. Morgan had such an open and friendly face – he was one of those people who it just felt good to be around. She watched him as he bustled about, confident in her kitchen.

'Now, would you like to eat in here or out on the patio? It's a nice warm evening.'

'Oh, the patio, please. That's a great idea. The only fresh air I've had for the last week was the time it took to get George and Timothy in and out of the run.'

'Then the patio it is.'

'Oh my, I feel full fit to burst!'

'You've still got half of a sandwich to eat.'

'Morgan, if you'd sliced the bread a bit thinner, I may have managed both but these doorsteps would be a challenge at the best of times. I did finish all my soup though, surely I get brownie points for that?'

'Okay, fair point and yes, you do. I'll wrap the sandwich up and put it in the fridge so you can have it if you feel peckish later.'

'You're such a dad sometimes,' she teased.

'Is that a bad thing?'

'No, it's nice to be in the company of someone who considers others as you do. I like it.'

'Good. Now, talking about considering others, I have a favour to ask.'

'Oh, right. Well, after the way you've cared for me this evening, short of asking me to run naked through the town, it's going to be hard to refuse whatever it is.'

'Well, your modesty is safe for now but if that's something we could maybe consider for the future…'

'Ha ha! Very funny! Spit out your request, dude, before I decide your good deeds are null and void.'

'Give me a second.'

Morgan stood, picked the dirty plates up from the table and took them back indoors. He returned a moment later with a carrier bag in his hand. She looked at it and had a vague recollection of him walking in with it when he'd arrived earlier.

He placed it on the table as he sat back down.

'I've put the kettle on for another brew so let me say what I have to say and then you can have a think while I make the tea.'

'Okay. I'm all four ears.'

She giggled when Morgan looked at her in surprise and then burst out laughing when it dawned on him that she was referring back to their silly conversation on that Saturday night.

'Hah! Very good! Well remembered. Anyway, what I would like to ask is, would you mind autographing some of your books? The town has an annual fair and part of the events is the obligatory raffle. I thought it would be nice if I could add the first three books of your series, signed by the author, as one of the prizes. It would be a welcome change to a sketch pad and coloured pencils or a free birthday or seasonal card every month for one year.'

'I see…'

'Kettle's boiled. Be back in a mo.'

Perrie opened the bag and pulled her books out. She hadn't looked at these in a long time. She was currently writing number fourteen in the series and her main character had moved on considerably from what she'd put the poor sod through in her first novel.

She turned her debut novel over and read the blurb on the back, remembering the agonies she'd gone through as she'd tried to condense her three-hundred pages of words into less than a dozen lines in order to whet the appetite of the agents she'd sent it out to. Thankfully, the publishers now did all that for her.

She placed it carefully on the table and picked the others up in turn, admiring the new covers they'd been graced with. Her agent had advised her they were being revamped but she hadn't seen the new ones yet. She liked them very much.

'Here we go! I've put less milk in yours this time,

now that you've finally eaten some proper food.'

'Thank you. That last one was awful.'

'You still drank it though.'

'I was thirsty.'

Morgan smiled as he took up his seat across from her.

'New covers, I see,' he said, nodding at the books in her hands.

'Yes, they do that every so often. Keeping up with market trends apparently.'

'And the favour?'

'Of course, I'll sign them for you although I'm not sure they'll be a popular prize.'

'Are you kidding me? These should see the ticket uptake double, nay… treble!'

'Seriously?'

'Yes, seriously! I'm not the only one who loves your work and the television series based on them is the talk of the town for weeks when it's being aired.'

'I see! Wow! And what does the money go towards? Charities?'

'A combination of things – buildings in the town that require work to be done, maintaining the town infrastructure so that the tourists keep coming and any charity which requires a boost. For example, three years back, one of our older residents had incurable cancer and her biggest regret was that she'd never been abroad so we used the money from the fair that year to send her to Paris for five days.'

'Oh, what a lovely thing to do. Did she enjoy herself?'

'Totally. She tried everything and returned home a complete Francophile. It's been said that her last words to her family were, "It's not goodbye, it is au revoir, mes enfants!" You have to admire the style she went out in.'

'You do indeed! Then, I would be honoured to sign these books for you. Leave them with me.'

'Thank you, I really appreciate it.'

'It's the least I can do. Now,' she let out a large yawn, 'I think I need to go to bed. I feel like I'm about to fall asleep over the table. It's just come on all of a sudden.'

'That's because you've eaten. Anyway, I need to go and pick up Daisy. Any later and she'll be falling asleep in playgroup tomorrow. Although she's such a little chatterbox, I suspect they'd appreciate the silence.'

'Aw, bless her. Look, if I'm feeling livelier by Saturday, why don't you both come over after you've finished work and we can all hang out. I've missed her and I'm sure she's missed Timmy. She can play with him in the run for a bit or, if the weather's bad, bring a couple of her favourite DVDs and she can watch them on the sofa with her boy snuggled up with her.'

'She would love that. I won't say anything though just in case you still feel off-colour. You can confirm with me on Saturday.'

'I'm sure it'll all be fine...' Another large yawn brought tears to her eyes. 'Oh, my goodness, I'm so sorry.'

'It's fine, I'm gone!' Morgan gave her a grin as he picked up the mugs from the table and followed her back inside.

He collected his jacket from the back of the kitchen chair and made his way to the front door where he shrugged it on.

'Thank you for everything you've done this evening, Morgan, I'm grateful.'

'No need to be, I just wish I'd come round sooner. I was worried that I may have upset you last week and wanted to give you some space.'

'It would take far more than that for you to upset me.'

'Well…'

She watched as he shuffled his feet awkwardly but before she could say anything further, another yawn made its escape.

'Right, you, get off to your bed. And when you find your phone, let me know about Saturday.'

Not giving her a chance to speak, he leant down, kissed her cheek and walked out the door, only this time he closed it firmly behind him, not giving her the opportunity to hover until he was out the gate.

Perrie went back to the kitchen, replenished the cats' water bowls, put on the dishwasher, locked the back door and made her way up the stairs to bed.

She pulled back the covers and got in with absolutely no expectation of sleeping but ten minutes had barely passed before she was out for the count and the morning sunlight was peeking around the curtains when she next opened her eyes.

TWENTY-TWO

Perrie took a sip of her wine and savoured it for a moment before swallowing while enjoying the feeling of relaxation making its way into her bones. It was over four weeks since she'd had her meltdown and true to her resolution, she'd made sure every moment had counted.

There had been long walks along the cliffs with George and Timothy and shorter walks with Morgan and Daisy. They'd spent a day on Lundy Island which had been a delight and the memory of seeing the wild dolphins following the ferry across would never be forgotten. There had been nights in when the three of them had all cosied up on the sofa and watched movies and a few nights out when Morgan's mum had extended her babysitting duties.

Perrie had even made her peace with Babs and they'd had a couple of nights out to the pub where they shared which actors they fancied – the argument over who had first dibs on Tom Hardy hadn't yet been settled – which TV soaps were better and other such light-hearted nonsense. They'd also discussed books and preferred genres but Perrie had kept her lips buttoned and hadn't shared her own writing secret.

Through all of this, she'd felt the closeness developing between herself and Morgan although the relationship hadn't progressed beyond a hug and a peck on the cheek when saying hello or goodbye. This, however, suited her just fine. Perrie knew she wasn't in the right place to deal with anything more. She glanced at Morgan, sitting over the table from her with a smile playing across his lips.

They were outside in her garden. Daisy was running around the grass pulling a cat toy behind her which Timothy was chasing. She would let out squeals of delight whenever he caught it and the sound had them both smiling. George, on the other hand, was prowling around the perimeter of the garden, having a good sniff and no doubt conducting a reconnaissance for possible escape routes. Perrie was one step ahead of him on this and had made sure the side and back gates were locked and secure.

She put her glass down on the mosaic-topped table and let her hand rest next to it. Morgan's hand was mere millimetres away and she could feel the heat from it on her fingers. The smallest of movements would see them touching...

'Oh, I know what I wanted to mention.'

He turned towards her suddenly and she quickly pulled her hand back.

'Err, yes?' She could feel the heat rising up her face and sincerely hoped her cheeks were not turning bright red and, if they were, then she double-hoped he couldn't see them given their shady spot on the patio.

'Do you still want to visit Smuggler's Cove? I've been keeping an eye on the tides and the perfect window to go down would be on Saturday afternoon, just after three.'

'Oh, yes please! I would love to see it. How much time would we have?'

'We'll have about three to four hours although I wouldn't want to keep Daisy out that long and I can't see that we'd be able to go without her – she's been desperate to visit. If she found out we'd gone and left her behind, she'd be really upset.'

'Of course, she should come along. If it wasn't for Daisy, I wouldn't have known about it. I wouldn't enjoy it half as much if I didn't have my little buddy with me.'

'In that case, I'll ask Ruth if she would mind covering the last couple of hours in the shop on her own and I'll leave early.'

'I'll put together a picnic for us to take down. I must also remember to bring my camera – I'm sure I'll be able to use the location in a book somewhere.'

'Is everything you see and do fodder for your books?'

Perrie thought for a moment. 'Yup! It pretty much is. My mind doesn't stop and the smallest of things can either find their way into my stories or be the inspiration behind the creation of one.'

'Don't you find it wearisome? Being unable to switch off?'

'Sometimes I do. But, on the other hand, it makes me more observant and I think I see things which I may otherwise miss if I wasn't trying to take everything in.'

'Is that why you took so many photographs on Lundy?'

'Sort of. I was trying to capture the essence of it, the bleak terrain, the proximity of the sea and so on. Then, when I need to describe an area of desolation and isolation, I can refer back to them. I have files upon files of photographs which I dip into when I need to ensure realism in what I'm describing.'

'Do you do the same with people?'

'To a lesser extent. I'll rarely describe the face of one person – I'm more likely to use the eye colour of one, the hair colour of another, the facial shape of a third.'

'So, you create a composite picture?'

'Exactly!'

Morgan gave her his little shy smile – the one he gave, she'd come to learn, when he was talking about something he wasn't quite sure of.

'Until I met you, I never put any thought into what it took to create the fabulous books you, and other authors, write. Now, I find the process fascinating and I'm intrigued by how it all comes together. I hope you don't mind me asking questions.'

'Not at all. It's nice for someone, other than my agent or publisher, to be interested.'

'I'm sure there'll be plenty to interest you on Saturday. Now,' he drained his glass and stood, 'I need to get someone small and curly home and into bed.'

'And I need to do an inventory of my fridge for our picnic.'

'Not too much, please,' he grinned, 'since I'm the one who'll be carrying it down.'

'Hey, I can do my share of the donkey work, you know.'

'I'm sure you can but you'll be in charge of Daisy and making sure she doesn't take a header down the steps!'

'Ah, okay then. I'll leave the magnum of Champagne on ice for another day.'

Between them, they rounded up the baby blonde and two large bundles of fur and Perrie wasn't quite sure which of them was the least trouble – they all wanted to stay out longer.

Eventually, everyone was sorted out and Daisy did her usual arm-fling around Perrie's legs when she said goodbye.

'G'night, Merida, thank you for letting me play with Timothy. I've kissed him bye-bye and now I kiss you bye-bye too.'

Perrie knelt down so Daisy could give her a kiss and another cuddle. She cuddled her back and relished again the feel of the little warm, squirmy body in her arms. There really was nothing to beat the feel of a child's embrace.

'Come on you, stop dragging it out. You need to get to bed!'

Morgan was smiling at Perrie as he spoke. They both knew this was one of Daisy's delaying tactics but it was a game they were happy to indulge her in.

When Perrie straightened up, Morgan leant in, kissed her cheek and gave her a hug too.

Was it wishful thinking or did he hold her just a few seconds longer than usual? He'd pulled away before she could be sure and they were both up the path and out the gate, waving as they went.

When they were out of sight, Perrie closed the door and leant her head against it.

In just over a week, she had to return to London and she hadn't yet broken the news to Morgan.
She'd definitely tell him on Saturday. When they returned from Smuggler's Cove. She wanted just one more carefree outing before everything had to change.

TWENTY-THREE

'Now, Daisy, hold on tightly to Perrie's hand and go slowly. Don't rush. The steps will be slippery so you need to be careful. Do you hear me?'

'Yes, Daddy. I'll be a good girl.'

Morgan bent down to give Daisy a cuddle.

'I know you will, darling, but I need you to understand that it's dangerous where we're going.'

'Morgan, if it's really that dangerous, we don't need to go. I don't want anyone to be in danger.'

'I'll assess how things look when we get there although I think it'll be fine.'

'When was the last time you went to the Cove?'

Morgan felt himself shrink a little under Perrie's direct gaze.

'Erm, about fifteen years ago... maybe.'

'So, you don't know what state these steps might be in? If they're still there at all!'

'Perrie, they've withstood the elements for a few hundred years, I don't think the last fifteen or so will have made that much difference.'

'Hmm, we'll see. Right,' Perrie held out her hand to Daisy, 'are we ready to rock and roll?'

'Yes, Merida, let's go on a venture. Just like in the film.'

The three of them set off and Morgan adjusted the rucksack on his back. Perrie had one too with her camera, notebook and the rug for them to sit on. As they chattered away, Morgan felt the sense of peace again that he'd come to realise now surrounded him when he was with Perrie. Her undemanding ways, gentle nature and quick wit had slowly made their way beneath his armour and under his skin and now he only ever wanted to be in her company. When they were apart, it felt like something was missing.

When Harriet had died, he was convinced he would never again meet anyone who could fill his being as she had done.

And yet, without being aware of it happening, someone had.

Perrie made him look forward to finishing work and going home. Knowing she was a five-minute walk from his front door gave him comfort. Daisy adored her and there was no question over the adoration being returned although he didn't know where he stood in the adoration stakes. Did he love Perrie? Did she love him? Did he want to love her – in *that* way? Did he want her to love him – in *that* way?

These questions had begun to circle in his mind over the last few days and he really couldn't say what answers he wanted to hear. Thankfully, there was no need to rush and they could take their time to reach the eventual outcome.

'Is it over there, Daddy?'

Daisy's voice brought him out of his head.

'That's right. On the other side of the hedge.'

'I like that we have a lifebuoy close to hand,' Perrie nodded in the direction of the red and white floatation aid that was secured to a post, 'should anything untoward occur.'

'Yes, and they're all regularly maintained too. The local parish council take their responsibilities rather seriously in matters of safety. If you do ever come across anything that is a concern, let me know and I'll pass it on. Broatie has an excellent safety record and we want it to stay that way. It's good for tourism.'

'I'll keep it in mind.'

Perrie smiled at him and his heart pattered just a little faster.

Morgan stepped off the wide cliff path, leading them over to the thick gorse bushes and hedging which ran close to the cliff edge.

'I'll go first.'

He looked about to ensure there was no one around watching and then pushed his way through the thicket. He put his rucksack on the grass and held his arms out for Perrie to lift and pass Daisy over. When she was beside him, he pulled the thick branches to the side for Perrie to pass through.

'The council put the gorse and hedging in ten years back to deter tourists from going too close to the edge and seeing steps down to the cove below. They couldn't afford to keep sending out the rescue boats to the idiots who got stuck!'

'Ah, right. Good idea. So only those who know about the cove know how to get there.'

'Correct. And those of us who know also understand the need to respect the movement of the sea.'

'Unless they're fifteen-year-old boys who come in on a boat…'

Perrie smirked at him.

'Aye, well, we don't talk about that in front of little ears.'

He walked over to where the cliff-edge was a little more worn and looked down, breathing a sigh of relief when he saw the carved-out steps still prominently in sight. The rope handrail going down the wall was still in situ although he could see it was thin and frayed in a few places. On the other side, where the steps became open to the drop below, a wooden banister had been put in. It, however, was in a poor state and he wouldn't be inclined to rely on it for support. The thick gorse and heather which grew alongside the uppermost steps blocked the view of the cove. He couldn't wait to hear Perrie's reaction when she stepped down at the point where all was revealed.

'Good news, ladies, the stairs are still here and are passable. I'll go first and kick the seaweed off the lower steps. Try not to step on it if you can because it will be slippy. There's a rope running down the wall side – I'd advise holding it but take care as I can see some places where it looks fragile. DO NOT touch the wooden banister on your left, however, as it appears to be exceptionally rickety and I suspect the slightest touch will see it break. Also, the steps are an uneven depth. An old ploy to cause problems for the King's soldiers in days of yore.'

'No problem, Morgan. We'll take it nice and slow, won't we, Daisy?'

'Yes, Merida. Can we count the steps as we go?'

'Of course, we can, there are rather a lot.'

They carefully descended the rocky old stairway, counting as they went. After twenty, only Perrie was counting although Daisy tried to join in. At step thirty-three, they stepped out of the little protective corridor provided by the hedging and the cove opened up below them.

'Oh WOW! That is stunning!' Perrie exclaimed and Morgan smiled to himself. It was a stunning view and all three of them paused for a moment to let it sink in.

'It's glorious!'

'I know! To be honest, it's so long since I've been here, I'd forgotten how breath-taking it is.'

'Can we keep going, Daddy, I want to build my sandcastle.'

Morgan laughed and it thrilled him that Perrie did too.

'Kids, eh?' she smiled, 'Views like this are wasted on them.'

'They are but in years to come, she'll learn to appreciate it.'

'I'm sure she will. Okay, Daisy, we'll get moving. Can you remember which number we'd reached?'

'Thirty-free.'

'Right, so this one must be thirty-four...'

The girls resumed their counting and it wasn't long until they were stepping down onto the soft sandy beach.

'Seventy-nine!'

'Wow! That's millions of steps!'

Perrie laughed.

'Now that's a five-year-old's logic for you!' she said, before turning slowly to look around.

The high rock face surrounded them on three sides, making the cove a lovely, private space and Morgan watched her face as she took it all in.

'Oh my! How amazing!'

'What is?'

'The steps we walked down. As we've moved away from the cliff, they've disappeared from view. Almost as though they've been absorbed back into the rockface they've been carved from.'

'So that any officials approaching by boat would be fooled into thinking this is nothing more than a small inlet.'

'Very clever. Is that,' she pointed up towards a large black hole halfway up the cliff-face they'd walked down, 'the smuggler's cave?'

'Yes, it is.'

'But, it's so high up. Surely the sea doesn't reach all the way up there?'

'At certain times of the year it does. On a spring tide, or in big storms, the water has been known to rise above it. You see where the gorse stops and the wooden banister begins?'

'Yeah.'

'That's the normal sea level when the tide is in. That's why there's no hedging down from that spot – it doesn't grow underwater.'

'No way!'

'Yes, way!' He smiled, pleased to have shown her something which had clearly impressed.

'So, how come we're able to get down here today? Does the tide really go out that far?'

'No. Most of the low tides still see the cove underwater. Today, however, we have what they call a "neap tide" which is a really low tide. They're not so frequent which is why today is a treat.'

'How much time do we have?'

'A few hours. I made sure we came down while the tide was still going out. It won't have turned yet so plenty of time for a picnic, a paddle, some sandcastle building… and photographs.'

Morgan added the latter as Perrie was already pulling her camera from her backpack.

'I need to get shots of these cliffs, they're amazing.'

'Feeling inspired?' He grinned as she began clicking

away.

'You bet I do! I would never have considered adding smuggling to my stories but I've already got a plot developing in my head.'

'What? Just like that? I thought you writers had to sit and drag every word out of your veins with a blunt spoon?'

Perrie's throaty, wholesome laugh danced around the cove, bouncing off the high, rocky cliffs.

'Morgan, there are plenty of occasions when that's exactly what it feels like but we also have times when the words are tripping over themselves to get onto the page and your fingers can't type fast enough.'

'I do admire people who can create like that. It's such a gift! I just don't have the imagination for it.'

'Yet you run an art shop?'

'You know the shop was Harriet's – she was the arty one. I did Business Studies and Finance at uni and, luckily, all the presentation material for those could be done on a computer. My input to the shop was to put together a business plan and a flow-chart to present to the bank when I expanded into greetings cards, gift wrappings and party products.'

'And there is your gift. You saw a gap in your local retail market and knew how to go about filling it. I would never have thought of that.'

Morgan smiled at her as he accepted her generous response. He'd never looked at it like that before. He always considered talented people to be sporty or musical or creative when, in fact, talent came in many guises.

'Daddy, can I paddle now?'

'In a little while. We need to sort out the picnic.'

'I can do that, Morgan. Give me a moment, Daisy, to put the rug down so we can get your shoes off without covering you in sand.'

Morgan slipped his trainers off while Perrie helped Daisy. Yet again, his heart did a little clench as he watched his daughter giggle when Perrie was pretending to tickle her feet.

'Right, squirt, are you ready?'

'Yes, Daddy.'

'Will you be joining us, Perrie?'

She grinned up at him from where she was kneeling on the rug, unpacking the various treats they'd brought for their al fresco tea.

'Absolutely! I just need to unpack all this because the towels are at the bottom of the bags. I'll be with you shortly. Go and enjoy some one-to-one time with Daisy.'

Morgan held out his hand to Daisy and listened to her chatter as they walked over the wet sand towards the waves that were gently lapping the shore.

'The sea's a long way away, Daddy.'

'It is, darling, that's because the tide is out. Remember I was explaining it to Perrie. But it'll only take us a few minutes to reach it.'

'Merida is coming too, isn't she?'

Daisy looked back over her shoulder.

'Yes, she's just sorting the picnic first.'

'Do you love Merida, Daddy?'

'Excuse me?'

Morgan looked at Daisy in shock and, by not watching where he was stepping, almost went face first onto the sand as his foot sank into a deeper-than-expected pool of water and he lost his balance. His arms flailed about as he tried to remain upright which Daisy clearly thought was hilarious judging by her laughter.

'Everything alright here? Need some assistance?'

A hand landed on his arm and he was pulled close against Perrie's side.

'Thank you. You've just saved my dignity. Another

few seconds and I'd have been walking home in rather wet clothing.'

Morgan could feel the heat from Perrie's body as it seeped through his T-shirt. Was that her heart beating faster against his chest or his own?

'What happened?'

'Unexpected rock-pool. I lost my balance although someone around here seems to think that it was very funny...'

He mock-glared at his daughter.

'Oh, Daddy,' she giggled, 'you looked just like the silly people in the cartoons.'

'Is that so? Well, I think the silliest people are the ones who get to the water last. Race you!'

And with those words, he set off running towards the waves and grinned with delight when he heard the laughter and shouting from the girls behind him.

Did he love Perrie? That he couldn't answer but he did know he was loving his life right now and it had been a very long time since he'd felt this way.

TWENTY-FOUR

'Up you get, Daisy.'

'Are you sure you'll be okay to carry her?'

Perrie watched with concern as Morgan crouched down to give Daisy a piggy-back up the cliff steps. She was shattered now after running around in the waves and building her sandcastles and Morgan had expressed his doubts that she'd be able to make it back up the seventy-nine steps under her own steam.

'I'll be fine but if I could just ask you to tie this strap around us, that would be a big help.'

He handed her a nylon strap with a buckle attached which she fed around Daisy's back, under her shoulder blades, and fastened across the top of Morgan's chest.

'And the purpose of this is what?' she asked.

'If Daisy falls asleep and loses her grip, she won't fall backwards.'

'Good call. I would never have thought of that.'

'My dad used to do it with me when I was her age.'

Perrie gathered up the remains of their belongings and packed it all into the bags again.

'Here, I can carry one.' Morgan held his hand out towards her.

'No, you cannot. You just concentrate on getting you and Daisy up those steps. Now that the food and drink is gone, there's no weight in them and I can manage perfectly well.'

'Okay, if you're sure? We'd better get a wriggle on – the tide is on its way back.'

Perrie led the way over the sand and stood back to let Morgan go up the stairs first. She looked up at the gaping hole, several feet above her head, and registered how much larger it was when viewed up close. Part of her wished it was more easily accessible as she'd love to explore it.

'Are you okay there, Morgan?'

They were halfway up the steps and Perrie was beginning to feel it in her thighs and calves. The differing heights of the steps were making the task considerably more tiring and she was only carrying the bags; it must be worse for Morgan with Daisy on his back.

'It's not the easiest climb I've made up these but I'm managing.'

'What about you, Daisy – are you okay on Daddy's back?'

'I'm okay, Merida, but feeling sleepy now.'

'Try and stay awake till we reach the top, that'll make it easier for Daddy.'

'I'll try…' came the drowsy reply.

Perrie kept a close eye on Daisy after that in case she had to come to Morgan's rescue when she did fall asleep. Fortunately, Daisy managed to hold out until they were almost at the top and Morgan was able to keep her in position until they were safely on the cliff-top.

'Here, let me take her weight while you undo the strap.'

Perrie stepped up behind him and put her arms around Daisy, ready to lift her off Morgan's back when he released the safety strap.

'I'll hold her while you push through the hedging and pass her across.'

'No need for that, Perrie, there's a path over there which comes out just up from our house.'

'Eh? So why—'

'— did I go through the thicket earlier?'

'Well, yeah!'

'I didn't want *somebody* to know there was an easy route to the steps. In a few more years, she'll be at that age where kids go off on "adventures" – I don't want rescuing her from the cove to be one of them.'

'Ah! Fair point. That was good forward thinking.'

Morgan grinned at he as took Daisy from her arms.

'Not really. I remember using it when I was that age and there's no way I want to see Daisy get into the same mischief I got up to!'

Perrie laughed as she helped to settle Daisy in his arms before picking up the bags again and following him onto the overgrown path which ran a bit closer to the cliff edge than she was entirely comfortable with. His preference for Daisy to remain unaware of its presence made more sense now as she walked along behind him. The path dipped down behind the hedging which hid them from the view of other cliff-top walkers. Perrie admired the glorious yellow of the flowering gorse and enjoyed the faint coconut scent while taking care not to get too close to the spiky branches. Not an easy feat when a steep drop was on her other side.

Soon, she could see the roof-top of her house and the path petered out close to the dry-stone wall that ran along the open land that lay opposite her cottage. Beyond and below were the rooftops and cottage gardens she'd admired from above in her first few days in the town.

'If you don't mind climbing over, Perrie, I can pass Daisy across.'

'No problem.'

She placed the bags on top of the wall and was soon on the other side. Her long legs and the easy footholds of the rough stonework had made light work of the climb. She took hold of Daisy who woke up as Morgan handed her over.

'Are we home now?'

'Nearly. Just a few more minutes.'

Daisy snuffled under her chin, still half-asleep, and they waited for Morgan to join them.

'What's the matter?'

Morgan, having climbed the wall, was now running his hands over it, pushing and prodding the stones in several areas.

'This wall needs to be redone. The stones are corroding from the salty air and it's becoming loose and unstable. If it topples, passers-by may be curious enough to stop for a look and find the path for the cove.'

'Which we've agreed would not be good.'

'No, it would not. I'll give the council a call on Monday and bring it to their attention.'

He took Daisy from her, cradling her in his arms and less than five minutes later, they were walking through Morgan's front door.

'I'll take her straight up. I'm sure her teeth won't fall out if she doesn't brush them this once. There's wine in the fridge, feel free to pour yourself a glass. I won't be long.'

'Actually, I really fancy a nice strong cup of tea.'

Morgan stopped on the stairs.

'D'you know what, so do I. Can I leave you to sort that while I get a little lady into her bed?'

'Of course.'

Perrie headed into the kitchen and by the time Morgan joined her at the little bistro table outside his back door, there was a pot of tea brewing and two mugs waiting to be filled.

'I found this in one of the cupboards – I hope you don't mind me using it.'

She noticed a small flicker cross Morgan's face when he looked down at it.

'No, not at all.'

'Are you sure? You seem a bit…'

'It's the first time it's been out since Harriet passed. There's no need for a teapot that size when there's only one of you to use it.'

'Oh, I'm so sorry. I didn't think.'

'No, please, don't apologise. Harriet loved this tea set and would be delighted to see it in service again.'

Not knowing the best way to answer that, Perrie, after giving the bright blue teapot with its vibrant yellow sunflowers a small swirl, poured the tea into the matching mugs.

They sat in silence for a time, appreciating the relative quiet of the evening. The birds continued to chirrup in the trees, some bumblebees hummed around the pots of lavender dotted about the garden and the faint swish of the sea could be heard in the distance. It was very peaceful and Perrie was happy to just sit and soak it up. Anything to help put off having to tell Morgan that she was heading back to London in a week's time.

The shadows were lengthening and the remaining dregs of tea in the pot had cooled down to barely lukewarm when Perrie drew in a deep breath.

'Thank you for showing me the cove, I had a lovely time.'

'My pleasure. Daisy enjoyed it too. Despite living in

a seaside town, we don't get to the beach that often. It's made me realise I need to make more of an effort to do simple things like this with her.'

'It must be difficult though – you work all week and when you can get to the beach with her, I expect it's filled with tourists. I've seen how busy it gets down there. You certainly wouldn't have the same space you had today, that's for sure.'

'No, it wouldn't be the same. If you like, we could visit again the next time the tides are right?'

'I'd like that, thank you.'

'Then I will keep an eye out for the tides being in our favour once more and let you know.'

'Smashing! Although, if they're favourable in the next few weeks, I'll have to give it a miss.'

'Why?'

Here we go, she thought, as her stomach churned.

'I have to return to London.'

'Oh! For how long?'

'Hopefully, no longer than two weeks but that could change. I won't know until I get there.'

'I see. Am I allowed to ask what is dragging you back?'

'What makes you think I'm being dragged back?'

'Your voice sounds more like you're dreading it and the expression on your face backs that up. You certainly don't look excited to be going.'

'I see! Oops! It's just some business that needs to be sorted out. I probably look reluctant because I've grown used to being in a small town and don't really relish the hustle and bustle of the busy London streets. Especially in the middle of summer when the tourist level, which is always high anyway, seems to treble.'

'Would you like me to look after the cats while you're gone? It would be no trouble.'

'Oh gosh, thank you for the offer but no, there's no need, they'll be coming with me.'

'You're not staying in a hotel then?'

'No, I'll be crashing at my sister's place. Her boys love the cats and they're probably more welcome than I am!'

They both laughed at this.

'Daisy will miss you, you know.'

'And I will miss Daisy.'

There was silence for a few minutes. Eventually Morgan spoke again.

'I'll miss you.'

His voice was quiet, almost a whisper. His hand crept over the table to cover hers.

Perrie looked into his eyes and her insides turned fluid. This was the part she'd been dreading. She knew she'd fallen for Morgan, despite her every effort not to, and she'd suspected of late that her feelings were reciprocated even though nothing had ever been put into words.

She gave his fingers a soft squeeze as she smiled gently at him.

'I'll miss you.' Not giving him a chance to respond, she carried on. 'I'll miss Broatie very much and will be wishing the days away until I can return. For now, however, I think I had better get home – I have two big furry beasts who will be waiting for their dinner.'

She stood and Morgan walked with her to the front door where she picked up the backpack she'd dropped there earlier.

'Will I… I mean… will we see you again before you go? I know Daisy would be upset if you went off without saying goodbye.'

'I'll be leaving next Saturday night. I figure if I head off about half-past seven, I should miss the worst of the traffic. I'm sure we can fit in a dinner before then.'

'And I'll have finished work so Daisy and I can wave you off, if that's alright with you?'

'Sure, why not. That would be nice. Anyway,' she looked at her watch, 'I need to get going.'

Morgan leaned past her to open the door and the citrus undertones of his aftershave floated around her. She breathed in the scent and felt herself go slightly giddy. She turned her head and found herself looking straight into his eyes. Her breath caught in her throat as she found herself locked in his gaze and with no desire to break it. Her hungry cats were forgotten as time seemed to come to a standstill and she felt herself falling into their shining blue depths.

When Morgan took a step nearer, closing the miniscule gap between them, Perrie found herself glued to the spot. She couldn't have moved if she'd wanted to – her feet were adamantly going nowhere which meant there was no avoiding the kiss coming her way. His lips came to rest upon hers, a touch so delicate it felt like a butterfly had briefly swept by. Gradually the pressure increased until his arms folded her into his chest and held her tightly against him. Of their own volition, her hands grasped the front of his sweatshirt, pulling him closer still.

She didn't know how long they were in their embrace but when he raised his head and released her lips, Perrie felt bereft and confused. It took a few seconds for her scattered senses to regroup and when she looked into Morgan's eyes, she saw the longing she was experiencing reflected in them.

'Erm, um…' she tried to speak without knowing what she could say.

'Ah, yes, err…'

She guessed that he too was feeling dumbfounded.

'I have to go. I'll text you in a couple of days to sort out dinner.'

'Of course, yes, sure.' He gave a small cough.

She moved to place a little peck on his cheek and with a smile, stepped out the door onto the pavement. She turned in the direction of her cottage and had taken a few steps before she heard the door close behind her.

When she knew she was out of Morgan's sight, Perrie's head dropped and tears formed in her eyes. She'd wanted so much to avoid this. She hadn't intended to become involved with anyone and her plan had been to live in solitude until she had to go to court. She didn't want anyone else getting caught up in the shit-show that her life had become. And yet, here she was, in love with a gorgeous, generous, caring man and his equally delightful daughter. Two innocents who now risked being hurt when they found out the truth.

TWENTY-FIVE

The seagulls shrieked loudly as they flew overhead above the cottage. Perrie looked at her watch and sighed when she saw that it was only just after five a.m. She was wide awake, had been for a while, and she knew there was no chance now of getting back to sleep. With a small huff of annoyance, the quilt was thrown back and she took herself off into the shower.

When she was dressed, she decided to take a walk through the town to the beachfront. It was as she walked down the hill and around the bend, that she realised she hadn't been out for a dawn walk in quite some time. In the past, it had been her favourite time of day to go out and walk before the rest of the world woke up and she was alone on the streets; the occasional milkman or early jogger her only contact with the rest of the human race.

Everything felt different at that time of day. Just like the muted sense of peace that comes when snow falls, the pre-dawn hour is filled with a soul-restoring solitude and helps to clear the mind. Whenever she'd come up against a difficult scene or chapter to write, walking at this time of the day always helped her to find the route she had to take.

As she walked down the hill past Babs' gallery and the olde-worlde sweet shop, Perrie was pleased to feel the same sense of peace here. Everything was still and quiet until she reached the esplanade and heard the sound of the fishermen getting ready to go out on the waves.

Their voices were carried over from the harbour on the still air and, although unable to make out what was being said, the sense of urgency to get out on the waves could not be missed. She took a seat on a wooden harbour bench and watched as, one by one, they sailed off and the voices grew distant until, eventually, the only sound was that of the gulls and the waves.

Perrie watched the sea roll in and out for a time, letting the soft, kissing sound of the gentle waves work their magic on her soul before twisting around on the bench to face the long row of shops which spent their days looking out towards the horizon.

At the far end, to her left, was the mini-supermarket which seemed to sell a little of everything and was always full of tourists and locals, replenishing their fresh supplies of milk and vegetables. Next to it was the clothes shop that seemed to sell only items of a nautical nature. Every window display that she'd passed had been a variance of tops with anchors embroidered upon navy-blue and white horizontal stripes, white skirts, navy trousers and blue and white boat shoes. These were always accompanied by small child-sized sailor outfits and Perrie couldn't help but feel sorry for the children who'd been squeezed into those over the years and whose photographs would come back to haunt them in later life. They were most probably nestled up beside the naked bath-tub pictures in a box that would once again see the light of day when the poor, unsuspecting innocent brought their first boyfriend or girlfriend home to meet their parents.

Alongside this den of childhood torture, stood Morgan's art supplies and gift shop. She hadn't appreciated the size of it until now as she'd never taken in this view before but she could see it had once been two units when compared to the other shops in the row. Two doors along stood The Ice Cream Parlour – standing out bright and colourful with its candy, pastel colours and vibrant green awnings. It had to be said, their ice-cream was to die for and she wished she could take some back for her nephews and Aggie but even the best cool box would struggle to keep it frozen on her journey back to London.

Her eyes continued to sweep along the row, acknowledging the little cafés and coffee bars which she'd sat in, consuming large frothy Cappuccinos along with slices of something delicious and homemade.

At the end of the row, on the corner which led back up the hill, was "Jasper's Jam Bar" – the largest pub in the town. They not only had their own little micro-brewery but was also the local music venue which made it very popular with both the tourists and the locals. From her spot on the bench, she could see the bunting that had been put up in preparation for the beer festival which the town hosted every other year and the pub was advertising their own sea shanty band who, according to the posters in the window, were award-winners although she hadn't yet had the pleasure of hearing them perform.

Across the road, taking up residence on the opposite corner, was the ubiquitous amusements arcade. Did a seaside town even qualify as such if it didn't have one of these? Memories came flooding back of her, Aggie and Marcus pleading with their parents to get them two-pence pieces from the Change booths so they could play on the tipping point machines. They'd never won back anything near to the amount they'd fed in but it had been quite the adrenaline rush when it looked like they were close. Their parents had always said the machines were fixed so as not to give out big wins but they'd chosen not to believe them. Ah, the joy of childhood belief in everything being good.

The next shop along was her favourite shop in the whole of the town. "The Beach Front" was one of those old-fashioned shops which were a treasure trove for children who had holiday savings to spend. They had buckets and spades of all shapes, sizes and colours piled up outside along with multi-coloured fishing nets for exploring rock-pools, inflatable plastic beach balls and Frisbees galore. Inside, it was packed to the gunnels with every kind of cheap, tacky, pocket-money priced toy you could imagine. Perrie had spotted toys in there that she hadn't seen since her own childhood. It had taken all of her willpower not to purchase one of the "Magic Pictures" drawing boards where you could draw a picture and then, with a quick left-right swipe of the little piece of cardboard at the bottom, your drawing would disappear and you had a clean slate to start all over again. She longed to get a couple for her nephews but figured that since they'd been raised with twenty-first century technology, they would find her childhood favourite to be rather lame.

She stared at "The Beach Front" for some time, taking in every little detail, right down to the Lyons Maid ice-cream sticker on the closed door. She knew that when they opened, the metal, swinging, pavement sign would be put out for all to see.

Eventually, her gaze moved along to the fifties-style diner which served all kinds of American burgers, hot-dogs and pancake breakfasts. It also vied with "The Ice Cream Parlour" for milkshakes and large ice-cream sundaes. Lastly, and taking up the final corner, was "Terry's Rock Shop" – a shop which sold almost every kind of sweet, tooth-rotting, sugary rock confection ever created. Terry sold traditional pink and white, peppermint-flavoured rock with "Broatie Bay" running through it, all the way up to the novelty rock such as large dummies, false teeth and giant lollipops. In between, he had rock of all flavours and colours and the open front display was a veritable rainbow.

Just then, the clock tower of the small church up on the hillside chimed seven o'clock and it was as if a celestial hand had flicked a switch and Perrie's pre-dawn solitude came to an end. The atmosphere around her changed in an instant as the metallic clang of the mini-market's shutters rolled up and the shopkeeper called out to the driver of the road-sweeper as he came around the corner. The cafés opened their doors, brought out the tables and chairs and put out signs advertising their all-day breakfasts which could be eaten-in or taken away in a large bap.

In no time at all, the area had once again become all hustle and bustle and the first raft of fishing boats which had gone out while she was still in her bed were now returning with the fishermen swarming around her as they emptied their hauls onto the harbour.

She stood, shook out her leg which had cramped due to the awkward angle she'd been sitting at and, returning the greetings being called out by the friendly workers, made her way back up towards the cottage, mentally ticking off the remaining tasks she had to do before taking George and Timothy for a last long walk along the cliffs. Hopefully, she'd manage to tire them out so they would sleep through most of the journey back to London.

TWENTY-SIX

Perrie had just put the cats in the Landy and was fastening their safety harnesses when her mobile rang. She snapped the last buckle into place and tugged the straps, checking they were secure, before she answered.

'I can see youuuu…' Morgan sang quietly in her ear.

She looked up and saw him waving from where he stood outside his garden gate. He was on his own and she was grateful for that. She'd had dinner with him and Daisy twice this week and after Daisy had gone to bed on Wednesday, they'd discussed at length the best way for her to leave that would be the least upsetting for the little girl. Neither wanted to risk the upset that would invariably come if they were to wave her goodbye as she drove off. Perrie was relieved about this as never mind Daisy losing control, it was herself she was worried about. She very much doubted she'd be able to stay composed when faced with the tears of a five-year-old. It had finally been agreed that a special treat of pizza on the sofa, with movies on the television, would be the best way forward and they'd been right.

As they'd sat together around the coffee table, with a selection of homemade pizzas in front of them, Perrie had shared the news of her trip with Daisy. When she'd finished explaining, Morgan had quickly – just as they'd planned – started the new Disney DVD which had been bought specially and it created the instant distraction they'd hoped for. By the time the credits began to roll, Daisy was practically asleep and had gone off to bed with a simple, 'Come back soon, my Merida'. There had been no tears or upset and it was mission accomplished.

When Morgan had come back down the stairs, he'd sat close to her on the sofa and taken her hands in his.

'Perrie, I don't want to put any pressure on you but I'm really going to miss you. It makes my head reel when I think of how my life has changed since you rolled into it. Literally!'

'Ha! Ha! Think you're funny?'

'Sure do,' he'd chortled before giving her his serious look again. 'I mean it though, Perrie, I had no interest in growing close to someone again – you know that – but somehow, with you, it happened.'

'Maybe it was because neither of us were looking for anything. Maybe that is what made something happen. I came here for peaceful solitude with the intention of just putting my head down and working.'

'Would you change any of it?'

'No, not a single second.'

'Me neither!'

Then he'd leant forward, placed his lips on hers and slowly kissed her.

'You're cheating!' she replied now, watching him pace back and forth. 'This wasn't what we agreed.'

'No, cheating would be me down there with you, kissing you goodbye.'

'You kissed me goodbye last night. Plenty of times!'

And had he ever!

Perrie couldn't remember ever being kissed in such a way that had made her head spin or her toes curl as they had when Morgan had pulled her into his arms and held her close.

'I could kiss you goodbye again now…'

'You could… but you can't.'

She stared up at where he was standing, putting her hand above her eyes to shade them from the bright sunlight. It was coming up for seven o'clock in the evening and the sun was just beginning to drop lower in the sky.

'Why not?'

'Because we did our goodbyes last night and said it would be easier this way – for all of us.'

'I've changed my mind.'

'Well, I haven't.'

'You're a hard, cruel woman, Perrie Lacey.'

'You'd better believe it, mister!'

There was a heavy pause for several seconds while she looked up at him and he gazed down at her. Eventually, she broke the silence.

'I have to go, Morgan.'

'I know.' His reply was quietly spoken.

She waved and was about to end the call when he suddenly spoke again, this time with an urgency in his voice.

'Perrie… please hurry home…'

His words brought a lump to her throat.

Home.

Was he right?

Was this now home?

Suddenly, she was grateful for the distance between them for he wouldn't be able to see the tears in her eyes.

'I'll be back as soon as I can. Goodbye.'

She ended the call, letting out the sob she'd been desperately holding back and placed the phone deep inside her handbag behind the driving seat so she wouldn't be tempted to phone him on her journey.

Just as she was getting into the car, she heard the church bell chimes. Seven o'clock again. They had been the quickest twelve hours and the moment she'd been dreading was now here. She started the car, let off the handbrake and slowly made her way out of the car park, watching Morgan in her rearview mirror until she rounded the bend and he disappeared from sight.

By the time she reached the main road, the tears were streaming down her face and her heart felt like it was being ripped apart. She had fallen in love with this town, with Morgan and with Daisy. She didn't want to leave.

Unfortunately, she had no choice.

TWENTY-SEVEN

Perrie opened her eyes and wondered where she was.
Why was it so quiet? And why was the sun to her right
and not her left?

It only took a few brief seconds for her to remember
why it was different – she was in the attic suite of her
sister's house in Wandsworth, London and not the cottage
on top of the cliffs.

Her heart plummeted with the realisation and her
stomach began to churn again at what lay ahead.

'No! Not today! Tomorrow! Don't think about it
until tomorrow,' she told herself firmly as she got out of
bed and revived herself with a cold shower.

Thirty minutes later she walked into the kitchen and
was immediately engulfed in four arms around her legs
and middle.

'Auntie Pea, Auntie Pea... you're here! We wanted
to come up to see you but Mummy wouldn't let us. She
said you'd had a long drive last night and needed to
sleep.'

Perrie smiled over at her sister, Aggie, sitting at the

kitchen table with a mug of something warm in her hand. Knowing Aggie as she did, Perrie would put her money on the "something warm" being a very strong, black Italian coffee. A quick glance towards the kitchen worktop confirmed this when she saw the cafetiere sitting there.

'They speak the truth. I refused to let the little brats come up and use you as an indoor trampoline. You can thank me later. For now, would you like a coffee?'

'Only if you have something that won't strip the enamel off my teeth!'

'You're in luck, Perrie, I bought some for you yesterday otherwise my darling wife would have you caffeine'd up to the eyeballs. How are you?'

'Hey, Graham, lovely to see you. I'm okay, all things considered, how are you?'

She leant in and gave her brother-in-law a hug. He was a sweet, kind man and she liked him a lot. Aggie's first husband had been a dickhead of gigantic proportions and Perrie was delighted that she'd struck gold second time around.

'Not so bad, thank you, Perrie. Here, take a seat, I'll sort out your coffee. How was your journey?'

'Fairly easy. It was definitely a good idea to leave when I did. Most of the tourists and day-trippers were already on their way home by then so the traffic wasn't bad at all.'

'Auntie Pea, look, we did drawings for you.'

Perrie looked at her nephews and exclaimed about how much they'd grown since she'd seen them last. At six and nine years old, they were shooting upwards at a rate of knots. There was no doubt they had the height that came from their mother's side of the family.

'Boys, I think it's time you took your father into the garden, or over to the park, for a game of football. He needs to work off the burger and chips he had for tea last night.'

'Really, darling? I thought we'd done—'

'Not in front of the sprogs, my love!'

Perrie sat and listened to the good-natured banter between Aggie and Graham. Her sister had always favoured a sharp tongue and a droll manner but she had a heart of gold. She also adored every hair on the heads of her husband and children. Her family was everything to her and that included her own brother and sister.

'Okay, now that they've gone, we need to talk.'

'Oh, do we have to? I was kind of hoping to get one last day before the circus begins.'

'I know, and I wish we could let it lie longer, but we have to get you prepared. Tomorrow's going to be a big day and you, my darling little sister, are the main star of the shit-show!'

'Do you have to put it quite like that, Aggie?'

'You know what I mean.'

'I do.' She let out a huge sigh. 'Okay, let's get on with it. What's first?'

'Your hair. Easiest to do it while the house is empty. Let me just pop this joint in the oven for later and then we can crack on.'

Within a few minutes, Perrie had a towel around her shoulders while Aggie washed her hair.

'Do you want me to take a couple of inches off the ends; they're looking a bit scraggy.'

'Yes, if you don't mind, thanks. It hasn't seen a pair of scissors since the last time you cut it.'

'Hmm, doesn't feel like it's seen a deep-condition either! I'll put some in and let it sit for a bit.'

'So, how are the shops doing? Is business good?'

'SHOPS? Wash your mouth out, you foul creature! They are salons, dear, salons! And they're doing exceptionally well, thank you for asking.'

Perrie smiled to herself – she loved winding Aggie up and referring to her up-and-coming salon chain, "Wands of Beauty", as shops was guaranteed to do just that.

'Do you get much opportunity to practise your art or is it all meetings and business now?'

'Oh, I make sure I keep my hand in. I visit one salon each week and work there for a day. It keeps the staff on their toes, ensures there's no slacking and I can check that everything is being done, and run properly. It also gives me the opportunity to try out the latest treatments, hair styles or beauty aids. New things come onto the market all the time and a good beautician and stylist makes sure they keep on top of them.'

'And you're definitely both of those!'

'D'you know,' Aggie leant over to check on the deep conditioner, 'I hated Mum no end for forcing me to stay on at college when I was all set to leave after Dekko asked me to marry him.'

'I recall,' Perrie answered dryly. 'You slammed every door in the house for about six months and barely had a civil word to say to our poor, long-suffering mother for almost a year!'

'It pained me no end to admit she was right though. Talk about a grovelling apology. After that bastard walked out, leaving me with a three-month baby in my arms and up to my neck in the debt he'd racked up, it was those skills that saved me.'

'And look where you are now – married to a lovely man who worships the ground you walk on, two fabulous children and a successful business. You worked hard for what you've got, Aggie, I do hope you take a moment each day to stop and appreciate it all.'

'A moment? Honey, it's the first thought in my head

in the morning and my last thought at night. After the crappola Dekko put me through, I'll never take anything for granted again. Now, enough about me – tell me more about Broatiescombe Bay. Is it as cute as I vaguely remember?'

'Probably cuter, to be honest. I have completely fallen in love with that town. The problem with childhood holidays is that your priorities are all about having fun and not about where the fun is taking place. My little cottage is absolutely glorious, the cats adore it and the run-space they have, and the room I have set up as my office has the best view right across the sea.'

'And what about the menfolk? Any nice fishermen caught your eye?'

'Aggie!' she giggled, 'no, they have not!'

'Why not? A gorgeous redhead like you should be fighting them off with their lobster pots!'

'I'm not in the right place for emotional involvement right now,' she sighed.

'Hey, kiddo,' Aggie gave her a hefty nudge, 'who said anything about emotion!'

'Oh, Aggie! You are incorrigible!'

'Damn right I am, little sis! And you need to be too! It would do you good. Now, get your head back over that sink so I can wash this out.'

Perrie did as she was ordered, glad that Aggie had changed the subject because she knew she'd have struggled to keep Morgan a secret once her big sister got the probing bit between her teeth.

The following morning, Perrie stood in her bedroom. Her

hair was now more blonde than red, thanks to Aggie's special touch, and had been swept up in a classy chignon. The subtle makeup which she'd gone without for months, had been applied, turning her cheekbones and eyes into stand-out features once again.

She tugged the black, fitted jacket gently along the bottom and turned slightly to check the black, slim-fitting suit skirt was sitting as it should. She twisted it slightly to get the seam in the right place.

Finally, her eyes swept down to her classy, black patent, Louboutin stilettos – the high heel adding more inches to her already impressive height.

Perrie Lacey turned to face the mirror full on. Juniper Halstead stared back out at her.

TWENTY-EIGHT

'Are you ready to go?'

'As I'm ever going to be, Aggie.'

'You really should eat something; it's going to be a long day.'

'I know, I know, but my stomach is churning worse than an ocean in a storm – anything I ate wouldn't be staying down for long.'

'I hear you. Probably a bit too much information there, but I get you. Come on then, let's be on our way. Goodness only knows what the traffic is going to be like.'

'At least you won't have to cross the river – that has to be a bonus.'

'In truth, it is but a small consolation.'

Aggie reversed her car out of the driveway and Perrie grasped the door handle tightly. It wasn't that her sister was a bad driver but she was a forceful one. Some might say aggressive but Perrie felt that was a bit strong although the driver she'd just cut up when her tyres had hit the public highway might beg to differ, if the hand gesture she'd caught a glimpse of was anything to go by.

The drive from Wandsworth Common to Southwark was no distance at all but it took on marathon proportions during a Monday morning rush hour. On one hand, Perrie was happy for the journey to never end, on the other, she just wanted this all over and done with. She looked out the window and stared at the people going about their normal lives – the joggers on Clapham Common, the schoolkids waiting for their friends so they could walk to school together, the workers standing at bus-stops, scrolling on their phones as they waited. Everything was so ordinary yet her life was perched on a knife-edge and she had no idea which way it was going to fall.

'Hey, kid, you okay?'

Aggie's hand came over to give hers a quick squeeze.

'Trying to be…'

'You've got this, Perrie. You know you have.'

'We'll see.'

'Anyway, the plan is that I'll drop you off outside, you go in while I park the car and then I'll come back to be with you.'

'Where are you parking up?'

'Graham called in a favour with one of his clients who has an office in the area – they've kindly said we can use one of their visitors' parking spaces for as long as we need to.'

'Wow! That was a result.'

'Tell me about it.'

Silence filled the car again and, very soon, they were driving along Tooley Street. Perrie's stomach went into overdrive as Aggie made the right-hand turn into Battle Bridge Lane. They followed the road round and there it was, Southwark Crown Court. Perrie felt faint as Aggie pulled up to the drop-off point.

'Come on, Pea, pull it together. Don't let them see

your weakness.'

Together they looked out the window and Perrie was horrified at the size of the media pack, being held back – thankfully – by sturdy, metal barriers.

'Oh, Aggie, I can't face them again. Why are they allowed to be here?'

'They're here because it's a high-profile case and you CAN face them. You have no choice. Now, hurry up and get in there, I can't sit here any longer – there's a plod over there giving me the bad eye and as he has a fuck-off size gun in his hand, I'm not inclined to get into any verbal with him.'

Despite everything, Perrie managed a small laugh at Aggie's comment.

'Okay, I'm going. Please, be quick.'

She pushed the car door open, drew in a deep breath, and stepped out, pulling herself up to her full height. The extra heel inches earned their big bucks in that moment as they gave her an air of confidence she most certainly wasn't feeling.

With her head high, she strode up the three small steps and marched purposefully towards the entrance, ignoring the cat-calls from the press as they shouted at her to "look this way…", "Were the allegations true?", "Was she guilty?", "Had she known?"

As soon as the doors closed behind her, the noise was instantly muted. The young security guard checked her bag and watched carefully as she stepped through the metal scanner. His face was inscrutable when it beeped and she gave a nervous laugh while removing her earrings. The second pass-through went without a hitch and she quickly gathered up her things so the people queueing behind her could get to where they needed to be without any further delay.

She stood looking around until she found the

information on where she needed to be and when Aggie arrived beside her, ten minutes later, they scurried quickly along the corridor.

'Juniper, there you are! I was beginning to worry.'

'Sorry, Michael, Monday morning traffic, I'm afraid.'

She gave the bewigged barrister a small, apologetic smile.

'Well, you're here now. How are you? Do you remember all that we discussed? This morning will be spent sorting out the jury but hopefully, all being well, proceedings will get underway this afternoon. If anything changes, you'll be the first to know.'

'Thank you.'

'No problem. I need to go. Aggie.'

He tipped his head at them both and quick-stepped it along the corridor, his black robes billowing out behind him.

'So now we wait!'

As per Michael's prediction, several hours and a lunch-break had passed by before a court usher came out through the big, sturdy wooden door and called out, 'Juniper Halstead.'

Perrie gave Aggie a thin smile and followed him into the courtroom. As the usher directed her to where she needed to be, she had a quick glance around and saw Aggie slip into the public gallery.

Once she was sworn in, the usher stepped away and she saw him bow to the Judge before going back through the door they'd just entered.

The Judge looked down towards her and cleared his throat quietly before speaking.

'Doctor Halstead, before we begin, I need to

ascertain that you are fully aware of why you are here in court today.'

'I am, your Honour.'

'May I ask you, for the court records, to state the reason for your presence.'

'I'm here, your Honour, to give evidence against my husband.'

TWENTY-NINE

Did the silence in the room grow heavier after she'd spoken or was it her imagination? Was it more her own sense of relief to have finally arrived at this point and knowing that this nightmare – one way or another – would soon be over?

'Doctor Halstead.'

She looked up at the Judge sitting in his elevated position above the room, his fine red robes providing the necessary gravitas to his important position. She also noted he had a kindly face although there was strength in it which told her there would be no nonsense in his court while he was in charge.

'Would you like to stand or sit?'

'Oh, erm… sit, please, your Honour.'

The Judge gestured to the court usher who quickly moved a chair behind her. As she sat down, Perrie noticed how white her knuckles were and realised she'd been tightly gripping the wooden ledge of the witness stand.

'You may need to adjust the microphone to ensure we can hear you clearly.'

She pulled her chair forward, closer to the mic, and bent it down towards her.

'Thank you, your Honour.'

He smiled at her, acknowledging her discreet test that she could be heard.

He instructed counsel to begin proceedings. Michael, the prosecuting barrister, rose to his feet, gave her a smile which she guessed was supposed to put her at ease – not a chance! – picked up a pad from his desk, looked at it and then said, 'Doctor Halstead, for the purposes of providing the jury with the full information, please could you advise them as to what kind of doctor you are.'

She looked across to the panel of twelve sitting opposite her. She quickly counted – seven men and five women. Nathaniel wouldn't be happy with that; he wouldn't be able to charm the blokes the way he did the females.

'Certainly. I'm a Doctor of History and I hold a research position at Cambridge University.'

'So, just to clarify, not a medical doctor.'

'No, absolutely not. If you broke your leg, I'd be able to tell you how they'd have gone about healing it back in the fifteenth century but I'd be no use in actually helping you to walk again.'

A ripple of laughter ran around the court and Michael threw her a discreet wink. They'd rehearsed this bit a few times in their recent video calls as Michael had said it would help to make her human and, therefore, more believable. The evidence she was about to provide was paramount to the case and provided substantial support to that which would come after her.

'Doctor Halstead, you're here today to provide evidence against your husband, Nathaniel David Halstead, who has been charged with one count of manslaughter and seven counts of sexual abuse against minors. Do you still believe this to be true?'

'I do.'

'Very well. Please could you talk us through the events that have led you to this belief.'

Perrie hesitated for a moment. This was it – the point of no return. She glanced over at her husband and for a brief second, saw the Nate she'd fallen in love with all those years ago, not the Nathaniel he'd become later. He scowled when he caught her looking at him.

You stupid man, she thought, *if you had smiled, I would have been undone. Instead, you've just made this easier for me.*

She looked back at Michael.

'It was the tenth of April, last year—'

'You recall the date?'

'Yes, it was a friend's birthday and we were meeting her and her husband for a celebratory meal in a nearby restaurant. We were getting dressed to go out when Nathaniel's phone rang. He left the room to take the call.'

'Was he out of the room for long?'

'I'd take a guess at maybe twenty minutes or so.'

'Did you know who he was speaking with?'

'Not at the time but I'd guessed it was probably Rupert Barnes, his assistant. Most calls tended to be from him.'

'Was this unusual? Mr. Halstead's assistant calling him in the evening?'

'Not at all. As an MP, and one recently promoted to the cabinet, he would often receive calls at all hours of the day and evening.'

'So, when your husband returned to the room, how was he? What was his demeanour?'

An image flashed into her mind, of Nathaniel practically stumbling through the bedroom door. He'd been as white as the proverbial sheet and visibly trembling.

'He was in a state of upset and shaking noticeably. He told me to call my friend and cancel the dinner arrangement. I argued that it was too late notice to cancel and asked what was wrong. He barked at me, "Just fucking do as you're told!" and then walked back out of the room. He was talking on his phone again as he walked into his study along the hall and slammed the door behind him.'

'Did you cancel as you'd been instructed?'

'I did. I feigned sickness, probably mumbled something about a migraine, apologised profusely and promised to rearrange.'

'Did your husband often speak to you in this manner?'

Perrie leant forward and picked up the glass of water, taking a sip to give the appearance that she was thinking about her answer. Michael had drilled this into her – the next few minutes were crucial in her evidence. If she answered too strongly, there was a risk she'd be perceived as a wife out for revenge. She had to get her words and her tone just right. Enough for the jury to understand what kind of man Nathaniel had become without sounding like she was sticking the knife in.

'It wasn't the first time he'd used this tone on me but he did have a stressful job so—'

'Was he ever physically violent towards you?'

'No. Never. We did have a couple of occasions where we had to replace doors because he'd punched a hole in them and also some plaster repairs for the same reason. He did, I mean, does, have a temper but he's never been physically abusive towards me.'

'What about mentally abusive?'

'He could be controlling. As a politician's wife, he told me repeatedly that I had to present myself accordingly. My image reflected upon his image. Everything had to be just so because it all came down to the persona he projected to the public.'

'I see. So, going back to the night of the tenth of April, please can you take us through what happened after you cancelled your dinner.'

'I got changed into my comfortable sweats, went down to the kitchen, made a sandwich, poured a glass of wine and went through to watch television in the snug.'

'Can you recall what you watched?'

'Honestly? No, I can't. I was seething at having to cancel without any explanation and wasn't paying attention to what was on.'

'When did you see your husband next?'

'It was much later – maybe about eleven, eleven-thirty. I'd fallen asleep on the sofa. He woke me up and told me there was something important he needed to tell me.'

'And what was this "something important"?'

Perrie closed her eyes as the memory she still had a problem dealing with slammed into her brain.
'He told me that,' she replied quietly, 'one of the Sunday newspapers would be printing a story the next day. They were naming him as part of a paedophile ring and that he was also being implicated in the unsolved murder of a fourteen-year-old girl.'

THIRTY

Thirteen Months Earlier

Perrie stared at Nathaniel, unable to comprehend what he was saying. She was hearing the words but they just weren't making any sense in her head. Hysterical laughter from the television made her turn to look at it – some stupid, inane, reality show was playing across the screen. She knew she should switch it off but she didn't want to. Somehow, she couldn't bring herself to let go of that tiny bit of normality. The silence that would ensue would force her to accept, *to listen*, to Nathaniel and she didn't want to do that. Right now, she was hearing him but not listening to him. She couldn't – what he was telling her was simply too horrific for her to believe.

'Juniper, are you listening to me?'

'Fuck off, Nate!' She jumped up, glaring at him. 'You drop that bombshell on me and then add insult to injury by calling me a name you know I deplore because you think it reflects better on you! How many levels of stupid are you? Nothing is ever going to make this better.'

She stormed out the door only to storm back in again a second later to retrieve her wine glass although there weren't enough vineyards in the world that could make her forget what her husband had just told her.

He followed her through to the kitchen.

'Juni— Perrie, please, talk to me.'

'Talk to you? TALK to you? What the hell do you expect me to say, Nate?'

'Nathan—'

'Don't you fucking dare!' She pointed the neck of the bottle at him. 'You can drop your highfalutin notions right now! You might think using Nathaniel instead of Nate makes you appear more important but all it does is show you for what you are – a pompous, arrogant arsehole!'

'Really, Perrie, I don't think name-calling is going to resolve this situation.'

'Resolve this situation? Are you for bloody real? You've just told me you've been named as a member of a paedophile ring and implicated in an unsolved murder and now you're trying to "resolve" the situation. And you've just forced me to resort to using finger quotes, you bastard!' Her voice rose several octaves as she spoke.

'Perrie, please, calm down. We need to discuss this sensibly.'

She slammed the wine bottle down onto the marble worktop, placed her hands flat on either side of it and drew in several deep breaths. He was right, she did have to calm down because if she didn't, she was liable to run him through with her best Sabatier!

'So, Nate, please tell me exactly HOW you plan to *resolve* this situation because from where I'm standing, you and your career are pretty much done for. Some incidents can be recovered from – such as verbally abusing a policeman – but being called a kiddie-fiddler and accused of murder… I really don't fancy your chances!'

'Rupert is putting together a denial as we speak. We'll need to get the PM's approval for it tomorrow and then it can be released. We'll do the press-meet outside the gate on Monday morning – so I'll need you looking your best to help deflect some of the accusation – and then we can move on.'

'You really are a disillusioned fool if you think this is just going to go away on your say so. This is the kind of mud that sticks! Your precious career is over. Everything is gone!'

She watched him blanche as her words hit him like little daggers of truth.

'You need to stand by me, Perrie. If we present a united front, you know it'll make a difference. You need to tell the world that you believe I'm innocent of these terrible accusations.'

'Do I? Because it seems to have escaped your notice, Nate, that so far, you haven't actually told me if they are true or not.'

'Of course, they're not true.'

She glanced down before forcing herself to look into his eyes.

'Nate, I'm going to ask you this only once and you had better be honest with me – are these allegations true?'

'No, they're not true! I've told Rupert and now I'm telling you – they are lies. It's a smear campaign to discredit me.'

Perrie watched him closely and got her answer.

The bastard was lying to her!

In the end, the decision to stand by him in front of the

press was taken from her – the police turned up to arrest Nate at eight-thirty the following morning. At nine-thirty she left the house, glad of the springtime sunshine because it justified her need to wear a baseball cap and her sunglasses, and drove to the large, retail-park, supermarket a few miles away where no one local was likely to see her. There, she loaded her trolley up to the brim and grabbed a copy of the offending broadsheet on her way out the door.

Her timing couldn't have been better – she'd only been back in the house ten minutes when the media hounds began to turn up at her firmly closed gates. She'd been a politician's wife long enough to know how these things went and she knew they'd be camped out on the pavement for the next few days, trying to get her side of the story, hence the reason for the supermarket dash – getting the larder fully stocked until they buggered off.

After walking around the house, closing curtains and blinds, she made herself a pot of coffee, warmed up a croissant she really didn't want, and sat down at the table to read the article which had blown her world apart.

Fifteen minutes later, she was leaning over the sink, throwing up the small breakfast she'd just eaten.

She was wiping her mouth with some kitchen towel when her mobile rang. At first, she really didn't want to see who was calling but when it rang a second time, she checked the display and let out a small sigh of relief to see her big sister's name flashing up.

'Aggie!'

'Oh, Pea, I've just seen the news. It's awful. How are you, my pet?'

'Oh, Aggie, I... I... I don't know!'

'Look, give me an hour and I'll be there.'

'NO! Please, don't come over. I can't risk you being dragged into this.'

'Hey, I'm a big girl, I can cope with a few tawdry little sensationalist scumbags. The one with the moustache looks like he couldn't fight his way out of a wet paper bag!'

'It's not you I'm thinking of— Wait a minute... moustache? How do you know what they look like?'

'Because I'm sitting here looking at your front door on the twenty-four-hour news channel. The gates are closed, as is the garage door and your curtains are shut tight.'

Perrie's head dropped into her hand.

'The TV cameras are here too? That was quicker than I expected.'

'Sorry, Pea, it's the full circus out there, babes.'

'Look, as I was saying, you mustn't come over. I know you can look after yourself but think of the boys. He's their uncle – they'll get all sorts of crap at school once people make the connection. I can't do that to them. We must protect them the best we can.'

'Did you know? Did you have any idea?'

'AGGIE! How can you even ask such a thing?'

'Because everyone else will and you need to be ready for it.'

'No,' she sighed, 'I didn't know. Not even a tiny inkling.'

'Do you think it's true?'

She sighed again. 'Yes, it's true...'

'He admitted to it?' The incredulity was blatant in Aggie's voice.

'No, he denied it.'

'Then, how...'

'Because I know my husband!'

THIRTY-ONE

'Doctor Halstead, you say you "know your husband" –
please could you elaborate on that.'

'We've been together for over fifteen years and I
know when he's lying to me.'

'May I ask how?'

'He has a tell.'

'A tell?'

'Yes, a tell. An unconscious movement or reaction.
It's most often associated with card players but nearly all
humans have one or two little things that give them away
in certain situations.'

'And your husband has one?'

'Yes, he does.'

'Could you explain further, please?'

'When he lies, he scratches the back of his left
hand.'

The barrister turned towards the jury.

'Ladies and gentlemen of the jury, we're now about
to show you a short montage of the video from Mr.
Halstead's first police interview. Please watch it closely.

Doctor Halstead,' he turned back to face her, 'I believe the best screen for you to view this is that one there.'

He pointed to a screen placed on the table underneath the judge's bench. One of Michael's juniors scurried over and turned the screen to face her.

A moment later, she was watching Nate being interviewed. The detective doing the questioning was a woman and she could see her husband was doing his best to try and charm her. It was interesting to see the lack of response from the detective – not many women were immune to him.

The video played for about three minutes and whenever Nate was asked if he'd either had sex with under-age girls, had known the girls were under-age, or had met the young girl who'd been murdered, he denied that he had. Unfortunately for him, each time he'd been scratching his left hand harder than a dog with a bad dose of the fleas!

'Ladies and gentlemen of the jury,' Michael was speaking again, 'If I may direct you to the folders in front of you. Please could you open them at tab "C", page six.'

'Doctor Halstead,' the judge leant forward to address her, 'the folder in front of you is for your reference.'

'Thank you, your Honour.'

She opened the folder as Michael had directed and found herself looking at a blown-up photograph of Nate's left hand, the back of which had been scratched red-raw.

'Doctor Halstead, can you confirm if this is your husband's hand.'

'It is.'

'And you know this how?'

'His wedding ring – it's rather distinctive.'

She'd always hated his wedding band with the three tiny diamonds embedded in it. She'd thought it looked naff when they went out to buy their rings and had said as much. Nate, however, had always had a touch of the magpie about him and had a penchant for shiny things. He'd insisted on getting it and now it was coming back to bite him on the ass!

'Thank you, Doctor Halstead.'

'Counsellor, I'm looking at the time and wondering if this might be a convenient point to stop for the day?'

As the judge leant forward, Perrie threw a quick glance down at her watch and was shocked to see she'd been on the stand for over two hours. No wonder she felt so drained.

Michael concurred with the judge that they should halt proceedings for today and resume in the morning. After a few words of caution from His Honour that she should not talk about anything discussed within the courtroom that day, she was escorted back out to the corridor where she found Aggie already waiting for her.

'Hey, you,' she whispered, as her big sister pulled her into a hug and held her close.

'You did well, you're doing well.'

'I didn't sound like I was out for revenge, did I?'

'Not in the slightest. You were perfect.'

'I'm so not looking forward to tomorrow.'

'Really? You've faced the worst of it today. Tomorrow will be a cinch.'

'No, Aggie, it won't. Tomorrow will be hell because that's when I'll be facing Nate's defence barrister and he will be doing all that he can to discredit me and the evidence I've given.'

'But Michael is so nice.'

'Yeah, because I'm on his side. Anyway, can we please just get out of here...'

'Of course. Let me go and get the car. Wait till you see me pull up and then make a run for it.'

Fifteen minutes later, Perrie was bending forward in the

car, hiding her face from the journalists' cameras as Aggie spun around the turning circle and took her away from their glare as fast as she legally could.

THIRTY-TWO

'Daisy, dinner's nearly ready. Go and wash your hands, please.'

Morgan gave the sausages another turn on the grill, took the potatoes over to the sink to drain them and placed them back on the hob to steam for a moment or two before being mashed into oblivion! If Daisy came back in time, he'd let her do the honours since she enjoyed it so much.

He pulled open the cutlery drawer and took out two sets to lay on the table. Thoughts of Perrie came back into his mind – not that she'd been all that far from it since she'd left – and he had to work on holding back a loud sigh. He had to be strong and not let Daisy see how much he was missing their friend.

Just then, Daisy came running into the kitchen, exclaiming breathlessly, 'Daddy, Daddy, Merida's on the television!'

'Is she, darling?'

Trying to ascertain if the sausages were thoroughly cooked – always his biggest concern when he served them up – Morgan was only half-listening to his daughter.

'Yes, she is. Well… I think it is. She looks different. But it's definitely Merida.'

'Have they made a new cartoon of her? Maybe that's why she looks different. Or is she older now, not the young girl in the film?'

'What are you talking about, Daddy?'

Satisfied that his sausages wouldn't be causing any salmonella issues, Morgan took them off the grill.

'You said Merida looked different, so I was making suggestions as to why.'

'No, Daddy, not that Merida, OUR Merida! It was OUR Merida on the television.'

'What? You mean Perrie?'

'Yes!' Daisy gave him a look of impatience.

'Are you sure?'

'That's what I said. I'm sure it was our Merida but she looked different. It was on the boring growed-up programme.'

'You mean the news? She was on the news?'

'Yes.'

Morgan rushed through to the lounge but the commentator was now talking about the Premier League football match taking place that evening and had long moved on from his previous topic.

'Where are the buttons, Daisy? Let me rewind it.'

Typically, however, the remote control was nowhere to be seen and by the time it had been located between the cushions of the sofa, the next programme had begun and Morgan was aware of their dinner growing cold.

'We'll just need to ask Perrie when she returns if it was her, since you're not sure, won't we, squirt?'

He tousled her hair as he switched off the TV and walked with Daisy back into the kitchen.

'If it was our Merida, does that mean she's famous?'

'Hmm, maybe. It depends what she was on the news for. Did you listen to the talking?'

'No, Daddy, that's the boring stuff!'

He let out a small chuckle. Daisy wasn't far wrong there – most of the time, the news was boring stuff but he was intrigued to see who Daisy had mistaken for Perrie. He made a note to watch the next bulletin later that night.

The clock on the mantelpiece rang out its chimes, causing Morgan to look up at the time and put down the book he was reading. The football highlights would be on soon, he might as well check them out. He hadn't fancied watching the whole match, preferring instead to read the thriller he was finding quite engrossing.

He remembered Daisy's earlier comments about Perrie as he flicked on the TV and so scooted through a few channels until he came to one where the national news had just begun. The top story seemed to be about the trial of some MP who was accused of being part of a paedophile ring. He vaguely remembered the story breaking last year but he was still in a dark place after the loss of Harriet and hadn't paid too much attention to it. Being honest, he hadn't paid too much attention to anything at that time.

Harriet! Thinking of her brought back memories of when Jimmy Savile had turned out to be considerably less nice than the nation had been led to believe. Harriet had asked him about it, trying to get a man's perspective but he'd been unable to answer her questions for he couldn't understand it himself. Morgan shuddered even now at the thought as it was something he simply could not get his head around at all.

He looked down at the book by his side – could he squeeze another chapter in before the footie highlights?

"The trial of ex-MP, Nathaniel Halstead, began today when his wife, Doctor Juniper Halstead arrived at court to give evidence against him."

Morgan glanced up at the television disinterestedly and had already looked away when his brain caught up with what his eyes had just seen.

'What the hell?'

He grabbed the remote control, hit rewind and leant forward in his seat as the newscaster spoke again.

"The trial of ex-MP, Nathaniel Halstead, began today when his wife, Doctor Juniper Halstead arrived at court to give evidence against him."

He paused the screen at the point where the woman on it was looking right into the camera. His breath slowly left his body and he nearly forgot to breathe in again such was his shock and confusion. There was no mistaking that it was Perrie – Daisy had been right – but it wasn't *his* Perrie. Or *their* Perrie.

Perrie...

Juni*per*...

Finally, he got it! He'd always thought it was an unusual name but had never asked more on it. Its origins all made sense now although it was about the only thing that did.

Perrie was married.

He looked down. With his elbows resting on his knees, his hands were clenched tightly, hovering in the space in between.

She was married? To a – soon-to-be-convicted? – paedophile?

Why hadn't she told him? Did she honestly think he wouldn't find out?

He looked back up at the television and worked on taking in this Perrie who wasn't Perrie. A Perrie with blonde, smoothly styled hair – not an auburn, corkscrew curl in sight. A Perrie with smoky-eyed makeup on, giving her aquamarine eyes a feline quality. Perrie in a sharp suit and high-heeled shoes... no longer his wild and free neighbour and friend but someone who looked every inch like they were in control and with a stiff-upper-lip for good measure. He pressed the button to restart the programme and watched as Juniper – he couldn't think of this woman as being Perrie – rushed past the waiting journalists. She put her hand up at one point to deflect a camera and he noticed the rings shining on her wedding finger. Rings he was seeing for the first time.

He let the article end before switching the television off, getting up from the sofa and walking through to the dining room where his laptop sat on the table.

He booted it up and even though he knew it was a very bad idea, Morgan proceeded to trawl through the internet, looking for every article he could find on both Nathaniel Halstead and his lovely wife, Juniper.

He started off with reading through articles on their charity work, benefit dinners they had attended – Juniper had looked especially stunning in a long, black sheath dress at one of them – and projects they supported together.

While there were a number of articles on the two of them, when he typed in Nathaniel's name alone, there was an explosion of options for him to read. Morgan, out of curiosity, typed in Juniper's name on its own and found the search results greatly reduced. He ascertained she was a doctor of history at Cambridge University, held a position there as a researcher, was a co-author on a few historical papers which had been published and also three non-fiction books. As a historical researcher, he now understood how her novels were so detailed and seemed to impart information that he hadn't previously known.

When he tried searching for a link between Juniper

Halstead and J.P Lassiter, nothing whatsoever came up. In that respect, Perrie had been truthful.

Morgan deleted the search and went back to just Nathaniel's name. Judging by the thousands of items that appeared, it seemed he carried a rather large ego around with him. As an MP, Morgan had expected him to have a reasonable presence on the internet and social media but nothing quite as extensive as this. There were *reams* of photographs, some with his wife but many, many more without her.

Morgan enlarged a few and concurred that, with his brown eyes, sculpted cheekbones and so-blond-to-be-almost-white hair, Nathaniel Halstead was not an unattractive man. As an MP, he would no doubt be oozing with charm – try to find an MP who wasn't – but his weak chin and soft-looking lips suggested a man who would follow the herd, incapable of making decisions for himself.

All of this had Morgan wondering how on earth he could have ended up facing the charges now being directed at him. With those looks, he could have charmed the birds from the trees and the knickers off anyone in a ten-mile radius! He certainly didn't need to resort to abusing young girls.

His curiosity now in overdrive, Morgan searched on the allegations directed at Nathaniel. After reading for ten minutes, he really wished he hadn't looked – he felt sick to his stomach as he read about the young girl who'd been found murdered. She'd barely turned fourteen, had been beaten beyond recognition and sexually abused, quite violently, in every way possible.

His thoughts staggered this way and that, bouncing off the walls of his brain as it worked on comprehending what he'd read. It then made a leap that he really wished it hadn't – if Perrie, or Juniper, was giving evidence against Nathaniel then, surely, she must have known! When you're married, you know everything about your other half. Even more so when you've been together as long as the Halsteads had been. There had been no secrets between him and Harriet so Perrie… Juniper must have been aware of his actions and had done nothing to stop him!

How could she?

What kind of monster could condone this kind of behaviour from anyone, never mind her own husband? Had she loved him so much that she'd been prepared to ignore his crimes?

He felt his stomach begin to churn and he wondered if he was about to be sick but instead, he found himself running up the stairs to Daisy's bedroom, rushing through her door and taking his precious little girl in his arms, all the while berating himself for having left her – a number of times – alone in the hands of someone so evil.

'I'm so sorry, my baby girl, for putting you in danger. I promise I will never do that to you again.'
He didn't know how long he sat there, rocking a sleeping Daisy back and forth, but when he finally laid her down, his resolve had hardened and he knew she would never, ever see Perrie again.

THIRTY-THREE

'Here we go again!'

Perrie let out a massive sigh as Aggie turned the corner towards the courthouse. The media pack were still in situ.

'Hey, at least you have some armour today!'

'Seriously? You think these will make a difference?'

Perrie pointed towards the over-large, bug eye sunglasses she was now sporting. Aggie had been following the twitter feed on the case and somebody had mentioned Juniper's lack of sunglasses to hide her face. This had sent Aggie off on a hunt around the house to find the Victoria Beckham-inspired purchase of a pair of massive, face-hiding sunnies which had looked ludicrous on her and were eventually consigned to the back of a drawer somewhere.

'Hey, at least you look glamorous with those on. People thought I was an alien extra from Doctor Who when I wore them! Be grateful, wench!'

'I wish I could wear them in court...'

'Look, it might not be that bad.'

'And it could be considerably worse.'

Aggie pulled up beside the pavement.

'Same deal as yesterday, yeah? See you back inside in ten minutes?'

'Sure. See you then.'

'Once more unto the breach,' she said as she drew in a deep breath, preparing herself to run the gauntlet that was the press pack and into the relative safety of the courthouse.

Perrie schooled her face to hide her annoyance and disgust. She didn't know which sleaze-shop Nathaniel had dug this barrister out from but he brought a whole new meaning to the words obsequious and obnoxious. He was so slimy she was convinced he must leave a trail behind him when he walked.

She was also exhausted. Having already been questioned to the nth degree over their alcohol intake and use of drugs – or lack of in her case but finding out that Nate had become dependent on cocaine had been quite a shock – she'd now just spent the last half an hour being drilled on their sex life and asked to describe, in detail which she was far from comfortable sharing, what she and Nate had got up to in the bedroom… and everywhere else in the house going by the innuendo in the comments and questions she'd had to face.

Although, maybe if she had dressed up as a schoolgirl – as suggested by this creep – perhaps Nate would have been satisfied by that and wouldn't have gone off looking for the real deal. Nor had they indulged in any form of BDSM beneath or around the sheets so her husband's penchant for a bit of violence while getting it on was news to her. Yet again she wondered if the lack of "trying something a bit different" had been the catalyst that pushed Nate to cross the line.

She didn't have time to ponder the issue as the Slug was off and slithering again.

'Doctor Halstead, if we may, I'd like to discuss your journals in greater detail, please.'

I'll bet you do! she thought, *given that they are the key to this case.*

'I know you discussed these in length with the Prosecuting Counsel this morning but I'd like to go over some other aspects which were not brought up earlier.'

'Very well,' she replied.

'Can you tell us again why you feel the need to keep journals, or diaries as some people refer to them?'

'I'm a historian and I learnt at a young age the importance of diaries for providing information from our time to those who will come after us.'

'Would you care to elaborate further on that statement?'

'Erm, well… we were learning the history of The Great Fire of London at school and our teacher shared some details from the diary of Samuel Pepys. She told us that much of what we know from that period in time is down to the detailed information this gentleman had written. After that, I began to keep my own diary although I don't think future historians will be overly enthralled to read about a ten-year-old's crush on Robbie Williams.'

'So, you think you're the next Samuel Pepys, do you?'

The words "stupid imbecile" flashed through her mind as she smiled sweetly.

'Absolutely not. He was merely my inspiration. As

I'm sure he was for a lot of children who found the period of plague and fire in London to be fascinating.'

'Quite!'

Perrie waited while the Slug flicked through some papers on the desk in front of him. Finally, just as the tension in the room was about to peak, he looked up and said, 'Doctor Halstead, when you presented the police with the evidence against my client, you stated your journals were the key to proving he was not at home on the nights the allegations against him took place. Is that correct?'

'It is.'

'Yet, when I look at the dates of the allegations and I refer to your diaries of the same, I rarely see any mention of my client's movements within them.'

'Over time, our individual careers took us in different directions and our paths crossed less frequently so there was often little about our marriage to write about.'

'So how, may I ask, are you able to pinpoint the nights my client did not return to the marital home until late or at all if he is not actually named in your musings?'

The condescending smile he bestowed on her had Perrie almost grinding her teeth down to their roots.

It's time to take you down a peg or two, you supercilious little turd!

'Sir, if I may direct your attention to the extracts of my journals in the evidence folders we have been provided with,' she picked up the white A4 ring-binder sitting on the shelf in front of her and opened it at the relevant pages, 'you will note that every entry has an asterisk on the left-hand side, approximately a third of the way down the page. Also, this asterisk is alongside a blank line.'

'Yes, I see it. What of it?'

'On the nights my husband did not return home, I would find myself working later than I should, which meant I had less time to write in my journals. What I would do, therefore, is write the first part – my feelings and thoughts at that moment in time – before going to bed and then follow up with other newsworthy items the following day. I chose to enter the information in this manner for clarity.'

'Clarity?'

'Yes. If you write a journal before bedtime, your thoughts and emotions will differ from other times of the day. It may be because you are relaxed, in preparation for sleep, or that you are stressed due to layers of pressure placed upon you over the course of the day. As such, the items I consider to be worth noting in my diary before I switch off to sleep could be quite different to those I write about when I am fully awake and refreshed. I wanted to notate this for clarification purposes.'

'I see.'

'Furthermore,' she was on a roll now and intent on sending this slug back under whichever rock he'd crawled out from, 'you have my journals for the last ten years and you will see that all entries dating from when my husband was elected as an MP have been marked up in this manner and therefore preceding the timescale your client is being investigated across. I think you will also find that many of the notations correlate with your client's office diaries from which you will be able to see when he attended official functions or late-night voting in the house. And finally, although not discernible on the black and white photocopies we have been provided with, I write my secondary entries in blue pen, not the black pen of the first entry. Again, just another small notation for my own personal reference. This should, however, act as proof that I did not doctor my journals after the event of my husband's arrest. Or am I wrong in thinking that was going to be your next question?'

'Erm... urm... ah...' The Slug dithered over his paperwork, no doubt trying to find a way of clawing back the ground she'd removed from under him.

Perrie slipped a quick glance in Michael's direction, worried that she may have gone too far, but he was focusing on his own paperwork although the shaking in his shoulders suggested to her that he was trying very hard to keep his mirth under control.

A few minutes passed while the Slug continued to faff about with his paperwork. Eventually the judge leant forward.

'Counsel, do you have any further questions for Doctor Halstead? Or can we bring today's proceedings to a close?'

'I... err... I...'

'Yes?'

The Slug's shoulders dropped.

'No more questions, your Honour.'

'Very well.'

The judge looked towards Perrie and smiled kindly at her.

'Doctor Halstead, thank you for your time and the evidence you have given. There is a small chance you may need to be recalled for additional questioning but for now, you are free to leave.'

She stood and bowed her head towards him.

'Thank you, your Honour.'

With her head held high, she walked out of the court. She didn't look at Nate or even in his general direction. After all this, she never wanted to set eyes on him again.

Aggie met her in the corridor and she all but collapsed into her arms.

'There, there, Pea, it's over. You did it. We can go

home now.'

Perrie stepped back and looked her sister in the eye.

'It's over for now, Aggie. We need to wait and see if it's enough to put him away.'

'Let's hope it is,' she sighed, 'let's hope it is.'

THIRTY-FOUR

Perrie stood outside her Hampstead home, Aggie by her side.

'Have you missed it?' Aggie asked as they stood inside the gates looking up at the building Perrie had vacated over a year before.

'Actually, no, I haven't. Given how excited I was when we first moved in, I'm surprised by that.'

'Do you think it's been tainted by what's happened?'

'Yes, I do. I was a prisoner in here for weeks while the press hounded me daily to give interviews. For as long as I live, I will never forget that moment of being driven through those gates in the back of a police car as they took me away for questioning. I'm sure they were expecting me to defend Nate – it was certainly a surprise for them when I handed over my evidence against him.'

'Yeah, I never did ask you – it didn't feel right to discuss it when you came to hide at my place – what prompted you to make the connections with the dates?'

Perrie moved towards the front door, pulling the keys from her handbag.

'It was the newspaper article – it mentioned some dates when the group were believed to have met. Being a historian means collecting data and putting it together to create a larger, clearer picture of events in the past so it was an automatic response to refer to my journals to see what did or didn't add up. Unfortunately, the dates when Nate wasn't at home matched those in the paper.'

'How did that feel?'

Aggie asked the question as they stepped into the cool hallway of the house and Perrie closed the door behind them.

'I don't know, if I'm being truthful. I felt quite detached from everything – I suspect my way of dealing with the shock of it all was to treat it like one of my research projects.'

'And Nate?'

'Do you know, Aggie, of all the things I could have thought him possible of doing, this would never have made it onto the list. And given how long that list would be, that's saying something. Even now I struggle to believe it. That doesn't mean,' she gave her sister a hard look, 'I don't accept he's done this vile deed. I'm not like some wives who would bury their heads in the sand and go into full-on denial. I KNOW he's guilty to the core, it's just hard to come to terms with it.'

'I hear ya!'

Perrie stood in the hallway of the Hampstead house that had been her home for five years. They'd moved in the day after Nate had won the election that saw him become a Member of Parliament. He'd always reckoned fate had stuck a great big hand into the mix as his political career began to take off at the same time they moved into a better postcode.

Personally, she now wished they'd stayed in their little one-bed flat in Camberwell and that Nate had stuck with being a local councillor because the first day he'd set his highly-polished brogues in Westminster Hall was the day he began to change.

'Right,' she gave herself a little shake, she'd vowed she wasn't going to dwell on this today, 'let's get on with it. Shall we start at the top and just work our way down?'

'Sounds as good a plan as any!'

When Perrie next looked at her watch, over six hours had passed. She handed the parcel tape to Aggie and held down the lid on the last storage box as her sister sealed it into oblivion.

'Seriously, Aggie, do you think there's enough tape on there?'

'I can add more if you like?'

'Probably best not otherwise we'll be paying double the delivery costs!'

Aggie picked the box up and carried it out to join the stack in the hallway.

'Are you sure that's everything? Shall we do a quick sweep just to double-check?'

Perrie nodded. 'Okay, although Karen will do that when she comes in tomorrow and Friday to do the deep-clean.'

They walked through the rooms that were now empty of all personal items although most of the furniture was still in situ.

'I do have to ask, Pea, what on earth possessed you to buy this glass and chrome crap? It is *so* not you at all!'

'Nate chose it! He wanted to give the appearance of being a trendy MP with his finger on the pulse and felt that the furniture and styles my tastes ran to were old-fashioned, out-of-date and would give off the wrong vibe to visitors.'

'Well, you certainly had your fair share of those – do you think any of them really noticed the décor?'

'The men probably didn't but I often caught some of the wives having a good mooch – although whether they liked what they saw, I couldn't say.'

'And you're okay with Dad letting it out? It doesn't feel strange knowing that next week some unknown family is going to be sleeping in your bed or eating at your table?'

'Nope! Not at all. All my personal items have been removed along with the artwork that means anything to me and the few bits of furniture that I care for.'

'Is all of it going into storage?'

'Most of it although there are some things which I'll be taking back to Broatie with me. All of my baking stuff, for example, along with the little embroidered foot-stool I found at that flea-market in Montpellier. That has been much missed and it will look right at home in the cottage.'

Perrie also knew a certain little girl who would love sitting on it but she wasn't sharing *that* with Aggie. Daisy and Morgan were news for another time when this was over.

'Well, we'd better get a wriggle on and get this stuff loaded into the car.' Aggie looked at the boxes around them. 'The storage facility closes at eight and we're ripe for hitting the rush hour traffic. I really don't want to be lugging it all into the house tonight only to lug it back out again in the morning.'

'Okay then, come on.'

It didn't take long to get the car packed up and soon there was only one, smaller, pile of boxes left.

'Take some time to say goodbye. I'll wait for you in the car.'

Aggie gave Perrie's arm a gentle squeeze and

walked out the door, closing it quietly behind her.

With a small sigh, she walked over to the insignificant stack of boxes sitting by the stairs. They were off to Nate's parents' house in Peterborough tomorrow. Karen, the cleaner who now came with the house, would be signing them over to the delivery company tomorrow morning.

Perrie went through to the kitchen and looked out of the window into the vast garden and the swimming pool she'd loved swimming in every day that was now drained and covered up. It had been one of the few things she'd really enjoyed about living here. She gazed at it for a moment before turning and making her way back towards the front door.

It was funny, she mused, as she spun slowly round in the hallway, looking up to the ceiling and in through the open doors of the rooms off it, that when you take furniture out of the equation, how little the personal possessions add up to. Nate had been all about the flashy and bright – the latest model of car, the biggest television or the brand-new, hot-off-the-production-line Apple phone. He hadn't cared about the candy-floss stick from their first trip to the seaside or the photo-booth picture strip from the night he'd proposed. The little things that had meant so much to her had been meaningless to him.

And in the end, she had become meaningless too. She'd looked good on his arm at events and affairs and it had pleased him no end to refer to his wife, the doctor of history with Cambridge University, but how she felt in herself had ceased to be of interest to him. Once he'd set his sights on Westminster, she'd become a useful commodity, nothing more.

In that moment, the feeling of closure rushed through her. Soon this would all be over and she was more than ready to move on. Perrie walked to the door, stepped over the threshold and closed the heavy wooden panel with a bang. She got in the car and as they drove through the gates for the last time, she didn't once look back.

THIRTY-FIVE

Aggie's back garden was quiet and peaceful and Perrie was sitting out there, enjoying the moments before her nephews came home from school and the house would feel like two small hurricanes had landed.

She adored the boys to bits but they were noisy and boisterous which she wasn't used to and sometimes they left her head spinning.

'How do you cope?' she'd asked Aggie on Saturday afternoon when they'd come flying in from football practice, stormed the kitchen for food, rushed up the stairs to wash and change, stormed the kitchen again for more food and then went off to a birthday party with Graham.

'Easy,' had been her sister's reply, 'I worship at the temple.'

'Worship at the temple?'

'Yes, the temple of wine, the temple of gin, the temple of vodka... talking of which, it's after two o'clock and therefore a perfectly acceptable time to crack open said vino – are you joining me?'

Through her laughter, Perrie had replied, 'It would

be rude not to! Pour one for me!'

It was now Wednesday and the second week of the trial. Perrie was relieved that she hadn't been recalled and Michael had been on the phone to say it was now unlikely she would be. He'd been rather non-committal when she'd asked how things were going and she'd taken this to mean he didn't want to tempt fate by suggesting it was looking good for his side. It was now a case of waiting for him to call with the news that the jury had retired to consider their verdict.

She let her head fall back on the comfortable Adirondack chair, listening to the lazy hum of a bee in the nearby lavender pots and made a mental note to look into getting a couple of these chairs for the cottage – they were very relaxing and she was sure Morgan would like them.

Morgan!

Oh, how she'd missed him. Considerably more than she'd expected given all that was going on. There had been several times – okay, every single night – when she'd longed to pick up the phone and hear his voice, with its soft Devonshire burr, in her ear but she'd forced herself not to. He would ask her what she was doing or where she had been and she didn't want to lie to him – not now. She'd managed to avoid doing so thus far by evading personal questions and deflecting him away from anything where she'd have to tell an untruth. Only a few more days to go and she'd be able to tell him everything after which she could look to the future and make plans again without her recent worries of being spotted or recognised whenever she went out.

She closed her eyes and pictured him and Daisy, imagining the sound of the sea as the waves rolled up and down the shore, whispering to the sand while caressing it with their white foamy fingers. She missed the cries of the gulls as they swooped over the cottage, going to and from the cliff-tops in their never-ending quest for food. She even missed the constant buffeting of the wind which assaulted her every time she walked out the front door. Seaview Cottage had become quite dear to her and her heart ached as she realised that she couldn't wait to go back.

When she'd driven away from Broatiescombe Bay that Saturday night, she'd wondered how it would feel when she returned. She was beginning to think she had her answer, that maybe she would be going home.

Just then, her phone began to ring. She picked it up, looked at that screen and swiped to accept the call.

Less than thirty seconds later, she hung up.

The jury had retired.

When Aggie returned home from a day at one of her salons, Perrie was still sitting in the garden with George and Timothy lying on the grass next to her chair.

'Graham told me you were out here. He also said you wouldn't come in when he cooked dinner for the boys. What gives?'

She opened her eyes as Aggie settled herself in the chair next to her, the wine bottle and glasses clinking on the table when she set them down.

'The jury have gone in.'

'Ah, I see.'

Aggie took a long drink of her wine and topped up her glass before speaking again.

'What time?'

'Just after two-thirty.'

Aggie made a big show of looking at her watch.

'Hmm, well, as the little hand is pointing at the six and the big hand is pointing to the nine, I think we can safely say you're not going to be getting a verdict tonight. So, why don't you get that down your neck,' she nodded towards the untouched glass of wine on the table, 'while I go and order in a takeaway. Indian do you?'

Perrie picked up her glass, took a large gulp and smiled over at her sister.

'That would be perfect, thank you.'

Aggie stood, leant over and placed a kiss on her head.

'Have a few more gulps of the grape juice, Pea. It won't get rid of the butterflies in your stomach but it will knock them into a drunken stupor for a while.'

She couldn't help but smile as Aggie sashayed back into the house, calling loudly to her husband to dig out the "hot shop menu" while she got changed.

Perrie was once again in the garden, it was the only place where she was able to find a modicum of peace within herself, although this time, she wasn't alone. Aggie had cancelled the few meetings she'd pencilled in – 'Pea, I was prepared for this, I knew there was a good chance we'd be at this point by now so I made sure I didn't book anything important and the meetings I did book could be easily rescheduled,' – and they both sat in silence. The tension was heavy in the air around them. It was the third day since the jury had gone in and Perrie was like the proverbial cat on a hot tin roof. The smallest sound had her jumping a foot in the air and she'd snapped at Aggie and Graham on a number of occasions and even a couple of times at the cats. This was immediately followed by a flurry of apologies to them and smothering them with hugs and kisses although it did little to appease her guilt. Snapping at her sister was one thing but being short-tempered with her precious fur-babies was something else entirely. She hated Nate even more for making her feel and behave this way.

'Oh, dear goodness, will you just hurry up AND RING!'

'I don't think screaming at your phone will do any good,' Aggie drawled, as she wriggled in her chair, trying to stay lined up with the sunbeams blazing down from the sky.

At that moment, the sound of Poison's "Look What the Cat Dragged In" pierced the air and her mobile began vibrating on the table.

'Well, bugger me, I was wrong! Screaming does work!'

Perrie picked up the phone and stared at Michael's name on the screen. This was it. They'd agreed he would only call her once there was news.

'For fuck's sake, Perrie, answer the bloody call!'

She swiped the screen and just about managed to squeak out a 'Hello?'

She listened as Michael spoke in her ear, unable to speak herself. Her mouth had gone completely dry and her stomach was churning so furiously, she thought she was going to be sick.

When a few minutes had passed, where Michael had done all the talking and she'd done all the listening, she eventually whispered, 'Thank you. For everything you've done. Thank you.'

She ended the call and placed the phone carefully back on the table.

Aggie spun round on her chair to face her, took her hands in hers, and asked quietly, 'Well?'

Perrie looked into her sister's eyes, which were so similar to her own, and replied, 'Guilty! Guilty of all charges including manslaughter.'

Then she burst into tears!

THIRTY-SIX

Morgan sat staring at the television, waiting for the late
news to come on and as had been the case for the last two
weeks, he was glued to the screen, ready to soak up every
last detail of the Nathaniel Halstead court case. He knew
he'd become obsessed with it but he couldn't help
himself – he'd been guilt-tripping over allowing Daisy to
spend so much time with Perrie. After seeing Perrie on
the television last week, he'd spent several days trawling
the internet, pulling up every single article he could find
that concerned Juniper and / or Nathaniel Halstead and
had read them all avidly. He'd watched the news every
night after Daisy had gone to bed and had felt more than a
little nauseous when the reports coming back from the
journalists concerned the evidence being given by the
victims. These were young innocent girls who'd found
themselves in situations they didn't know how to get out
of – preyed upon and groomed by men who should have
known better.

From what Morgan had been able to ascertain, the
four men the police had charged were all successful

businessmen. Two were CEOs in large financial establishments in the City, one was an investment banker and Nathaniel Halstead was the fourth. As an upwardly-mobile, young MP, Halstead was the most visibly prominent member of the group and was attracting all the attention although Morgan would bet his house it was the kind of attention he didn't want. This was the one thing that shot down the old adage, "There's no such thing as bad publicity". Well, yes, actually, there is!

Despite scouring all the bulletins on every channel, there had been no further news of Perrie after the second day. He still hadn't heard from her and wasn't sure that he wanted to. His head kept telling him they would need to have a discussion but his heart and emotions were dead set against it.

He guessed she'd return to the cottage once the verdict was in but that thought then led him down the path of where she considered home to be. Would she come back to Broatiescombe Bay or would she now feel free to move on with her life? Had this just been some little passing interlude to while away the time until the case had gone to court?

He ran his hand through his thick blond hair, making it stand on end in some places. He'd barely slept since making his discovery and the shadows under his eyes were growing more noticeable by the day. Well, they must be because even Daisy had commented. He'd fobbed her off by telling her it was the heat keeping him awake at night and she'd been content with that. A five-year-old was never going to understand the pain and confusion he was dealing with.

How had he got Perrie so wrong?

Had he got her wrong?'

Was he doing her a disservice by thinking the worst of her?

But if she'd had nothing to hide, why hadn't she told him? That was always the sticking point when he tried to rationalise it all.

If she'd been innocent, if she *genuinely* hadn't known of her husband's actions, then why hadn't she shared this with him? Why had she allowed him to develop feelings for her when she was a married woman?

The final question that inevitably finished off his soul searching was one he just couldn't answer – if she could keep something of this magnitude a secret, what else was she not telling him?

The newscaster's voice brought him back out of his head.

"Today, the ex-Member of Parliament, Nathaniel Halstead, was found guilty of manslaughter along with seven counts of sexual assault on minors. Judge Buchanan has set the date for sentencing two weeks from today."

Morgan sat up as the newscaster went into the details.

The verdict had been given – did this mean Perrie was already on her way back?

He stood up from the sofa and began pacing up and down the lounge, the feeling of panic growing in his chest. How on earth was he going to deal with this one?

Perrie looked across the table at her sister and brother-in-law. Her nephews were staying with Graham's parents for the night to allow the adults to properly relax and talk openly – if they wanted to – about all that had occurred.

'Are you sure you're okay now, Pea?'

'I am, Aggie, honestly.' She couldn't ignore the look of concern on her sister's face. 'I know I scared you earlier but it was the release I needed. I've cried tears of shock, tears of anger and tears of worry over this whole shebang but these were finally tears of relief. Relief that it's all over and I can move on.'

'Cry? CRY? Perrie, you were on the edge of hysteria. You really had me going, I didn't know what to say or what to do.'

She reached across and took her sister's hand, 'you did exactly the right thing. You just held me and let me get it all out.'

'I can't even begin to imagine how bad it must have been for you,' Graham said.

'Graham, no one can. Until you're in a situation for yourself, you can't ever know.'

Perrie thought back to the six months she'd spent upstairs in Aggie and Graham's attic room before she'd gone to Broatie. Six months that had been spent in a perpetual tear-filled state as she'd wallowed in the pain Nate had dropped upon her.

'I'm so sorry I didn't do more for you—'

'No, Graham, please, don't apologise. You did more than enough. You and Aggie were so kind in allowing me to stay here and never once uttered a word of judgement in my direction. I owe you the biggest thank you I can possibly give. I'm also aware of how difficult it was for you, having me here in that state.'

'Oh, don't be so silly, it was nothing.'

'It was more than that and you know it. I heard you both having heated words one night and I could tell it wasn't the first time you'd had that particular conversation.'

The colour left her brother-in-law's face for a brief second before it flushed a brilliant shade of red.

'Oh, please tell me you didn't hear—

'Yes, Graham, I did and I'm glad that I did because I needed to hear it. I was indulging in a pity-party for one and had no intention of giving it up until I heard you both arguing. That was the wake-up kick in the pants I needed to make me take back control of my life. You guys never argue and the realisation that you were doing so over me really hit home. I can't even remember why I was coming down the stairs but I do know I did a U-turn right there and then, went back to my room and sparked up the laptop. By the following morning, I'd provisionally booked my hideaway cottage in Broatiescombe Bay along with the croft in Scotland. Michael had already voiced his worries over my safety, as you both know, and it motivated me to take on board his concerns. And it turned out to be the best thing I could have done. So, please, you did absolutely nothing wrong. I mean that.'

Graham placed his hand on hers and gave it a gentle squeeze. As she sat there, holding hands across the table with her sister and Graham, Perrie felt truly at peace for the first time in a great many years.

THIRTY-SEVEN

'Here, don't forget your groceries.'

'Oh, smashing, thank you, Aggie.'

Perrie took the bag of shopping and put it in the cool box which was in the footwell behind the passenger seat. She plugged it in to ensure her cheese and milk didn't turn on the journey because it was going to be another hot one today.

'There you go, is that how you wanted them?'

'Oh, that's perfect, Graham, thank you.'

He'd put down the middle seats in the Land Rover so she could lay out cool mats for George and Timothy to lie on if they got too hot. She'd have the air-con going and had put sun shades on the windows but she was concerned it might not be enough with their big heavy coats. She placed a non-spill drinking bowl within easy reach for them and poured some water into it.

'Honestly, Pea, you look after those cats better than the old Queen's Corgis!'

'Just ensuring they have a comfortable journey.'

'Now, have you checked you've got everything?'

'I have. A quick loo-stop and then I'll be off.'

'Have a safe trip, Perrie. Look after yourself.'

She accepted the hug Graham bestowed on her and hugged him back just as tightly.

'Thank you again, so much, for everything. I appreciate it more than there are words to say. And thank you also for looking after my big sister – she's not always as tough as she likes to think she is.'

'Oh, don't you worry, I've more than got the low-down there.'

He gave her a wink as he pulled away and she smiled at him, knowing he'd always put Aggie's best interests' way before his own. He went indoors and left the two women to say their goodbyes.

'Hey, little sis,' Aggie reached up and tucked one of her curls behind her ear. Her hair was back to its rich, auburn state and the straighteners had been returned to her sister. If she never saw another pair in her life, it would be too soon. Juniper Halstead had breathed her last. Perrie Lacey was back to stay.

'Hey, big sis.' She embraced the wonderful woman who'd been by her side all through this ordeal. She'd loved her, cared for her and had never once judged her.

'Are you sure you want to return to Broatie? You haven't said much about it while you've been here.'

'My mind has been rather taken up with the trial and, I don't know if this makes sense or not, but I didn't want to taint how I feel about Broatie by talking about it while I was in the middle of this mess.'

'Yeah, that makes sense. I can see what you mean.'

'And to answer your question, I can't wait to get back. I love it there. I adore the cottage; the location is fabulous – I can see right across the sea from my desk – and the cats adore having their fabulous run. Even with carrying this burden, I've felt content there. Now this is all over, I'm looking forward to being able to relax and finally be at peace.'

'And is there any other reason that might be calling you back?'

'Such as?' Perrie knew exactly what Aggie was getting at but she was buggered if she was going to let on about Morgan. Apart from not having something concrete to tell her, Aggie wouldn't let up with the questions if she thought there was even a hint of romance in the air.

'You know, a young man perhaps…'

She laughed as her sister gave her a nudge with her elbow while winking suggestively.

'Aggie, behave yourself! Let the dust settle first before you start trying to pair me off with some other poor unfortunate.'

'Poor unfortunate, my arse! Any man would be lucky to have you; something Nathaniel Halstead managed to forget.'

'Yes, well, he's a thing of the past now and from this moment onwards, his name will never be mentioned again. Deal?'

'Deal!'

'Right. If you can stay here with the cats for a moment, I'll go to the loo and then be gone. I'm hoping that I've timed it just right to avoid the traffic at either end.'

'What time are you expecting to be there by?'

'All being well, just before seven.'

Aggie nodded. 'Text me when you arrive, so I know you've got there in one piece.'

'I will, I promise.'

Perrie quickly trotted inside to make one last use of the facilities and less than ten minutes later, was waving goodbye as she pulled off the driveway.

As she turned towards the main road, she felt butterflies of excitement in her stomach. Excitement at returning to Broatie but even more at seeing Morgan. She couldn't wait to show him just how much she'd missed him.

THIRTY-EIGHT

As she pulled into her space in the car park below the cottage, Perrie looked at the time – six-thirty! – and smiled, pleased to have arrived almost exactly when she'd hoped to.

'Hey, boys,' she looked in the mirror as she straightened up, 'we're back!'

There was no response until she got out of the car at which point the cats must have either got a whiff of the sea air or heard the gulls shrieking because, by the time she got to the back door to let them out, they were up and standing to attention, waiting impatiently for her to undo their harnesses.

She clipped on their leads and they jumped down, stretching out while she unplugged the chiller, put the still-chilled goods back in the carrier bag with the rest of her groceries and grabbed the rucksack with her bare essentials from behind the driver's seat. She elbowed the door closed and managed to click the lock before George and Timothy began tugging her towards the steps up to the cliff-top and the cottage.

'Okay, okay, you two. Stop pulling, I'm coming.'

She made her way up the stairs to the back gate, pleased she'd made the decision to empty the rest of her boxed-up belongings from the car tomorrow. The car park was a safe place known only by the locals so she had no concerns about theft.

'How about you guys go out in the run for a bit, eh? Burn off some of your energy since you've been sound asleep for the last four and a half hours!'

Perrie let out a grunt as she dropped her rucksack and shopping bag on the kitchen table. She'd only been away two weeks yet climbing those steps had felt like she was crawling up the side of Everest again!

'Okay, kettle on first, loo visit, make cuppa then message Morgan to let him know I'm back!'

She was sitting at the kitchen table, savouring her first sips of tea and thinking of how to word her text when there was a hammering on the front door, causing her to jump and spill tea on the table. 'What the blazes…'

She walked through to the dining room and from behind the curtain, peeked out the window. Her unexpected caller had their back to her but she'd recognise that thick blond wavy hair and trim, sturdy figure anywhere – even if she hadn't seen it for two weeks.

'Morgan!'

The butterflies were back doing loop-the-loops in her stomach as Perrie hurried to the door to let him in. He must have been keeping a watch out for her to be here so quickly.

She paused briefly to pick up the post on the mat before she flung the door open, her biggest and brightest smile lighting up her face as she did so.

'Hey, you must be a mind-reader, I was just about to tex—'

'We need to talk!'

Morgan stormed past her and marched into the kitchen.

'Er, come in, why don't you!' she muttered to his rapidly disappearing back.

She closed the door and the excited butterflies stopped mid-loop as they suddenly felt the need to check out the lay of the land. Something wasn't right here. She followed him through the cottage, dropping the post on the dining table as she walked past.

'So, you're back then, I see!'

'Well, yes, obviously.'

'Were you planning to let me know?'

'Morgan, what gives? I parked up less than thirty minutes ago. I didn't think you'd begrudge me a cup of tea after I'd been driving for almost five hours. Talking of which, would you like one?'

She walked over to refill the kettle.

'No, Perrie, or should I say *Juniper*, what I want are some answers!'

Her hand froze on the tap. He knew! He'd found out before she'd had the opportunity to tell him herself. In that instant, she felt her blood run cold and her hand began to shake.

She took a deep breath to steady herself, finished refilling the kettle and switched it on before turning around to face him, picking up a cloth to wipe the spilt tea at the same time. When she saw his face, she was sorely tempted to turn away again – his anger was palpable and emanating from every pore.

'So, you know then?' she said quietly.

'It was a bit difficult to miss when you were plastered all over the television!'

'An exaggeration but I get your point.'

'Were you ever intending to tell me? Or were you

just playing me for a fool?'

She was in the process of wiping the table but stopped and rounded on him when he said this.

'What? Why on earth would you think that?'

'You're married, Perrie! Didn't you think that was something I might want to know?'

'For crying out loud, Morgan, you've seen who my husband is – did you honestly think I'd want to own up to that?'

'Humph! More likely you didn't want me to know your past so you could get close to my daughter.'

For a second time, her blood turned to ice but this time, the shaking that followed was for an entirely different reason. The ice in her veins rapidly turned hot and now Morgan wasn't the only one fit to bust a gut.

'What the HELL did you just say?'

'You heard me!'

'I'm really hoping I didn't, Morgan Daniels, because I do not want to hear you say that you think I was in any way involved.'

'You're telling me you weren't?'

'No, I wasn't!'

'Why did you give evidence against him if you weren't guilty yourself and trying to cut a deal?'

Perrie's mouth dropped open upon hearing this as she tried to make sense of what Morgan was saying.

'Are you suggesting I turned on my husband to save myself?'

'Why else would you give evidence against him?'

'Because I could, Morgan! Because I had information that would help to put him away behind bars for a very long time. Hopefully, for the rest of his life!'

From nowhere, a wave of exhaustion came over her and she sat back down in the chair she'd been sitting on before he'd arrived.

'Morgan,' she looked up at him, still glowering above her, 'please, sit down. Have some tea and speak to me rationally. I get that you have questions and I am more than prepared to answer them but not like this. You don't get to shout at me and you certainly don't get to judge me either.'

'When my daughter is threatened, I am perfectly entitled to make any damn judgement call I please.'

'Right! That does it.'

The fiery temper that came with her fiery hair couldn't be contained a moment longer. She stood up, placed her hands on the table and all but screamed in his face.

'I've had enough of this. I have just lived through what has possibly been the hardest two weeks of my life and I didn't come back here to be hauled over the coals by some opinionated asshole who has decided to be judge and jury on my life! I've already faced both of those in the last fourteen days and I have no intention of doing it again to please you so get out. Now! Leave!'

'Oh, I'm going alright!'

Morgan strode back to the front door, stopping only to turn and throw one last question her way.

'Why did you lie to me, Perrie? Why did you let me think we could be something special?'

'I never lied to you, Morgan. Not once!'

He looked at her for a moment before replying, 'No, I suppose you didn't. You just didn't trust me with the truth.'

With that, he walked out the door, slamming it hard behind him.

Perrie stood looking at the space where he'd been standing.

A sob caught in her throat as she whispered, 'I didn't tell you… because I couldn't.'

THIRTY-NINE

Morgan felt no better for slamming the cottage door behind him and giving the gate at the top of the path the same treatment didn't help either.

He turned towards his house but then stopped. Daisy was staying with his mum tonight so there was no reason to go home. What would he do once there? Probably drown his sorrows in beer or wine and then regret it in the morning.

He did an about turn and set off towards the cliffs. Maybe putting a couple of miles between him and Perrie would be the best thing right now.

He all but stomped his way across the open grassland, barely grunting out a greeting to the few walkers he met coming the other way. He could still feel his anger running through him in waves and his thinking was... well... he wasn't thinking. He couldn't. His head felt like it was full of thick, dense blackness. A blackness made up of pain, hurt, and resentment.

He walked and walked and walked and even when the sun was slipping down under the horizon, he walked some more until, eventually, he simply ground to a halt.

He stood for a few moments, just staring ahead until with a shake of his head, he looked around to get his bearings and figure out where he was.

'Aw, you have got to be kidding me! Seriously?'

His heart sank when he saw the lighthouse just up ahead. It was about four miles from his house to the lighthouse which meant he now had a four mile walk home again – in the dark!

He got his phone out to check the charge. Only twenty percent – it looked like he'd be jogging home not walking if there was to be any hope of getting there before the torch on the mobile died on him.

'Oh, Morgan, you're a right daft twat, you know that don't you?'

He took himself over to sit on a large boulder which gave him an uninterrupted view across the sea. It wasn't the first time he'd found himself sitting here and he suspected it wasn't going to be the last. From his first teenage tantrum to the death of his wife, he always ended up in this spot. It seemed to be some kind of default setting within him that he came here when he had troubles which needed soothing. He'd spent too many hours in this place after Harriet had died, some of them contemplating if throwing himself on the rocks below would make it all feel better. He couldn't believe he was here again.

He let out a large sigh as he pulled his legs up, wrapped his arms around his shins and rested his chin on his knees. What on earth had come over him? His intention had been to go to Perrie's cottage, let her know he'd seen the news coverage and then give her the chance to explain herself before telling her that it was better for them all if they saw less of each other. Even if she was innocent of any crime, he knew he'd never relax fully while she was around Daisy.

But while that may have been his plan, it had all gone to cock the minute he'd arrived at her door. Somewhere between his front door and hers, a red mist had come down over him and he'd arrived at the cottage like some avenging hound from hell. He felt his face grow hot as he thought of how he'd marched into her home like he had every right to do so and then demanded that she explain herself.

Except... even as he'd demanded this, he hadn't given her a chance to speak. He'd just waded right on in with all his suppositions, cobbled together from what he'd read on the internet and gleaned from the news reports. He'd thrown his accusations around and had awarded Perrie no opportunity to give him the actual facts.

At that moment, his memory decided to thrust at him the appalled look on her face when he'd accused her of being a risk to Daisy. He let out a deep groan of disgust. While he may have thought it, and still did to an extent, there had been no need to let Perrie know this was how he felt. It had been a step too far and he knew he'd hurt her which had never been his aim.

Guilt and unease clawed at his insides. He could see now that he'd behaved totally irrationally. The resentment over the secrets which hadn't been shared had grown rapidly with each passing day since he'd learnt of, what he considered to be, Perrie's deception. He'd fed it with his obsessive internet searches and had allowed it to become a monster which had consumed him. Such was his anger at having been kept in the dark, he'd even convinced himself that Perrie had to be guilty of the same crime as her husband in some way or another.

Time crept on as Morgan sat on his rock, watching distant ships sail by until he eventually accepted what his head and heart were telling him. He didn't want to believe it, and a wave of searing hot shame rushed through his body when he finally did – he'd lashed out at Perrie because he *had* wanted to hurt her. He *had* wanted to inflict pain on her. His desire had been to see her wounded as he had been wounded when he'd found out she was married.

Because finding out that the woman you have fallen deeply in love with is married, hurts like absolute hell!

FORTY

Perrie let out a groan as she turned over for what felt like the millionth time since she'd come to bed. The clock on the bedside table told her it was a little after four in the morning. Just as it had told her when it was a little after one, a little after two and a little after three! Coming to the conclusion that sleep was going to continue to be in short supply, she threw back the quilt, stuck her feet in her slippers and headed towards the shower.

A short time later she was standing in the kitchen with a mug of strong coffee in one hand and her tablet in the other. She'd recently come across a recipe for a twelve-layer chocolate cake and right now, she needed something that would command her full attention. She'd been so angry the night before, after Morgan had stormed out, that she'd ended up burning it off by dragging up the boxes from the car and emptying all her baking equipment into several kitchen cupboards. Now that she had all her gear to hand, she searched the internet again to find the website, and the attention-demanding cake, then checked the ingredients against what was in her cupboard.

There were a couple of items she didn't have but she was sure she could work around those with some alternatives. Tweaking recipes was half the fun.

She pulled out the mixing bowls and was soon beating the living daylights out of her cake mix. Sure, she could have used the electric mixer but that wouldn't have helped to vent the frustration and residual anger from her encounter with Morgan the night before.

She couldn't get over the way he'd stormed in and behaved the way he had. Okay, she totally got that he was pissed off over finding out about her past from the television rather than from her own lips but to pass judgement on her without allowing her a chance to say her piece... well, that was just bang out of order!

His stinking temper aside, however, the thing that had cut through her the most was when he'd accused her of being a potential harm to Daisy. He didn't know her at all if he thought her capable of hurting a single hair on the head of that little girl.

Soon, the cake mix was weighed out into the baking tins and in the oven. As she waited, Perrie cleaned up her first mess before beginning on the second. It was a double-edged sword working with chocolate – to achieve the rich, decadent, sin-filled delight usually meant creating one heck of a mess first and, as this recipe called for both a chocolate cream filling AND a chocolate ganache, the mess was going to be twofold!

Time ticked by and soon she had two bowls of gooey filling waiting to be layered over the sponges once they'd cooled enough to be cut without crumbling. She tapped her fingers on the worktop, impatient to get on but even with the sponges chilling in the fridge, she still had a good fifteen-minute wait.

'Argh, sod this!'

By the time the chocolate sponges were ready for the

next step in her creation, a dozen fruit and cherry scones were baking away in the oven.

While she carefully cut the sponges, Perrie thought back to when baking had gone from being an occasional moment of madness to her therapy-alternative. It had begun about six months after Nate had entered parliament as an MP. He'd come home one night in a foul mood and she'd borne the brunt of it. He'd shouted and raged over something so insignificant she couldn't even recall what it was before locking himself away in his study for the rest of the night. She'd been so upset, she'd been unable to concentrate on anything – reading, television or the games she played on the computer. It was while in the kitchen, looking for some chamomile tea to help her relax, she'd spied the bag of flour in a cupboard. The next thing she knew, she'd found an online recipe for a Victoria sponge – the only cake she had all the ingredients for – and by the time she was dusting some icing sugar over the finished article, her earlier turmoil had eased. After that, she'd created her "Bakery Cupboard" and had stocked it up with a vast array of ingredients to ensure she'd be able to bake whatever took her fancy.

It also helped that she seemed to have a natural skill because the recipients of her wares were always quick to give praise and help themselves to seconds. Nate was sure he had so many constituents attend his surgeries because of the tasty treats she supplied him with. What a pity the daft twat hadn't sussed out that it was his continuing erratic behaviour which was forcing her to spend more time with her head in the oven. It was a damn good thing it hadn't been a gas one!

The ping-ping from the timer told her it was time to rescue the scones so she lay down her chocolate-covered spatula to bring them out and put them on the cooling rack. She debated for a moment on switching the oven off but decided to leave it on. While she felt calmer than she had an hour ago, she wasn't yet fully unwound.

It was gone eight o'clock by the time she finally sat down with her second mug of coffee. The Epic Chocolate Tower had turned out well, the scones were rather tasty – she was eating one with her coffee – and the lemon muffins, with a secret curd filling, would soon be cool enough to go into the freezer tubs.

When she checked the freezer for space, she was surprised at how empty of baked goods it was. That was when she realised how happy she was here in Broatiescombe Bay. The lack of baking meant she hadn't been stressed and therefore hadn't required her "therapy" time. Perrie also couldn't help but wonder if the situation with Morgan would change that. Had he and Daisy been the only reason she'd de-stressed since moving into the cottage or was it the distance between her and London, and leaving the reason for her stress, Nate, behind that had soothed her internal unrest.

Well, she thought with a sigh, she was about to find out because it didn't look like she'd be hanging out with Morgan and Daisy anytime soon.

FORTY-ONE

The sound of her mobile ringing pulled Perrie away from
the pitted muddy streets of Cambridge in the fourteenth
century and back into the twenty-first. She blinked a few
times to let her eyes adjust from staring at the old, faded,
medieval text in front of her before looking at her screen
to see who was calling. A small surge of hope flared up
that it might be Morgan but it quickly died when she saw
it was Sue from the bakery.

'Hi, Perrie, how are you doing?'

'Hi, Sue, I'm doing grand thank you, I hope you and
Alex are too.'

'Yeah, we're great. It's the height of the season so
the B&B is booked to capacity and the bakery is queued
out from opening time to closing time. We're knackered
but not complaining.'

'Ah, that's wonderful to hear – not that you're
knackered, obviously, but that business is good.'

'Cheers. Now, as it's the first of the month, I'm just
giving you my usual monthly check-in call to ensure all is
well with the cottage and that you don't have any

concerns.'

'Nothing to report, thank you. All is well and living here continues to be a delight.'

'Excellent! Just one last thing – your six-month rental period expires at the end of next month and I was curious as to whether you'd given any thought to your plans after that.'

Immediately, Perrie's thoughts went towards Sue trying to evict her. Had she also seen the news and didn't want the wife of a child-molester living on her premises?

With a feeling of trepidation she replied, 'To be honest, Sue, I hadn't thought that far ahead yet. Is that a problem for you? Do you need me to vacate at the end of September because you have someone else moving in?'

There, she'd given her landlady the perfect excuse to get rid of her without making it awkward for them both.

'Oh, my goodness, no! It's no problem at all. You've been the perfect tenant and, truth be told, I'd be thrilled if you extended your rental and stayed longer. Knowing how much you love the cottage gives me great peace of mind and I know it's in good hands.'

Perrie sat up in surprise. She had not been expecting this response.

'I see. Wow! Thank you. I'll let you know as soon as I decide what my future plans are.'

'Well, I'm happy to let it roll along on a monthly basis. You might change your mind once you've experienced a few of our winter squalls!' Sue laughed as she said this and Perrie found herself joining in although more from relief than the thought of being exposed to vicious wintry winds coming in off the sea.

They exchanged a few more pleasantries before hanging up and as she put the phone down on the desk, she realised how late it was.

'Bugger!'

She jumped up and ran down the stairs to bring the cats in from the run and get them fed. That was the downside of summer nights – they stayed lighter for longer and she found herself often working later than she'd intended.

'Mental note to self,' she muttered as she went out to the run, 'set the blooming alarm on your phone, woman!'

The cats had their noses buried deeply in their food bowls when she came back in from cleaning the litter trays out in the run. She was in the middle of washing her hands and thinking she should really eat something but didn't know what to have when the door knocker clanged loudly down the hallway. As she was drying her hands, it clanged again.

'Okay, okay, I'm coming!' she called out as she rushed to answer. She really hoped it wasn't Morgan gearing up for a second dance around the boxing ring because she simply wasn't in the mood to face him again.

Upon opening the door, however, she got the second surprise of the evening.

'Hey, gorgeous, how ya doing?'

Perrie stepped back in shock as Babs barrelled past her with a carrier bag in each hand and scurried through to the kitchen.

'Do come in!' she muttered once again, as she began to wonder if this was how everyone in this town behaved.

'Hi, Babs, lovely to… err… see you.'

Babs turned to her and, having dumped the two bags on the kitchen worktop, placed her hands on her hips and gave her a smile.

'Right! I'm here bearing gifts. Wine,' she pointed at one bag, 'and Chinese takeaway.' She pointed at the other.

'But, why? I don't understand.'

Babs stepped towards her and took hold of both her

hands.

'Because I now know what your darkness was and I figured you could do with a friend by your side.'

'How do you know that?'

Perrie's voice was almost a whisper. In the aftermath of Nate's fall from grace, almost everyone she'd known or believed to have been a friend, had turned their backs on her and disowned her. It was that which had been hardest to bear rather than what Nate had been accused of although that hadn't exactly been a party either.

'Well, judging from the look on Morgan's face as he walked past the gallery this morning and which was still on his face as he walked by again this evening, I'm guessing he didn't take the news of you being married too well and he's probably got a right strop going on which means he's not here for you when you need him to be.'

'Well, you got the being married bit right... but aren't you worried I might be a danger to your daughter or something? Do you really want to hang out with the wife of a convicted killer?'

Just then a thought went through her mind. A horrible thought but it was there all the same and she felt compelled to voice it.

'Say, you're not just here to get the low-down on all that happened so you can go back and gossip with your mates or sell your story to the papers, are you?'

Babs looked at her for a brief second before she burst out laughing.

'Oh, sweet-cheeks, I don't give a blind shit if you never mention a word about your husband or how crap your life has been for the last year. I'm simply here to let you know that just because you're some kind of minor celebrity it doesn't mean you get first dibs on Tom Hardy!'

Perrie looked at Babs, with her crazy dark hair,

happy smiling face and paint-splattered dungarees and, as she returned the smile, she said, 'Look, girlfriend, we've been through this already and that man is mine, all mine!'

'Oh yeah! Well, there's a tub of sweet and sour pork in that bag there and if you want to see any of it, you will have to concede your position.'

'There's a Chinese takeaway in Broatie? I haven't seen that? I love Chinese grub.'

'So, how about I set the table and you sort out the plates. Shall we go posh and eat at the dining table?'

'Sounds good to me. The cutlery and mats are in that drawer there.'

Perrie's head was buried in the cupboard as she bent down to pull out plates and bowls when she heard Babs say something.

'Sorry, what was that?'

'I said, where do you want me to put this pile of post?'

'Oh, I'd forgotten about that. Just stick it on the counter there, I'll get to it later. It'll just be junk mail and bills.'

'Well, unless British Gas have started sending out their bills in lush cream embossed envelopes...'

'What?'

She stood up quickly and walked over to Babs, taking the mail from her and looking at the envelope now positioned on the top.

'Do... do you mind if I open this now?'

'Course not, go ahead. I'll sort out the wine. I got two bottles of that rosé you like.'

'Thanks, Babs. The glasses are in the cupboard above the dishwasher.'

She looked at the envelope in her hand and, dropping the others on the counter, slipped her finger in the corner and proceeded to slowly prise it open. Her heart pounded in her chest as she hoped it contained the news she'd been waiting an age to hear.

Aware that she was holding her breath, she pulled out the sheaf of papers and opening them up, read quickly and then again slowly, absorbing the words contained within. She gripped the counter-top as a wave of light-headedness came across her.

'Hey, Perrie, are you okay? You've gone pale...'

'I'm okay, Babs. Where's that wine?'

She took the glass Babs handed to her and gulped down half of the contents before putting it back down on the worktop.

'Seriously, Perrie, is everything alright?'

'Oh, everything is more than alright! Things couldn't be more right!'

She handed the paperwork over to Babs.

'It's my Decree Nisi! In six weeks, I'll be shot of that evil bastard forever!'

FORTY-TWO

'Am I right in guessing Morgan doesn't know about this?'

Babs nodded at the paperwork now lying at the far end of the table as she spooned some fried rice onto her plate.

'No, he doesn't. If he hadn't stormed in, shouting the odds before storming back out again, he would know because I have finally been given the all-clear to talk about... well... things.'

'The all-clear? I don't follow?'

'When I came down here, I was sort of in hiding. The police didn't know if the paedophile ring was only the four people they'd arrested or if there were bigger fish behind it. With Nate being the most prominent member, and my testimony being so vital, there were concerns for my safety so they and Michael, the prosecutor, thought it might be better for me to be inconspicuous for a time.'

'Wow! That must have been tough.'

'Not really. I was staying with my sister but it wasn't ideal. I didn't want to go back to Cambridge and I really didn't want to go to Spain to my parents, so Broatie was perfect. I could hide away, wallow in self-pity and lick my wounds. The isolated location of the cottage was exactly what I wanted. I simply never thought a gorgeous, kind, gentle man with the most adorable little bundle of five-year-old joy would come along and cock up my plans.'

'Life, eh? Always likes to throw you the curve ball!'

Perrie gave a small smile at that one.

'Doesn't it just!'

'I have to be honest though, if my folks stayed out in Spain, I'd have been out there in a flash! Have they lived there long?'

'About six years – give or take. They moved out not long before Nate became an MP. My dad suffers from arthritis so it's better for him. He won big on one of those accumulator things on the horses when I was a kid and he used the money to buy some old properties which he renovated and sold for a tidy profit. He did this for a number of years and made a lot of money from it. He then decided he needed to diversify so went down the route of sell one, keep one, and now has quite the portfolio of properties around the country which includes the house Nate and I lived in. I think it always stuck in Nate's craw a bit – that we didn't own the house. He thought my dad should have gifted it to us. What he doesn't know is that my dad wanted to and I declined the offer.'

'Why would you do that?'

'I don't know. I've never been quite sure why. Just some deep-down instinct kept telling me to refuse it although Dad has said he plans to gift it to me on my fortieth birthday whether I want it or not!'

'Oh, the hardship!'

Perrie burst out laughing at Babs' droll response.

'I know! It's a bummer, right?'

They laughed together as she topped up the wine glasses and reloaded her plate from the bowls in front of her.

'I have to say, Babs, this food is delicious.'

'Ain't it just! I'll get you one of the menus the next time I'm passing and I'll show you where to find the shop. I'm sure Mr. and Mrs. Cheung will be delighted to have another happy customer.'

'Hmmm, I'm not so sure about that. Besides, I'll probably be moving on in the next month or so.'

'What?' Babs' fork stopped halfway to her mouth. 'Why?'

Perrie gave a little shrug and looked down at her plate. Without warning, her eyes filled with tears and she blinked hard to try and dispel them.

'I'm the wife of a convicted child molester and killer – while you might be okay with that, I'm guessing the rest of the town won't be so happy to have me living here among them.'

'You think?'

'Well, yeah! As Morgan pointed out, I was on the national news, how could I have thought that people wouldn't see me and find out the truth?'

'Look, Perrie, I won't lie, your secret is out of the bag around here. Yes, almost everyone knows and also, yes, it was the topic of a few discussions for a day or two but I can tell you this, no one will hold it against you. Okay, maybe one or two idiots might, but the majority of the town are very open-minded and rarely pass judgement on others.'

'But—'

'No, no buts! You're not the first person to arrive in Broatie with a big bag full of troubles on their back and you sure as hell ain't gonna be the last. We're a right little bay of lost souls here – I keep telling them they should paint that below the "Welcome" sign in the car park!'

'Who else came here to forget?'

'Ah, sorry, sweetie, not my stories to tell. We won't talk about you and we don't talk about them.'

'I'm sure none of them were married to a paedophile though.'

'It doesn't matter. Those people had their issues when they came here and the town gave them the space and time which allowed them to get better. Some came and left again, some came and stayed. The stayers are now valued members of the community and their past is exactly that – the past! You can have the same if you want it. And you're forgetting one small point…'

'Which is?'

'In six weeks from now, you'll be an ex-wife! After which, you can really move on.'

'But, Morgan – what about him?'

'He'll come round – he's just being bloke'ish. Although, you won't get a second bite of that cherry if you skip town now, will ya?'

'S'pose not…'

'Perrie,' Babs put her fork down and laid her hand over Perrie's, 'right now, you need to work on looking after yourself. Give yourself some time to unwind from the weight of the burden you've carried. Find your equilibrium and then you'll be in a better place to deal with Morgan when he's ready to get off his high horse. Okay? Don't make any decisions just yet.'

Perrie looked at this lovely woman who had been more supportive of her in the last two months than the so-called friends she'd known for years but who'd gone running off towards the horizon as soon as there had been a whiff of trouble or scandal. A lump jumped up in her throat and she had to work on pushing it back down again.

'Thank you for being so kind, Babs, it means a lot. I promise not to make any rash decisions.'

'Cool! Now, on a complete subject change, what's the gig on being a historical researcher?'

'If you've finished eating, I'll show you.'

'Oh, my goodness! That's amazing. This book is really over four-hundred years old?'

'It sure is.'

Babs lightly touched the page in front of her with her finger.

'So, how or why do you have it?'

'History is all about research and what I do is read and collate the information I find. That box over there,' Perrie pointed to the far corner, 'contains a number of volumes that were recently found hidden away behind a false wall in an old house in Cambridge. They were donated to the university and my job for now is to read them, decipher them, make notes and decide how they fit in with what we already know from that period of time.'

'I thought we already knew everything.'

'We know quite a bit about high-ranking officials and the royal courts because these were always well documented but it's the information we can glean from journals, written by lesser officials, clergymen, scholars and so on that really tells us how life was for ordinary people who lived ordinary lives. Little things like a bill of goods, a shopping receipt to you or I, can say so much about the wealth, or lack of, of a family. An old barber's ledger informs us not only who had haircuts but who also had bad teeth or required limbs to be amputated because those were services the local barber also offered.'

'No way! A barber was allowed to cut your leg off?'

'If required, yes he was.'

'Blimey, who knew?'

'So, what I'm doing now, is not just reading those books but also comparing them with other books of the same period and location. If we're lucky, we'll get more than one person's view of an incident, or incidents, and this gives a more rounded description of what really happened. It's not just history but also a never-ending puzzle.'

'And I can tell you love it! I swear, Perrie, if my history teacher at school had been as enthusiastic as you are, I would have been more inclined to pay attention.'

'You're too kind. Now, as a thank you for letting me drone on, do you have any space after all that Chinese food for some chocolate cake? I made a rather large one this morning and some help eating it would not go amiss!'

'Hmm, let me see...' Babs put her finger on her chin, looked up to the ceiling and mused aloud, 'is today the day when I finally develop the willpower to refuse chocolate cake? Err... nope! It's not! Lead me to it!' she grinned, already walking towards the door of the study.

When Perrie brought the cake out of the cupboard, Babs used several fruity words to describe how awesome she thought it was.

'And you're telling me you made this at seven o'clock this morning?'

'I couldn't sleep and baking helps me to unwind. Is it okay? It's the first time I've done that recipe and I had to tweak it a bit to fit with the ingredients I had in.'

'Peffie, it's mucking gofgeous!'

Perrie smiled as Babs tried to speak through the huge bite of chocolatey gooeyness in her mouth.

'I'll take that as a "yes" shall I?' she grinned.

'Oh, hell, it's a yes! This is sublime. I don't think I've ever tasted anything like it. You know, if you ever get bored with reading your old books, you could give Mrs Campbell a run for her money. I mean, that cake you did for Daisy's birthday was unbelievable. You really raised the bar there and I think Mrs. Campbell is almost wishing she hadn't agreed so readily for you to step in because everyone has been asking her to make cakes on that level and the poor dear just isn't of that standard.'

'Oh no, that's not good. I just wanted to give Daisy something special – I never gave any thought to the consequences.'

'Hey, don't fret it but…'

The sneaky cheeky look on Babs' face made Perrie smile even though she had an inkling on what might be coming.

'But what?'

'It's Sarah's birthday in a couple of weeks and she's having a party – of course! God forbid that we didn't – and I was wondering how cheeky you would think I was if I asked a massive favour of you. Like… would you make a cake for her? PLEEEEEEASE!'

It took a great deal of effort to keep her face straight and appear cross but somehow Perrie managed it.

'Well, I really don't think it would be appropriate. Poor Mrs. Campbell is already under the cosh and it wouldn't be fair to make matters worse. No, I don't think I could, sorry.'

'What if I said Nancy Wilson and her mother will be attending…'

'Oh, why didn't you say sooner? Of course, I'll do it! Just the one cake?'

Both women burst out laughing and it was a few minutes before they could speak again.

'Look, if you really don't want to do it—'

'Babs, it would be my pleasure, honestly, it would. I know Sarah is good friends with Daisy so it would be nice for them both to have special birthday cakes. Is there anything specific she would like? What is she into? Peppa Pig? Paw Patrol? Dinosaurs?'

'Ermm... The Incredible Hulk!'

Perrie couldn't stop the snort of wine that came shooting out her nose at that. As she wiped up the mess she'd made, while Babs hooted with laughter, she replied, while shaking her head, 'D'ya know, with you as her mother, that really shouldn't have surprised me! No problem, leave it with me.'

FORTY-THREE

Perrie carefully balanced the two cake tins on top of each other and slung her "bag of tricks" across her chest. The base of Sarah's cake had been delivered last night and now she was taking over the rest of it. The piece de resistance was securely tucked up in the tins and she would be assembling on site as trying to carry the finished article up and down the hills of the town would have been a logistical nightmare. Instead, she'd finish creating it in the privacy of Babs' little fudge kitchen where the cake would stay hidden until the moment of the big reveal.

She checked all the windows and doors were closed and then checked the time. It was just gone ten – she should be safe to walk past Morgan's house having worked out that this should be one of his working Saturdays but there was always a chance he could have swapped them.

There had been no contact between them since the night she'd returned from London and she was missing both his and Daisy's company. Now that they were absent, she was realising just how much time they'd spent together. The dinners they'd innocently shared as friends had quietly grown to be much more than that and she no longer enjoyed her own company as much as she once had.

'Okay, boys, you both be good now. I won't be gone long and you can go into your run when I get back.'

Timothy raised his head from where he lay on the cool kitchen floor and gave her a look as if to say, 'Fine, Mum, see you later.' George didn't even deign to raise an eyelid of acknowledgement!

'Every time,' she muttered, picking up the tins and juggling her way through the front door, making sure to lock it behind her.

The early morning heat hit her as she stepped out of the porch. August was turning out to be a scorcher and she was glad she was spending it in Broatie because London would be unbearable in this. The sea breeze helped to take the edge off but if you found yourself in a spot that was sheltered from the wind, you got the full effect of the sun beating down and it was like being in a furnace. Or close to one!

As she drew nearer to Morgan's house, Perrie had to adjust her grip on the cake tins as her hands were becoming sweaty and she didn't know if it was from the heat or nerves that Morgan might happen to step out of his front door just as she walked by. Fate could be a bit of a bitch like that at times.

This time, however, it was clearly too hot for Fate to make the effort because Perrie made it past without anything untoward occurring. She was mostly relieved but a little devil was sitting on her shoulder asking her if she was disappointed and she couldn't say no with any certainty.

The thought of this played on her mind until she

reached the bottom of the hill and had to manoeuvre her way through the already bustling main street. By the time she was knocking on Babs' door, she was feeling more than a little frazzled.

'Hey, you're here. Excellent! Maybe Sarah will shut up now. She's been nagging my ears off about the lack of birthday cake and I was beginning to wish I had the gift of magic so I could put her on mute!'

Perrie laughed as she followed Babs through to her fudge kitchen. It was the space, Babs had explained, where she made her fudge, and as she sold the sweet delight to the public, it had to meet Health & Safety criteria. She'd moved her own utensils to one side and the worktops were clear for Perrie to work on.

'Right then, shoo! Leave me to get on with this.'

'Do you want a drink of anything? Tea, coffee, wine...'

'Wine? It's not even ten-thirty!'

'I need to get my Dutch courage up to speed so I can cope with all the kids later.'

'Where's Sarah?'

'Upstairs with her cousin who had a sleepover last night. The deal is I babysit Jade, and Jade's mum, Sarah's aunt on her dad's side, will man my shop today so I can be here for this.'

'Aw, that's nice of her to do that.'

'Yeah, everyone is good at mucking in and helping out around here. It's a great community – you'd benefit from staying here you know!'

'Hey, think you could lay that hint on a little thicker there, Babs, I'm not sure I quite caught it!' Perrie laughed along with her friend as she pushed her out of the small space and closed the door firmly behind her. Babs' voice came through the wooden panel, 'You never answered my question – do you want a drink?'

'No, thank you, I'm good for now.'

She opened the tins sitting on the worktop, took out the cakes inside and then laid the contents of her bag along the second counter behind her.

'Right, girl, time to get to it!'

An hour later she straightened up, rubbed the small of her back and stepped back to admire her handiwork. Perrie gave a little smile of pleasure. Everything had come together just as she'd hoped.

When Babs had first broached the idea of the cake, Perrie's initial idea had been a bog-standard sponge cut in the shape of the Hulk but with a day or two of thought, she decided she could do a fully standing, 3-D version. She'd toyed with the idea of a melting-type middle – after all, Daisy had had the pink M&M's – but that would have weakened the structure so she opted to go for a slightly heavier muffin mix heavily laced with chocolate chips, fudge pieces and jelly babies. The cakes had turned out well and had held together when she cut them into the shapes she required. After coating all the elements of the beast in vibrant green fondant, all that had been left for her to do this morning was stick him together using wooden skewers and then place him on the base cake which she'd decorated to look like a semi-demolished road bridge. Around him she'd placed six of his Avengers compatriots, the figures made from marzipan, and these held the birthday candles.

She couldn't help but feel proud of this one and had just snapped a couple of pictures on her phone when there was a gentle tap on the door.

'Hey, Perrie, how are you doing? Is it safe to enter?'

'Sure, come on in.'

'OH-MY-BLESSED-GIDDY-AUNT! That is

AMAZING! I cannot believe you made this!'

Babs bent down to take a closer look.

'I love these little Marvel figures, that is such a cool idea.'

'Thank you.'

'No Deadpool, I see.'

'I didn't think he was quite appropriate for a kids' birthday party. Now, if it had been your cake…'

'You already know what I want.'

'I do?'

'Yeah! Me, Tom Hardy, a big bowl of chocolate icing and a locked room!'

Perrie's laughter filled the room.

'Babs Middleton, you are incorrigible!'

'Yeah, I know!'

Shaking her head, while still laughing, Perrie gathered up the remains of her tools and accoutrements, put them back in her bag and looked around to ensure she hadn't missed anything. She'd wrapped the dirty items in plastic bags to be washed when she got home. Babs was busy getting ready for the party and Perrie didn't want to be in the way.

'Right then, is there anything I can help you with before I head off? Any sandwiches needing to be made or sausage rolls to come out of the oven?'

'What do you mean "head off"? Aren't you staying for the party?'

'I…err…I didn't want to cause you any embarrassment with the parents of Sarah's guests so I was going to leave before anyone arrived.'

'Why would I be embarrassed?'

'Because of… well… you know…'

Perrie felt her face grow flushed and hot under Babs' scrutiny. In fairness, the odd foray she'd made out to the local shops in the last two weeks had been considerably more pleasant than she'd expected but this event today was quite different. This was a child's birthday party and parents were likely to be less tolerant of her situation – as she'd found out only too well since Nate's dirty washing had been hung out to dry in public.

'Perrie,' Babs glared at her, 'I've already told you that the town won't judge you on the actions of someone else and anyone who does, will get the sharp side of my tongue, let me tell you. Now, you are here as an invited guest and I would love for you to stay and have some chilling time. You've earned it after creating that!'

She inclined her head towards the cake.

'Well, if you're quite sure… I confess, I would love to see Sarah's reaction to her cake. It's that first moment of surprise which makes all the effort worthwhile.'

'I'm quite sure. Now, do you think you're ready for that glass of wine? The little darlings will be here in less than thirty minutes which doesn't give much time for the numb state of gently inebriated to set in.'

'Oh, go on then! My work here is done and I no longer need a steady hand.'

FORTY-FOUR

Perrie hung back in the kitchen area of Bab's open-plan room as Sarah's little friends began to arrive. The first few parents, much to her surprise, had smiled at her – albeit with a hint of awkwardness – and asked her how she was doing. Their quiet acceptance helped her to relax a little and the tight grip on her wine glass eased off. She was trying to ward off the mildly curious questions of one mother who was trying to find out if she'd made Sarah's birthday cake and did it match up to Daisy's when there was a squeal of 'Merida' and a small blonde-haired bundle threw itself into her arms.

Unable to prevent herself, Perrie picked Daisy up and held her tightly. The arms around her neck squeezed back just as hard. For a moment, she lost herself in Daisy's little girl smell and soaked up the sensation of holding her again. She loved the bones of this child and not being able to see or speak to her had hurt more than she'd cared to accept.

'Merida, where have you been? Why have you not visited me? Don't you want to be my friend anymore?'

Before she could reply, a strident voice rang out across the room.

'What the hell is SHE doing here?'

While Perrie was grateful for the intervention that prevented her from having to find acceptable answers to Daisy's questions, seeing Cleo Wilson glaring at her across the room was not the interruption she would have chosen. She lowered Daisy to the floor and gently pushed her behind her.

'Perrie is here as my friend, Cleo.'

Babs stepped forward and returned the irate mother's stare.

'What? So, you're consorting with child-molesters now, are you?'

'You know fine well Perrie had nothing to do with that.'

'So you say! We all know how those kinds of things are never contained to just one family member. If her husband was at it, you can be damn sure she knew and was in on it too!'

'I see! That's how it works, is it, Cleo? Well, in that case, since your husband managed to boff just about every single woman in this town, and a few married ones too, before he moved on to work his way down the coastline, that must mean that you're also…'

Babs left the rest of her sentence hanging in the air while Cleo turned a deep shade of scarlet.

Perrie looked on along with the rest of the adults in the room but where a few of the other women were sniggering at Cleo being put in her place, she didn't feel comfortable with it being done so publicly, even though she knew Babs was defending her from a place of friendship.

'Cleo,' she called over, 'can I get you a glass of wine? We've got all the colours here, which would you prefer?'

One woman muttered, 'A nice bit of red to match her face would be good,' but quailed when Perrie turned towards her and gave her a hard look.

'Erm, white would be nice, please. Thank you.'

She poured the drink and took it over to Cleo who had the decency to look ashamed as she took it from her.

'Look,' Perrie whispered quietly, 'I do understand your concern – you're just a mother looking out for her child – but I assure you my husband's behaviour is no reflection of my own. I can't prove that to you; you will need to decide if you trust me or not. Whichever you choose, is your prerogative.'

'I'm sorry. Babs made a valid point. It was wrong of me to think that way.'

She could see how difficult it was for Cleo to back down and admit she was wrong. Perrie guessed it was a position she didn't find herself in all too often. Not if the way she'd behaved at Daisy's party had been anything to go by.

She gave the woman a small nod, letting her know her apology had been accepted and made her way back to the corner of the kitchen she'd been standing in before Cleo had kicked off.

'Nicely handled!'

Spinning round, Perrie came face-to-face with Hettie, Daisy's grandmother.

'Oh, hi, Hettie, I didn't see you arrive.'

'Well, you did have your face full of Daisy when I walked in.'

'I'm sorry. She came flying over and I couldn't be so cruel as to refuse her a cuddle.'

'And nor should you. The child adores you and would have been devastated if you'd ignored her. Not exactly the best start to a birthday party.'

'But Morgan—'

'Is not here!'

'But you know how he feels about me seeing Daisy?'

'I do but like I said, he's not here.'

'Daisy's bound to tell him she saw me.'

'We'll cross that bridge when we get to it.' Hettie patted her on the arm. 'He's just being a typically stubborn bloke, letting his ego get the better of him. Give him time; he'll come round and forgive you.'

'Excuse me? Forgive *me*? I don't think so! After the things he said to me, the way he behaved and to think me capable of hurting anyone, never mind a child… if anyone around here is doing any forgiving, it'll be me!'

This was something that had been going round and round Perrie's head for the last few days. She'd been so busy beating herself up for not having shared her past with Morgan, that she'd lost sight of the bigger picture – the fact he'd been so quick to think badly of her!

'Good girl! Well done you!'

She couldn't have done a good job of hiding her surprise at Hettie's words because the older woman chuckled and patted her arm again.

'It'll do the young lummox some good to have someone stand up to him. Harriet rarely ever did.'

'Oh!'

There wasn't much she could say to that. She knew very little about Harriet and saying, 'So, tell me all I need to know about your dead wife…' wasn't that easy to slip into casual conversation.

Hettie looked up at her and took a sip of wine before speaking again.

'Harriet was a gorgeous girl but also rather fey. She was quite ethereal in both looks and personality. She bent with the wind and was always happy to go with the flow.

In all of her life, I only knew her to dig her heels in over two issues – the first was when I wanted to sell the art shop after her father died. It was his place and I couldn't run two businesses. She was adamant that I keep it until she'd graduated from art school and then she'd take over running it. I put a manager in place for two years and sure enough, as soon as she'd finished her course, she stepped in and took it on.'

'I see. And the second?'

'When they wanted her to abort her baby so she could have treatment for her cancer.'

A sharp gasp escaped from Perrie's lips.

'Oh my! That must have been a horrific choice to make.'

'Not for her it wasn't. Morgan pleaded with her to follow the doctors' advice but she was having none of it. Point blank refused to even think about it. She wasn't aborting her baby for anyone.'

'Do you think it might have saved her if she had?'

'She was only four months into the pregnancy when they found out so five months without treatment gave that tumour plenty of time to get a good foothold on her innards! We can't say for definite that earlier treatment would have helped but I don't think it could have made things any worse.'

'Do you wish she'd followed the doctors' recommendation?'

'How can I? Look at the gift she left behind. What if she'd aborted and the treatment hadn't worked? It would have been a double loss. As a mother, I fully understood her decision but as *her* mother, it broke my heart to watch her fight against a disease that still takes away more people than it should.'

'I'm so sorry.'

This time, it was she who put her hand on Hettie's

arm and squeezed it gently.

'It is what it is, love. Time moves on and people can either go with it or root themselves in the past and wallow in what-might-have-beens. The latter is not the best option but it's where Morgan was until you showed up.'

'Really?'

'Yup! Sure, he was dating other women, but he was just scratching an itch if you ask me—'

Perrie began coughing as the mouthful of wine she'd just taken went down the wrong way. Of all the things she'd expected Hettie to come out with, that hadn't been one of them.

'— as they were the wrong sorts of women. Not the kind you settle down with so it wasn't too difficult to see the way his head was thinking. You, however, you're different. Something about you poked the bear and made him waken up.'

'I think it was more likely my filthy red-headed temper and my potty-mouth in front of Daisy that did it!'

'Whatever it was, it brought back the man we used to know.'

'Then we'd better hope he gets his act together and comes up with a good way of apologising to me otherwise he'll be back to dating the wrong sorts again! And he's not got long as my rental is up at the end of September.'

'Oh, right! So soon? Are you thinking of leaving us? I'm sure Sue would be happy to extend the lease if you wanted it.'

'She's already made the offer.'

'But you're not sure?'

'No, I'm not. I do love being here, I won't deny that, but this falling out with Morgan has left a bitter-taste and I can't help but wonder if it would be better to find something similar in another location and start again.

This time it would be without the secret baggage.'

'You could do that but I think someone would be beyond distraught if you did.'

Perrie followed Hettie's gaze and saw Daisy picking up a drink from the nearby table.

'She'll miss you like blazes if you leave.'

'But, if Morgan continues to keep his distance, it'll be harder for her to see me around and not be allowed to talk to me. Leaving may actually be the best thing for her in the long run.'

'Aye, perhaps it would, when you put it like that.'

There was silence between them for a moment and Perrie was wondering what to say next when Hettie suddenly turned and looked her up and down.

'So, are you planning on going back to your city-self?'

'I'm sorry? I'm not sure what you mean?'

'The blonde hair, sharp suits, face covered in muck and your feet on stilts!'

'Ah, no, absolutely not! What you see is the real me. That persona was what my husband thought a politician's wife should look like. I hated it.'

'So why wear it when you went to court? Why not be yourself and stick two fingers up at him by doing so?'

'Because it was my disguise! I know that the people who know me recognised me on the television but strangers won't now that I've dispensed with it. From now on, what you see in front of you is how it will always be.'

'I should hope so! It was a sacrilege doing that to your hair. It's perfect and glorious as it is – be sure to keep it that way.'

'I intend to!'

'Good! And on the subject of glorious red things – is there any merlot left in that bottle or do we need to crack open another one?'

Perrie picked up the bottle of wine.

'I think we're in luck.'

'Then pour it out, lass! These screaming kids are giving me a headache and I need something to dull the pain.'

That night, Perrie lay in bed and thought back over the day. Babs had apologised for making the scene with Cleo.

'I'm not sorry for calling Cleo out on her behaviour – I'm still pissed that she thought she could come into my home and behave like that. How dare she try to cause an upset at my kid's party. I am sorry, however, that it put you in an uncomfortable situation; that was not my intention.'

Perrie had reassured Babs while pointing out that, in a perverse kind of way, it had probably worked in her favour as it had made the other parents stop and think. The initial awkwardness which had been present when they'd arrived was dispelled and everyone had been considerably more pleasant towards her after that.

Then there had been Hettie's revelations about her daughter. She'd been curious to know more about Harriet but hadn't felt comfortable asking anyone. When you know a person has died in tragic circumstances, it doesn't feel right to poke about, trying to find out more.

She turned onto her side, pushed the single sheet off her shoulders in an attempt to cool down and switched off the bedside light. Lying in the dark, with sleep gradually creeping over her, Perrie became aware that the hard, tight, knot of anxiety, which had lived in the pit of her stomach for over a year, felt just a touch smaller tonight. Her new start was underway and a smile sat on the corners of her mouth as she fell into a deep slumber.

FORTY-FIVE

Over the days that followed, the heat continued to build and by Thursday, Perrie was sitting at her desk, with the windows in front of her open as wide as they would go, trying to catch the breeze off the sea. This heatwave, however, was cooking everything including the usually refreshing, often bracing, coastal winds. The forecasters had said the weather would break within the next twenty-four to forty-eight hours but were unable to be more specific due to the way the jet-stream was moving. This was of little comfort to her and the rest of the country.

Currently, she had the thermal blackout window blind rolled up but it would be pulled down shortly to try and keep the room cool as the sun moved round to the front of the cottage and proceeded to bake the rooms from that angle. She looked at the bottles of once-frozen water standing in front of her desktop fan and realised they were now fully melted. It was time to swap them over. She'd read an article online that said placing bottles of frozen water in front of a fan gave off cooler air and in desperation, she'd given it a try and had been impressed to find it did work. She now had a dozen small bottles which were rotated to ensure she always had a modicum of cool air nearby.

She stood, stretching out her back which had seized up while she'd been hunched over her desk, totally engrossed in a small journal which was giving a wonderfully detailed account of life in London in the middle of the sixteenth century. The writer, from what she'd been able to discern so far, was an affluent stationer who'd moved his business from Cambridge to London with a view to taking advantage of the recent increase in the written and printed word. She was finding it utterly intriguing and had already made copious notes. Taking a note of the time, Perrie decided to have a small break and was about to gather up the bottles when she had the thought to pull the blind down now. She was leaning over the desk when some movement below caught her attention and she looked down to see a man working on the drystone wall opposite. She'd forgotten to ask Morgan if he'd reported it to the council but the sight of the gentleman below suggested he had. As she watched, he picked up a bottle of water and drained it dry, chucking the empty bottle into his tool bag.

Perrie felt sorry for him because there was no shelter along that stretch and the sun was blazing down on him. She turned on her heel and rushed down the stairs.

A few minutes later, she was trotting across the grass with a cool bag in her hand.

'Excuse me, sir...'

The workman turned round and, close up, she saw he was an older chap a little taller than herself. Under his baseball cap, he hid a leathery-brown face that was home to a pair of bright, twinkling blue eyes with pale white lines fluttering out on either side which suggested he was a man who smiled often.

'Aye, lass?'

'I noticed that you appeared to have finished your drink so I've brought over some chilled lemon water to keep you going.'

'Oh my, that's most kind of ye. Thank you.'

'It's my pleasure. It must be quite draining working in this heat.'

'Aye, it is that.'

Now that she was standing next to the wall, she saw that the gap was decidedly larger than it had appeared from the top of the house.

'You're never going to get that all repaired today, are you?'

'Nay, unfortunately not. Had it been cooler, possibly, but in this heat, I've got no chance. I'll be here until the back of one and then I'll have to call it a day. I'd be down with the heatstroke if I tried to keep going after that. Especially here where the sun is in every corner.'

'Will it be safe leaving it open like that?'

She recalled Morgan's concern about people taking advantage of the easy access to the path leading to the cove steps.

'Aye, it'll be fine. I've got one of those metal fence-things which I'll place across the gap and I've got the warning tape with "Danger! Keep Out" emblazoned along it.'

'Won't that grab the attention of anyone walking by?'

'It would but you don't get too many going on to the cliffs this way. They usually take the top path across from the car park which brings them out further along so they bypass this section. It's only the locals who come up this way and they know to avoid this section.'

'Fair enough. Well, I'll let you get on. When you leave, you can just drop the bag in the porch of the cottage.'

'Cheers again, lass.'

She smiled and made her way back into the cottage, relieved to return to the relatively cool interior – redheads and blistering sunlight was not a match made in heaven!

She slipped her shoes off and walked barefoot through to the shaded kitchen, enjoying the feel of the cool laminate on her toes. In the kitchen, the cats were lying stretched out to their fullest length. Timothy was taking up every inch of his blue cool mat but George wasn't so keen on them and tended to lie half on and half off his.

'Hey, babies, now the sun has moved round, your run will be cooling off. I'll go and put the air-con unit on and you can go out shortly.'

As she pulled back the door curtain and stepped down into the garden, a rueful smile crossed her lips when she recalled the grunts and groans of the delivery men a couple of days back when the small air-conditioning unit she'd ordered had arrived. She'd directed them to the little car park, figuring it would be easier all round to bring it up the stairs on the dolly trolley than have the local sleigh lads having to pull it up the hill at the front. The delivery men were not happy but as she'd paid extra for delivery and placement, they'd had no choice but to get on with it. She was sure the tip she gave them for a couple of drinks afterwards had made up for the inconvenience.

When she opened the door to the run and stepped inside, Perrie was pleased to find it wasn't as hot as she'd been expecting. She'd left the shutters on and pulled out the awnings to keep the front as shaded as possible. One thing she had to say for the previous tenant, Mr. Rogers, he'd really thought of everything when it came to his birds and now Timothy and George were also enjoying those same benefits.

She topped up the reservoir on the air-con unit, switched it on and enjoyed a few guilty moments in front of it before going back into the cottage.

'We'll give that half-an-hour, boys, and then you can go out. While we wait, I'm going to make myself a cup of tea and a sandwich for lunch because we all know that if I go back upstairs to my desk now, I'll get lost in that diary and you'll still be sitting in here come teatime!'

Timothy responded to her chatter with a lazy swish of his tail while George shuffled over to the other half of his cool mat. Even when she took the ham from the fridge, there was no reaction from either of them – a clear indicator of how the heat was bothering them. Normally, they'd be bowling her over for a piece of ham, especially when it was slices of the extra special "off the bone" cut.

As the kettle boiled for her tea, Perrie woke up her tablet. She might as well use this short downtime to check her emails. She skipped through her inbox and opened up one from Aggie, reading it while she put her sandwich together and dunked a refreshing green tea and lemon teabag in a mug. Her sister had written to thank her for the birthday gift of a hot air balloon ride and to say how much she and Graham would enjoy that. She also passed on a little gossip that their brother, Marcus, had met a young lady and she suspected this one might be serious but she was keeping her lip buttoned as she didn't want to scare him off the idea. Perrie had to chuckle when she read that – Aggie keeping her mouth closed and her opinions to herself was no mean feat.

She read a few other emails, typed out a couple of replies and then closed the tablet up. After she'd rinsed her cup and returned her lunch ingredients to the fridge, she took the cats out to the run which was now completely shaded and deliciously cool. She turned the air-con down to a lower setting and left her boys clambering up one of their tall trees as she secured the door behind her, making sure the bolt was properly engaged.

Back in the kitchen, Perrie grabbed three more bottles of frozen water from the freezer and made her way up the stairs to her desk, stopping along the way to pull down blinds and close curtains in the bedrooms at the front of the cottage in an attempt to keep the house cool. When she sat back down at her desk and opened the old diary, the stationer's next entry went on to describe the unbearable heat as the city of London endured one of the hottest spells it had ever known and as she herself could feel the sweat trickling down her own back, Perrie couldn't help but sympathise.

FORTY-SIX

'Daaaaaaddy, it's tooooooo hot!'

'I know, poppet, but I can't do anything about it.'

'Can't we go swimming again? That made it better yesterday.'

Morgan looked down at Daisy from the top of his ladder.

'I would love to but I need to get this wallpaper down. I promised you I would redecorate your bedroom when I took my week's holiday, didn't I?'

'Yes, you did.' A large sigh accompanied Daisy's reply.

'Well, I can't do that if we go swimming and you'll be looking at this baby paper for another three or four months.'

Morgan couldn't believe he was stuck up a ladder, with a boiling wallpaper steamer in his hand on what was probably the hottest day of the year. What were the bloody chances?

Daisy had been harping on about the "baby" wallpaper in her bedroom for a while now and he'd promised her he would change it when he was on holiday. It was too much to do at the weekend – especially when he only got two full days every few weeks. He didn't object to repapering the room because it was long overdue having not been touched since he and Harriet had done it up in the weeks before Daisy was born. Part of him wondered if that was why he'd dragged his feet over doing the redecoration – it was one of the last projects that he and Harriet had done together where things had been almost "normal". As soon as Daisy was born, her mum had been whisked off to begin treatment for her cancer and their lives hadn't been "normal" again.

Pushing the memories away, Morgan looked down again at Daisy who was standing kicking the door frame.

'Look, why don't you go and get an ice-lolly from the freezer and watch one of your Disney films? You could put on "Brave" – that's your favourite one, isn't it?'

'Not anymore. I want my real Merida, not the pretend one.'

'Well, it's not possible to see Perrie right now—'

'Why not? She's back from the place she went to. She was at Sarah's party. Why has she not been here to see me?'

'She's not been to visit because she has to work. You need to give her space to do the things she needs to do.'

'It's not fair!'

Daisy kicked the door frame harder this time before turning on her heel and thumping off down the stairs.

Morgan tried not to let out a sigh of his own while his guilt kicked him in the stomach. He felt bad for giving Daisy such evasive answers when she asked about Perrie but didn't think it was right to tell her the truth. How could he? When she kept telling him – and boy, did she keep telling him – that she was missing her Merida, how could he say he was missing her too without going into the reasons of why she wasn't here? How could he even begin to try and explain the complex nature of why he wasn't talking to Perrie right now? He could barely explain it to himself, never mind to a five-year-old child. In the weeks since he'd stormed out of Seaview Cottage, he'd tried to come to terms with the emotions inside him but no matter how much soul-searching he did, he kept coming back to the same thing – he loved Perrie but he didn't trust her. And how, he asked time and again, could he be with someone he no longer trusted?

His head dropped down and he gripped the top of the ladder tightly for several seconds while drawing in deep breaths, swallowing hard a few times in an attempt to dislodge the lump in his throat.

Finally, he gave himself a small shake and returning his attention to the wall, gathered up the scraper and proceeded to vent his frustrations upon the pastel pink wallpaper.

Morgan was unaware of how much the room had darkened as he scraped off the last piece of paper and looked around him to check he hadn't missed a bit. He'd been gathering up the soggy, old wallpaper into binbags as he'd been working so there was barely any mess to clean off the floor. All he had to do now was give the walls a quick wash-down with some sugar soap to make sure there was no paste residue clinging to them and they could dry off overnight, ready for the new paper to go up in the morning. Daisy was chuffed to bits with the wallpaper he'd found that had stars and planets all over it and despite her whinging earlier, couldn't wait for it to go up.

He looked at his watch and gasped when he saw the time. It was after seven o'clock! How on earth had it taken this long? More to the point, why hadn't Daisy been up to moan that it was teatime and that she was hungry? Most likely because, he thought to himself, the little monkey had eaten more than one ice-lolly and was now either feeling sick from all the sugar or was feeling full and didn't want any dinner. His money was on the first option.

He took the paper-scraper and the steamer into the bathroom to clean and cartoon voices floated up the stairs from the lounge as he crossed the landing. Once he'd sorted these, he would make some dinner and then wash the walls once a certain young madam was in bed.

He walked down the stairs a couple of minutes later, a bag full of wet, sticky wallpaper in one hand and the steamer in the other.

'Hey, poppet, what do you want for dinner? It's later than I thought so do you fancy fish-finger sandwiches?' he called out, as he passed by the lounge door.

He put the steamer next to the cellar door and opened the back door to drop the binbag outside.

'Hey, Daisy, have you fallen asleep in there?'

Morgan washed his hands at the sink and wandered into the lounge, wiping them dry on the towel as he walked.

'Daisy, I—'

He stopped.

Daisy wasn't sprawled across the sofa as he'd expected.

He looked behind it and then behind the chairs. Was she playing hide-and-seek?

'Daisy, where are you? Are you playing a game?'

He ran up the stairs to his own bedroom, flung the door open and rushed in but there was no Daisy in there. He pushed the floor length curtains to the side but she wasn't hiding behind them. Nor was she in the wardrobe or under the bed.

By now, his heart was beginning to thump hard in his chest. Where the hell was she? He checked the little box room where she was due to sleep that night, just in case she'd grown tired of waiting for him to finish up and had taken herself off to bed but she wasn't there either.

Morgan was trying to quell the rapidly building panic inside him. A cold sweat broke out on his back and a trembling, jittery sensation passed through him. A thought flew into his head – the only place he hadn't looked was the cellar but she didn't like going down there and usually avoided it. That, however, didn't prevent him from checking anyway but to no avail.

As he ran up the cellar stairs, he heard a loud rumble overhead but it didn't register through his fear.

The garden! He hadn't looked out in the garden.

His brain tried to tell him he'd have seen her there when he put the rubbish bag out but his reasoning said he hadn't been paying attention and needed to check.

The kitchen door was yanked open but the garden was empty.

It took him barely a dozen steps to cross the lawn to the small garden shed but even as he approached, he could see it was firmly padlocked. There was no way she could be in there.

He stood in the middle of the lawn, running his hand over his head, when thunder rumbled again. This time louder and sounding even more menacing.

The air around him was growing thicker and heavier by the minute. He'd witnessed enough coastal storms to know how frightening and severe they could be and the one now brewing had all the ingredients to be a big one.

The fear already running through his body intensified. A mighty storm was imminent and his daughter was nowhere to be found.

FORTY-SEVEN

Perrie sat up with a start.

'Huh?'

She'd been completely engrossed in the words within the stationer's diary, having left the twenty-first century well behind as she'd time travelled in her head to the sixteenth century and was now wondering what had disturbed her?

She checked her phone but it was on silent meaning it hadn't been that and the alarm she'd set to bring the cats in from the run wasn't due to go off for another twenty minutes. So, what had broken her concentration?

Her answer came a few seconds later when a loud rumble crashed in the sky above her.

'Ah, I'll bet that's what did it.'

She looked to the window and realised there were no stray sunbeams trying to squeeze around the sides of the blind. She rolled it up and looked out into a dark, charcoal grey, heavy void. The sensation was akin to the air being sucked out of the room. Everything was still as life itself waited for the storm to begin.

Perrie reluctantly pulled the windows closed. While the rain would clear the air and freshen the atmosphere, she didn't need her work desk getting soaked in the process.

She was just switching off her desk light when another, even louder, rumble came and she rushed over to the door. The boys were still out in the run and she wanted them indoors before the rain began. As a rule, they'd never been too bothered by thunderstorms but that was back in London – she didn't know what they were like around here and she'd be happier with them both in the house before she found out.

She was halfway down the stairs when loud banging suddenly came from the front door.

She jumped down the last few steps and opened it to find Morgan, looking utterly distraught, on the doorstep.

'What the—'

'Is she here? Tell me she's with you.'

'I don't understa—'

'Daisy! Is she here with you?'

He pushed past her and walked into the lounge, calling as he went, 'Daisy? Daisy, are you here? Time to come home now…'

'Morgan, she's not here. What's going on?'

He turned to look at her, fear etched across his face.

'I can't find Daisy. I was… I was working upstairs, I thought she was watching the television – that's where I told her to be – but I lost track of time. When I came down, she was gone.'

'Have you looked everywhere in the house for her?'

'OF COURSE, I'VE LOOKED EVERYWHERE!'

He turned, barged her out of the way and made his way to the kitchen.

'Morgan, she's not here. I've been in all day – upstairs for most of it – and I can assure you she hasn't

272

been to see me.'

'I'm sorry, I'm sorry. I didn't mean to shout but…'

'It's okay, I understand. Look, give me a minute to get the cats in from the run and I'll come with you to look for her. While I'm doing that, have you called your mum or Hettie to check she's not made her way to them?'

'No, no, I haven't. I didn't think she'd go that far. That's why I came here, because you're so close.'

'Well, call them. I'll be quick.'

Perrie slipped her garden shoes on and stepped out onto the patio. Thunder rumbled again, the air so dense, it almost hurt to breathe and the sky had turned from dark grey to black in the few minutes since she'd closed the attic windows. The outdoor security light came on as she darted over to the run, glad now that she'd left the shutters up earlier, and pushed back the bolt on the door.

As soon as she stepped inside, she could sense something wasn't right. Everything felt wrong. She looked around before letting out a scream.

'MORGAN!'

He was beside her before she had time to draw in a breath to call him again.

'I'm here, what is it? Is she here?'

She looked down through the run before turning to face him.

'Timothy – he's gone! And,' she pointed behind him, 'so is his harness.'

Just then, an almighty crack of lightning split the sky above them and the heavens opened, the rain bouncing on the hard, sun-caked ground as it poured down.

FORTY-EIGHT

'Did you speak to your mum and Hettie?'

'No, I can't get a signal. The static in the air is probably playing havoc with them.'

Perrie stopped tying up her boots to pull her mobile out to look at it.

'No, mine's got nothing either. Look, use the cottage phone, it's just over there.'

Morgan stepped over to use the landline as she finished fastening her boots. He'd barely begun to tap the numbers into the cordless handset when the cottage was plunged into darkness. The buttons glowed in the dark so Perrie knew where he was standing but with no power going into the main unit, the handset was now useless.

'Argh! I don't believe this!'

'Look, I've got some battery-operated lanterns here. Hang on…'

She switched on the torch on her phone and walked through the kitchen to the understairs cupboard where she pulled out a couple of camping lights. Lifting the handles upwards, she yanked the base down and suddenly the room lit up.

'Whoa! That's bright!'

She threw her hand over her eyes, not expecting the light to be so powerful.

'That's LED lighting for you.'

This time, she opened the second one with a bit more caution and handed it to Morgan.

'These are pretty nifty. We should be able to see reasonably well.'

'Actually, I was thinking...'

'Yes?'

She looked at him, waiting for him to continue.

'It might be a good idea to leave one on the windowsill so that, if we miss her and she comes by this way, she'll see the light and follow it.'

'I'd say that's an excellent idea.'

Perrie walked over to the deep-set window in the dining room and placed the lantern on the wide, wooden sill. She moved the curtains well away to ensure the light could shine through every pane.

She used the light from the second lamp to put a bowl of food down for George and added some powder which would help him to relax despite the noise outside.

'Right, are you ready?' she asked.

Morgan nodded.

'Then let's go.'

As they stepped out into the porch, she left the door on the latch so that, if Daisy did come back, she'd be able to get indoors to safety.

They were walking up the path when a loud bang made them jump. Perrie looked round and saw the gate at the side of the cottage swinging furiously in the wind.

'Now we know how she got in and out without going through the house. I must have forgotten to lock it after I watered the plants last night.'

Morgan didn't respond and she followed along behind him until they were out on the cliff path. This was the first time she'd been over the cliffs in the late evening and the blackness swirled around her despite the bright light being carried by Morgan.

'Do you think she'd have gone out onto the cliffs?' She had to shout as the wind was fierce with no walls to shelter them.

'It's all I can think of. I can't see that she'd take the cat down into the town and you usually walk them on the cliffs, don't you?'

'Yes, I do. And she's walked with me many times so she knows the route I'd usually take.'

'Then we'll go that way and hopefully find the pair of them sheltering under a bush somewhere.'

Through the driving rain they walked, the force behind the droplets making them feel like needles when they hit their skin. The wind was so strong on the open and exposed cliffs that they were bent almost double as they pushed against it. Whenever they called Daisy's name, their words were ripped from their lips and stolen away. When Morgan told her to walk behind him again, so he could give her some shelter, he had to repeat himself twice before she could hear him.

They came to a halt when Perrie tapped him on the shoulder to tell him that this was where she usually turned to go back whenever she'd had Daisy with her.

'It's not that far…'

'I was always worried about her little legs,' she yelled into his ear, 'I wouldn't have been able to carry her and have two strong cats pulling me along.'

They held the lantern up and swung it round, shouting and calling Daisy's name but the sound was muted in the dense rain.

'We should go on a little further to see if she kept

walking to find somewhere to hide. She's really scared of storms.'

'Okay, you lead and I'll follow.'

They kept on going and when the lamplight reflected off the lifebuoy that stood by the gorse which hid the steps down to the cove, Perrie suddenly had a thought. She grabbed Morgan's arm and pointed over to where they'd passed through the undergrowth.

'Do you think she might have gone towards the cove?'

Morgan's eyes widened at her words.

'Surely not…'

'It's worth a look, just to be sure.'

Together they ran over to the thick hedging and as before, Morgan pushed through it first, holding it back for Perrie to follow him.

'DAISY!'

'DAISY!'

They yelled as loudly as they could while tiptoeing cautiously towards the edge, lifting the lamp up high, and holding hands tightly to prevent the wind from blowing them over and down onto the rocks below. For the briefest of seconds, the wind dropped and Perrie thought she heard something.

'Morgan, did you hear that?' She grabbed his arm with her free hand.

'What?'

'I'm sure I heard something. Come…'

Holding on tightly to the gorse bushes, and ignoring the jagging pain in her hand from the thorns, she stepped over the edge and onto the top of the stairs that led down to the cove.

'Morgan, can you hold the lantern up and over here, please.'

He came to stand beside her, lifting the lamp up high

above their heads.

'DAISY!' he yelled.

'Daddeeeeeee,' was the faint wail that came back towards them.

They walked down a handful of the stone steps, keeping the lantern raised high and when the light reflected off the angry seawater below, they saw Daisy, halfway down the stairs, up to her shoulders in seawater and clinging onto the old wooden banister for dear life. 'Daddeeeeee,' she wailed again, 'help me!'

FORTY-NINE

'Oh, good Lord, Daisy…' Morgan moaned with both relief and fear. 'I'm coming, baby girl, I'm coming. Keep holding on, don't let go.'

'Daddy, my hands hurt, I don't think I can.'

'You have to, poppet, you have to. Just a little bit longer.'

He was about to head down the steps into the water when he felt Perrie grabbing his arm.

'What are you doing? I need to get to her?'

'I know you do, Morgan, but give me a minute to go and grab the lifebuoy – please? If you get swept off your feet while she's in your arms, I could lose both of you. Be sensible. Just wait…'

She was back off up the steps before he could reply and as much as he wanted to hurry down to Daisy, he saw the sense in her words.

As promised, Perrie was back beside him barely two minutes later although they'd felt more like two hours as he continued to shout encouragement to Daisy.

'Here, take this with you and put it over Daisy when

you get to her. There's enough line here for me to pull you both back to safety.'

'Thank you, Perrie.'

He quickly kissed her on the forehead and passed the lantern to her before taking the lifebuoy and moving as rapidly as he could down the steps. When he reached the waterline, he had to slow down and feel his way with his feet. Perrie had followed him down and held the lantern up high, enabling him to see better.

'I'm nearly there, Daisy, just another few seconds…'

As he'd expected, the next step down was one of the deeper ones and the water was now up to his chest. Morgan pushed off and did a couple of breast strokes which brought him next to Daisy.

'Hey, sweetie-pie, what's a nice girl like you doing hanging around an old stinky place like this?'

'Oh, Daddy, I'm sorry.'

She let go of the banister and threw her arms tightly around his neck. Her movement took him by surprise and he felt himself dip down further in the water.

'Daisy, you need to let me put this over your head and then Perrie's going to pull us back to safety.'

'Merida's here?'

'Yes, she is and she's been very worried about you. Now, put your hands up in the air… it's okay, I'm holding you… there you go. Slip your arms through those ropes… good girl. Now, fold them across your chest. Excellent. That'll keep you all safe and you won't slip through because the ropes will hold you secure. Hold tight, I'm about to give Perrie the signal to pull us back.'

'Daddy, wait. You have to save Timothy. Please… don't let him die.'

'Eh? What?'

With the immense relief of finding Daisy, he'd completely forgotten about the cat she'd effectively stolen.

'Where is he?'

'Over there, Daddy. Oh, please, you have to save him.'

Morgan looked over and his heart sank. He could just about see the large bundle of fur floating next to some overhanging branches on the other side of the banister.

'I don't think—'

'Daddy, you must! Please…'

'Okay, you go back to Perrie and tell her to take you straight home to the cottage. I'll be right behind you. Let her know I'm getting Timothy.'

He gave the rope a sharp tug and felt the pull of the line as Perrie began drawing Daisy towards her. He watched with his heart in his mouth until his little girl was safely in Perrie's arms. He saw them talking and then saw Perrie looking out towards him as she half-hung, half-stuffed the lantern onto one of the gorse bushes, ensuring he still had some light. A second light appeared a few seconds later and he realised she was using the torch on her mobile to help them home.

Once he saw her take Daisy's hand and head up the stairs, he pulled himself over the top of the banister and held tight against the battering of the waves at his back.

He'd purposely waited for Daisy to leave before attempting to rescue the large cat because from the way he was floating in the water, Morgan was dreading getting closer, almost certain that Timothy was dead.

He only needed a few strong swim strokes to reach Timothy but it took several minutes to untangle his harness from where it had wrapped around the branch for the seawater had made the wet leather difficult to undo.

The cat's face wasn't in the water as Morgan had first thought but there were no visible signs of life. He slipped the loop of the leather lead over his hand and onto his wrist, wrapping it round twice to ensure he had a good grip and then, holding the large animal carefully against his chest with Timothy's face and front paws over his shoulder to stop him slipping into the water, he turned around and with only one arm free, began to slowly make his way towards the light Perrie had left behind, using that as a guide to the steps and fighting against the pull of the waves trying to drag them both out to the vast expanse of the sea. He wished now that he'd thought to ask Perrie to throw the lifebuoy back, it would have made this easier.

He could feel himself beginning to tire and was relieved when he managed to get across to the wooden handrail and felt the steps under his feet again. He leant against the cliff face for a few seconds, moving the weight of the water-logged cat further up over his shoulder, and got his breath back.

He stood like that for longer than he'd initially intended and it was the cold creeping up his body which forced him to move.

'C'mon, Timmy old chap, we can do this.'

He was inwardly sniggering at his unwitting use of Famous Five jargon as he moved forward when, at that moment, a large wave swept in and buffeted hard against him. He instinctively threw his arm out to grab a hold of the banister but the rickety old piece of wood broke beneath his hand, causing him to stumble and cry out in pain when his foot went out from underneath him on the submerged steps. He let out a yell as he fell backwards into the water.

Immediately, the sea swallowed him up and pulled him under.

Still holding on tightly to Timothy, he managed to push himself back up above the water, breaking through the surface just in time to see a large wave coming towards him.

With neither the time to swim away or steady himself in preparation to meet it, the wave picked Morgan up and slammed him hard against the solid, jagged rocks of the cliff face.

He briefly registered the pain in his skull before everything went black.

FIFTY

Perrie paused at the top of the steps for a moment, debating which route to take home before deciding she'd rather be scratched to pieces by the gorse bushes than take the narrow path they'd used previously. It had been precarious enough in broad daylight, no way was she doing it in the dark and especially not with Daisy in her arms.

'Can you wrap your legs around me, Daisy? I don't want you to be hurt by the gorse.'

The little girl shifted in her arms, wrapping her legs around Perrie's waist, tightening her hold around her neck and burrowing her face into her shoulder.

She tried to pull the edges of her jacket together in order to afford Daisy some protection from the elements but it wasn't easy as the wind was still blowing strongly and she simply couldn't hold Daisy, her mobile and the jacket all at the same time.

As the wind whipped the jacket behind her again, she looked to the sea below, trying to spot Morgan, hoping he was on his way up the steps but there was no sign of him. She didn't want to go and leave him behind but she also knew she had to get Daisy out of her wet clothes as quickly as possible.

With another quick glance, and still no Morgan, Perrie waded into the thick scratchy bushes, focusing her thoughts on ignoring the pain as the thorny evergreen grabbed her jeans and thrust its little spikey daggers through the material into her legs.

Once on the other side, she quickly made her way to the cliff path which would lead her home. She was all too aware of how little charge was left on her phone but if the light was snuffed out before she got home, she knew this path well enough by now that it should lead her back to the cottage even in the depth of darkness.

She stumbled along as quickly as she could, talking quietly to Daisy the whole time and trying not to let the lack of response panic her.

They were about five minutes from home when her mobile died, plunging them into darkness. Perrie stopped in her tracks, allowing her senses a couple of seconds to adjust to the black night now surrounding them. The thunder was still rumbling in the distance and the lightning was no longer flashing overhead although the rain continued to hammer down upon them.

When she moved forward again, her steps were cautious and she used the toe of her right foot to keep them on the path, checking it against the grass by the side. It felt like the longest two minutes she'd ever known but when they eased around the bend in the path, Perrie saw the smallest pinprick of light ahead of them.

'Oh, bless you, Morgan, for your wonderful idea...' she muttered aloud, realising she was seeing the light from the lantern Morgan had suggested she put in the window.

Using it as her guide, she was able to speed up her

steps and soon they were safely indoors.

She took Daisy into the kitchen and placed her gently on the floor, next to George. As she straightened up, Perrie dithered on what to do next – get Daisy out of her wet clothes, put some water to heat on the, thankfully, gas hob or go into the lounge to light the wood-burning stove – which she hadn't yet used but was laid ready to go – so the room could be warming up while she sorted Daisy out…

She decided to do the lounge first followed by hot water and undressing Daisy.

'Daisy,' she bent down to the little girl, 'I'm just going to get a towel and some dry clothing for you so I need you to just wait here till I get back. I've only got one lantern which I'll need to take with me but George is here to keep you company so there's no need to be afraid. Can you do that? Are you okay for me to leave you for a few minutes?'

Daisy didn't look at her but gave a small nod.

'Okay, good girl.'

Perrie placed a kiss on her forehead before rushing off to begin finding ways of warming them up. It didn't take long to get the wood-burner on the go. Aggie had one in her lounge so she knew what was what there. When she was happy it was underway, she ran up the stairs and grabbed a T-shirt, socks and a cardigan to dress Daisy in and then went to the airing cupboard for a towel.

She struggled to get the big bath towel she wanted out from under the pile of smaller towels above it and the clothes in her arms fell to the floor.

'Bugger!'

When she bent down to pick them up, however, a smile spread across her face.

'Oh, you beauty!' she exclaimed, as her gaze fell upon another camping lantern sitting under the lower shelf.

She pulled it open and was relieved when it lit up.

The new lantern was deposited on the windowsill up in her roof-top study, giving Morgan a homing-signal to follow.

When she returned to the kitchen, Daisy was still where Perrie had left her. Grateful that she now had an extra lantern, she placed it on the kitchen worktop then took another moment to put a couple of pans of water – a small one and a larger one – on the hob to warm up wishing, on this occasion, that the cottage wasn't fitted with a combi-boiler which required electricity to work, before helping Daisy up and battling to get the wet clothes off her.

'Daisy, you need to help me here, sweetie. Lift your arms so I can get your tops off.'

Her heart squeezed like a vice as the little girl, doing as she'd been asked, began to cry.

'I'm so sorry, Merida. I'm so sorry. I didn't mean to hurt Timothy.'

'Hush, now. Shhhhh, don't worry about that. Let's just focus on getting you warm and dry.'

Daisy continued to sob as Perrie poured the small pan of water into the dish basin and washed as much of the sand and sea-salt off her little body as she could. After drying her briskly in an attempt to warm her up, she dressed her in the clothes she'd brought down.

'Sit here a minute, Daisy. I'm just going to sort out a hot-water bottle for you'

The little girl was placed safely up on one of the breakfast-bar stools before Perrie lifted the second pot of water from the hob, decanted it into a jug which was then poured into a hot-water bottle that was wrapped in a towel before being handed over.

'Okay, little one, let's go and see how warm and

cosy the lounge is now.'

She picked Daisy up and carried her through, stopping at the window for a brief second to see if there was any sign of Morgan but there was nothing beyond the impenetrable darkness.

'Here you go,' she placed the child on the sofa across from the wood-burner, 'you snuggle into that corner, hold onto the water bottle and we'll wrap this throw around you. There, it's just like being in a little den. You can pretend you're a baby bear cub, all cosied up in its cave.'

A quiet sigh of relief slipped from Perrie's lips when Daisy gave a tiny giggle. She'd had a terrible fright and Perrie didn't want it to have any adverse effects. People often didn't realise how these things could stick with a child.

'Now, would little Daisy bear-cub like some hot-chocolate to warm up her tummy?'

'With mallows?' came the whispered reply.

'Of course, with marshmallows. Is there any other way? And, just because it's a special night, I'll even put extra on.'

'More than four?'

Perrie smiled, knowing how strict Morgan was with Daisy's sugar intake.

'Definitely more than four but don't tell your daddy or he'll give me a telling off.'

'Pinkie secret?'

Daisy stuck her hand out from under the throw, her little finger raised in the air.

'Pinkie secret!'

As their fingers entwined, Perrie couldn't prevent herself from pulling Daisy into her arms and holding her close. They'd been lucky tonight. The thought of how differently this could have turned out made her shudder and she held the little girl just that bit tighter.

She had another look out of the lounge window as she passed by but there was still no sign of Morgan. Where on earth was he? A glance at her watch told her it was over an hour since they'd pulled Daisy from the water – he should have been here by now.

Perrie felt the panic she'd successfully managed to suppress earlier proceed to rise up again. With the power cut still ongoing, she had no phones to call anyone for help. She couldn't go out and get help from any neighbours as Daisy was in no state to be dragged back outside tonight and she couldn't leave her behind on her own.

Her hand trembled as the milk pot was placed down on the hob.

A deep cold sense of foreboding landed in the pit of her stomach as the awareness of her helplessness grew and she could do nothing to prevent it.

FIFTY-ONE

'Owwwwwwwwwwwwwwwww!'

Morgan felt the echo of his groan in every bone of his body. His head felt like it had been used as a football by a team of ogres and he was sure his body had become the punchbag for every boxer in the land.

He lay still as every movement caused him pain. His brain was a maelstrom of confusion and he had to force himself to take some deep breaths, regardless of how much it hurt, in order to settle his thoughts and get some idea of what was what.

He tried to open his eyes but his eyelids were just too heavy and he couldn't do it, so with the gift of sight currently not an option, the next thing to try was touch.

He was lying on his left side with his left arm stretched out above his head. Under his hand he could feel cold stone and a grainy texture – sand? His back was pushing against a jagged surface and his right hand was holding something furry against his stomach.

Something furry and warm.

Something furry, warm and purring.

He tried again to open his eyes and was marginally successful on his second attempt. He glanced down and found a pair of bright golden eyes staring back at him.

'Hey, Timothy,' he croaked, and felt the cat's purr deepen. The sensation of it flowed through him and was strangely comforting. He closed his eyes again and let the soft vibrations envelop him for a short time.

The cat moved and stretched itself out lengthways against him. He felt its warmth seep through him as he slipped back into darkness.

When he came round the second time, his brain was more receptive to the thinking thing and Morgan recalled what had happened. This time, he opened his eyes with more ease and saw he was in the smuggler's cave. Daylight was creeping in through the mouth at the front and he'd spent enough summer nights in here as a teenager to know the time was early morning.

He moved slightly to get away from the rocky wall at his back and in doing so, woke up the cat who was still sharing its body heat with him. Timothy got to his feet, displaying the enviable elegance that all cats have, stretched out all his limbs, sat down right in front of Morgan and yawned widely, displaying every tooth while treating Morgan to a blast of cat breath.

'Urgh! Timothy! At the risk of sounding ungrateful – did you have to?'

With no small amount of caution, he pulled himself up into a sitting position, grimacing as he did so. Everywhere ached but his head was vying for the number one spot on the pain chart. He raised his hand and felt the large, tender bump on the back of it. As he touched it, the memory of how he obtained it came back to him.

This was quickly followed by the question of how

the hell he'd ended up in the cave.

Timothy stood and moved away to sniff the boulders opposite and in doing so, jerked Morgan's arm.

He looked down and saw the lead attached to the cat's harness was still wrapped around his wrist. When he looked closer, he could see bruising and a couple of welts underneath on his skin, almost as though the lead had been pulled tight against his arm.

'How the—' he muttered.

He looked at the cat, well, the cat's backside as that was the angle he was currently being offered, and back at his wrist.

'Surely not?'

Was it possible? Had Timothy somehow dragged them both in here? But how could he have managed it?

Morgan looked back towards the mouth of the cave and could see some small pools of water dotted about. This suggested the water level had either been high enough to come into the cave or another large wave had thrown them inside.

He looked back at the cat, incredulity swamping him as the idea that Timothy may have saved his life hit home.

'Timmy, what did you do last night?'

The cat turned at the sound of his name, gave Morgan a "wouldn't you like to know" look and then went back to sniffing his boulders.

'Okay, mate, keep your secrets but I think it's time we got out of here and went home. I suspect there may be a couple of young ladies sitting waiting while being rather worried about our wellbeing.'

He reached into his pocket with absolutely no expectation of his phone still working and was not disappointed. The seawater had done its worst and the mobile was now a thing of history.

'It looks, Timothy, as though we're going to have to rescue ourselves again.'

He used the rock face to help him up and waited a moment to let the feeling of nausea pass before he attempted to walk.

Unfortunately, this proved to be easier thought of than done when a bolt of pain shot up through his leg when he tried to put his weight on his left foot – the same foot that had gone from under him last night.

'Bugger!' he exclaimed, as he gripped the wall tightly to avoid falling over.

He took a moment to let the pain pass and then hopped over the cave to Timothy's boulders. With the wall and rocks on his left side, he could use them as support to get him to the opening.

'Come on, Timmy, let's try and get home.'

He was puffing by the time he reached the cave mouth and when he looked down, the small stretch of sand that was visible when the tide was out, shone in the ever-brightening sunlight.

'Damn it!'

The plan, such as it was, had been to lower himself down into the water, swim to the steps and make their way home, albeit slowly thanks to his ankle. Now he'd have to wait ages for the tide to come in again.

'Bollocking shitting bollocks!'

He sat down with his legs hanging out over the cave opening and Timothy sat beside him.

He looked at the cat and was sure there was a look of disapproval on his face. What was it with this damn cat and his ability to express himself with a mere twitch of an eyebrow or turn of his lip?

'Okay, I apologise for the language. I just want to get home, hold my daughter in my arms,' he gave the cat a little nudge, 'hold your mother in my arms and then have something to eat followed by a nice long soak in a hot bath. Is that too much to ask?'

This time Timothy didn't even bother to look at him and just sat gazing out towards the horizon.

Morgan leant to the side and rested his head against the rock. Memories of his teenage days crept up upon him and he smiled as he recalled the first time he'd tried alcohol in here with his mates, Adam and Paul. He'd also been with them when they'd attempted their first puff on a cigarette. He chuckled as he remembered them all coughing so hard, they'd ended up vomiting all over the ropes.

The ropes!

Morgan sat upright.

How could he have forgotten?

He levered himself up, using the rocky wall again for assistance, and hobbled back over to Timothy's boulders.

Was it possible? Could they still be here?

He leant over and dropped his hand down into the crevice behind, hoping against hope that no one else had ever discovered their secret hiding place and removed their secret escape route.

His hand landed on something rough and he grabbed it, pulling it up and feeling the relief and joy rush through him as the tangle of rough-hewn rope saw daylight again for the first time in almost twenty years.

Morgan sat down and pulled the rope towards him. It hadn't felt this heavy when there had been three of them carrying it.

He checked it over and was thrilled to find it just as sturdy as the day Adam had pinched it from his father's boating shed. They'd sat up here together, tying in the knots at regular intervals so that, if they did ever miscalculate the tides, they'd have another means of getting out of the cove.

Deciding it was easier to crawl than walk, Morgan made his way back to cave mouth and found the old iron ring the original smugglers had hammered into the wall so they could tie their boats up. He threaded the rope through and tied it up. It took a couple of attempts to remember the non-slip knot Adam had taught him but he got there in the end and was satisfied it would take his weight and that of the hefty furry beast sitting watching him.

He threw the rope over and looked down to see the end of it dangling about three feet above the sand strip.

'Right-ho, Timothy, it's time for you to trust me. You've done your rescue, now it's my turn. Come here, boy.'

He sat down next to the rope and when Timothy walked over to him, he picked him up and draped him across the back of his neck and shoulders, just like a big fur stole. He held him in position for a moment while whispering to him not to move and to trust him. Morgan didn't know if the cat understood what he was telling him but when he took his hands away, Timothy didn't move. The claws dug in as Morgan turned over onto his hands and knees, straddled the rope and then moved into position to begin the arduous climb down.

He paused to take a deep breath, knowing that what he was about to do registered very highly on the totally bonkers scale. After all, who in their right mind would attempt to scale down a cliff-face with a dodgy ankle and a ten-kilo cat perched across their shoulders?
One thing was for sure, he thought as he began moving, it was a sport that was never going to make it into the Olympics!

FIFTY-TWO

Perrie woke up with a start!

She lay for a moment, gathering her thoughts on why she was lying on the sofa with Daisy and George and not in her bed with George and Timothy.

Timothy!

Morgan!

The events of the previous night came rushing back to her.

She moved her arm and managed to turn her wrist to see her watch. It was just after six in the morning.

Immediately, the worry that Morgan hadn't returned home hit her and she eased herself off the sofa, taking care not to disturb the little girl who was out for the count.

The wood-burner had more or less gone out, just a few embers glowed as she tip-toed past and slipped out of the room. In the hallway, she pulled on a pair of trainers and stepped out the front door, making her way up the garden path to the gate to look out towards the cliff-path. She didn't know what she was expecting to see but nothing was what she got. The cliff top was devoid of any human life. A couple of rabbits bobbed around but soon disappeared when they sensed her presence.

Perrie stood waiting for several minutes, watching while the warm sun began to dry the dew on the grass. Not wanting to leave Daisy alone for too long, she turned and walked towards the cottage. She was just about to step over the threshold when something made her stop. A feeling inside her had her turning around and running back to the gate. She looked along the cliff-path again but still there was nothing.

Her heart plummeted down to her feet and the sorrow she felt was overwhelming. She'd been so sure this time...

She'd just turned away to walk down the garden path a second time when something caught the corner of her eye. She turned her head slightly to see a bundle of fur strutting round the bend, followed a mere second later by a man hobbling along, using what looked like a tree branch as a crutch.

In an instant she was through the gate and running along the path, her vibrant red hair streaming behind her.

When she reached them, she bent down, scooped Timothy up into her arms and then threw herself into Morgan's, practically sending the poor bloke flying.

'I was so worried, where have you been? Why are you so late back? What happened?'

She didn't give Morgan a chance to speak as she rained kisses down upon them both. Her relief at seeing them whirled and swirled around her before flowing out through her pores and into the soft breeze from the sea.

She tightened her hold on Morgan and he let out a groan of pain.

'Oh, I'm sorry, I'm sorry. Come, let's get you back to the cottage.'

She went to his side, took the long stick from him and laid it alongside the path – no doubt some dog would think Christmas has arrived when it found it. She put her shoulder under Morgan's armpit and gave him a little hoist up, effectively taking all the weight off his leg.

'How's Daisy? Is she okay?'

Perrie ached to see the worry on his face.

'She's absolutely fine and currently sound asleep on the sofa. Now, stop worrying and let me help you.'

With Perrie half carrying him, it took just over a minute for them to make it back indoors. They were in the kitchen with Perrie helping Morgan onto a chair when there was a small click and the fridge in the corner began to hum again.

'Oh, what a result. Let me get the boiler back up and running and then you can have a soak in a warm, salt bath.'

'Can we leave out the salt – I've had enough of saltwater for now.'

'Sure, I'll put in mustard instead.'

'Mustard? I'm not a rump of beef, you know.'

She gave a small smirk as she replied, 'I'm well aware of that but you'll thank me afterwards. Trust me.'

She ran up the stairs, started up the boiler and after giving it a couple of minutes to get going, began running the bath, making sure to put a good hefty dollop of mustard powder into the water. After getting more towels out of the airing cupboard and putting them on the warming towel rail to heat up, she went back to the kitchen and helped Morgan up to the bathroom.

'Take your time and shout on me when you're done. I'll come and help you back down. I've put a pair of joggies in there for you and a polo shirt. There are some advantages to being tall with a penchant for men's sports tops – in this case, you won't look too daft wearing my clothes!'

She closed the door and went back down the stairs, checking on Daisy as she passed the lounge and was happy to see her still all cosied up in the throw.

Ten minutes later, the cat paddling pool had been filled with warm soapy water and Timothy was also getting a good wash, with careful attention being given to between his toes and orifices. The smallest grain of sand could cause an infection and that was the last thing he needed after what he'd been through.

While she rinsed him off and gave his coat a good brush, Perrie wondered what on earth had happened after she'd left to bring Daisy home. She knew Morgan had stayed behind to save her cat but she hadn't expected it to take over eight hours. She couldn't wait to hear what he had to tell her.

FIFTY-THREE

'Who wants another Danish pastry? There's plenty for everyone.'

Perrie held the piled high plate as Morgan and Daisy dived in for seconds.

When Morgan had come out of the bathroom earlier, he'd almost collapsed from exhaustion so she'd helped him into her bedroom and ordered him to get some sleep.

She was far too wound up to sit still while the rest of the house slept – Timothy was in his cat bed with George curled up next to him – so she did what she always did when stressed; she baked!

The smell of warm croissants and pain au raisins had filled the cottage by the time her unexpected guests returned from the land of nod. While Morgan and Daisy shared some moments together, Perrie had gone to their house and brought back fresh clothes and toiletries.

A house-call was then made to the local doctor and they were waiting for him to arrive while they ate.

'Oh, this is soooo good. I don't think I've ever enjoyed a cup of coffee as much as this.'

With a smile, she topped up Morgan's mug before getting up to make another pot.

While she waited for the kettle to boil, Morgan turned to Daisy.

'Sweetheart, we're not going to give you a telling off because you've had such a terrible fright, but you need to tell us why you went off with Timothy. You know you're not allowed to leave the house on your own and you *absolutely* should not have taken Timothy out of the garden, especially without telling Perrie. That was very wrong.'

The little girl's eyes filled with tears again and Perrie's throat constricted with sadness at seeing her upset. She wanted to step in and tell Morgan to leave things be but it wasn't her place to do so. She turned away and busied herself with making the coffee, her ears straining to hear Daisy's reply.

'I'm so sorry, Daddy, I didn't mean to be naughty. I was watching "Brave" like you told me to but it made me 'member my Merida and I was missing her very, very much. I hadn't seen Timothy for ages too so I thought that it would be okay to visit as the cottage is so close to home. When I got here, I saw the garden gate was open and went in. I did come inside to see Merida but she was busy with a book upstairs and I didn't want to interrupt. You always told me not to interrupt peoples when they have books open. So, I came downstairs and went to see Timothy in his run. When I saw his harness on the wall, I thought it would be nice to take him for a walk along the path we usually go on but then I saw the hole in the wall and remembered the path we'd used to come home from the pretty picnic place and thought Timothy would like to see it before he went away.'

'What do you mean, "Before he went away"?'

Perrie placed the coffee pot on the table and sat

down as Morgan looked at her in confusion while he waited for Daisy to answer his question.

'I heard Merida tell Granny Hettie, at Sarah's birthday party, that she was leaving next month in Stember. I didn't want him to go away without me saying goodbye and giving him a big cuddle, so I came to see him.'

She turned to face Perrie.

'I'm sorry, Merida, I didn't mean to hurt Timothy. I love him. It was a naccident.'

Perrie couldn't stand to see Daisy so sad. She rose from her seat, gathered Daisy into her arms and sat back down, placing the girl on her knee.

'Daisy, I know you'd never do anything to hurt Timothy. It was a big, bad mistake and I'm sure you'll never do it again, will you?'

'No! Never ever ever! Cross my heart and hope to die!'

She made a criss-cross sign on her little chest and Perrie wrapped her arms tightly around her and held her close. She placed a soft kiss on her head before saying, 'Why don't you take Timothy out into the garden for a little while? He's still rather tired so you could snuggle up on the lounger and tell him a story. I've already put the umbrella up so just make sure you stay in the shade.'

With a big smile, Daisy slipped off her lap, went over to the cats and whispered in Timothy's ear. Just as she was about to walk out the back door, Daisy stopped and looked back at Perrie.

'Timothy saved me from the sea. He's a good cat.'

'What do you mean, darling, that Timothy saved you?'

The child turned to her father.

'When the sea came back, we were on the sand. I couldn't get up the steps quickly and the water reached

302

me. It was pulling me away but then Timothy pushed me to the wooden rail and I was able to hold onto it until you came to save me. Timothy is very clever.'

Daisy gave them a smile before skipping out the back door. A moment later, her voice floated back in the window as she began telling the cat a story about three bears who liked porridge.

'Is Daisy telling me that your cat can swim?'

'Both of my cats can swim although Timmy likes it more than George. My house in London had a pool and the three of us would swim together almost every day. Timothy was always the last to get out. He's really rather good in the water.'

'But... I thought cats didn't like water...'

'These guys are Norwegian Forest Cats – they love water and have no fear of it. That's why I chose them. I was worried about the swimming pool and the potential for something untoward occurring but when I was researching the different breeds and saw how strong the NFCs are, it made perfect sense to go for them.'

'So, is it possible that Timothy could also have saved me?'

'What do you mean?'

Morgan relayed his adventure to her and how he woke up in the cave. He showed her the bruising on his wrist as he explained his theory that Timothy had somehow pulled him into the cave.

'Do you think he could have done that?'

'They are quite strong and very good climbers. If he had some buoyancy behind him from the waves, I think it's safe to assume that he did. I can't see any other reasonable explanation.'

They sat in silence after that until Morgan said, 'What did Daisy mean about you going away?'

'My lease is up at the end of September. I was telling

Hettie and Daisy must have overheard. I did see her close by but she gave no indication that she'd heard me.'

'And… are you leaving?'

Perrie paused before replying, trying to think of how to answer him.

'I don't know,' she said with a sigh. 'I really don't know.'

'Why would you leave, I thought you liked it here?'

'I do like it, I love it. But… well… if you and I are no longer able to be the friends we once were, then it will be too painful to stay.'

'Perrie,' he placed his hand over hers and gave it a tender squeeze, 'Daisy is not the only one who owes you an apology, I do too. I behaved like a total asshole. I went from knowing very little about you to knowing everything about you but none of it came from you. I found out through watching the late-night news. The night you left was the night I realised I was falling in love with you. Forty-eight hours later, everything shattered into smithereens when I found out you were married. It cut me right through and I lost all sense of reason. I confess that I trawled the internet like a madman, trying to dredge up any little bit of information on you that I could. I know I should have waited until you returned but…' He gave a small shrug. 'May I plead temporary insanity?'

'I came home, ready to tell you all my secrets and explain why I'd had to keep you in the dark. It wasn't my choice. The police suspected I might be in danger. I came here to "disappear"!'

The colour drained from his face.

'You were a fugitive?'

'In a sense. I had to keep quiet for your safety as well as my own.'

'Oh no, now I feel even worse for being such a twat!

You were in fear of your life and then I go and behave like some over-possessive, ego-filled wanker! No wonder you want to leave. I'm not exactly someone worth sticking around for.'

Morgan took his hand away and sat back in his chair, a look of intense dismay on his face.

Perrie watched him struggle as he acknowledged what he'd done and the hard shell she'd put up around her heart, the shell that had already begun to crack earlier that morning, now dissolved and slipped away.

She leant across the table and took a hold of his hand, returning the gentle squeeze he'd given hers.

'Do you still love me?'

He looked at her. 'I'm sorry?'

'Do you still love me?'

She looked into his eyes as she waited for him to answer. Her chest was tight and she tried not to think of how she'd react if he said no.

'Yes, Perrie, I do still love you. More and more each day. The less I saw of you, the deeper my love became. It's true what they say, absence really does make the heart grow fonder.'

For the second time in a few hours, she felt relief course through her. He loved her! That was all she needed to hear.

'Okay, then let me tell you a story...'

For the next hour she talked while he listened. She told him about how she'd met Nate when she'd been at uni – he was the brother of a friend – but nothing had occurred between them until two years later when they'd bumped into each other in London. She explained that they'd been happy until he decided his career was in politics and that's when things began to change, growing worse when they found out why they couldn't have children.

'It would appear my body was more in tune with Nate's real nature than I was. The reason I couldn't conceive was because my body kept killing his sperm.'

'I'm sorry, you what?'

She chuckled at the look of disbelief on his face.

'Honestly, it's a thing. It's rare but it's a thing. Women can develop antisperm antibodies which means we kill off the sperm resulting in no pregnancy.'

'Could IVF bypass that?'

'Probably but Nate wouldn't give it headspace. It was the natural way or not at all for him. He wasn't interested in scientific options.'

'What an arse!'

'Yup, I know!'

'Well, I'm happy to try anything. I know you want a child so you just tell me what I need to do.'

'Jumping the gun a bit there, aren't you?'

'Nope!' He took her hand and pulled her towards him across the table until her face was level with his.

'If you think for a single second that I am ever going to let you go, you had better think again, Perrie Lacey. I love you. I love watching you with my daughter. I TRUST you with my daughter. I'm sorry I ever said otherwise, it was so wrong of me to do that. If you can forgive me for that, I promise I will love you till the end of time. And maybe a couple of days after that to be on the safe side.'

'I forgive you, Morgan Daniels. I love you too much to hold anything against you.'

He took her face in his hands and just as he was about to kiss her, there was a knock on the door.

'Seriously? Who is that?'

Morgan released her and pulled back in disgust.

'It's the doctor,' Perrie said, with a smile when she returned. 'I want that bump on your head checked out before you say anything more!'

She left the kitchen to allow some privacy while the doctor looked both Morgan and Daisy over. She was actually glad of the interruption for it had been getting intense there and she needed a moment to get her breath back. Morgan saying he'd do anything she needed so she could try for her own child had been more than a little unexpected. Something which had been off the table for so long had suddenly come back to it and it was making her feel excited, scared and confused all at the same time. The fact that he'd made such an offer, however, had removed her last line of defence. If he wanted a relationship with her, then she was all in.

When the doctor came out, he stopped for a moment to pass on some instructions.

'His ankle is sprained. Not too badly, so I've put an inflatable boot on it. He needs to keep the boot on for ten days and stay off his feet for the same amount of time. His head injury is quite nasty but he's not displaying any signs of concussion. I would just ask that you, or someone, keeps an eye on him for the next couple of days, just in case.'

'Thank you, Doctor, for coming out. I'll watch over him.'

She let him out and then stepped back into the kitchen.

'I hear you're not allowed to be alone for the next few days.'

'Yeah, so the man says.'

'I guess you'd better stay here then.'

'Are you sure? It won't be a problem?'

'It's not a problem. Now, where were we before we were rudely interrupted…'

'I think I was just about to kiss you.'

'Oh, yes, so you were…'

307

Pulling over a chair, she sat down in front of him and looked into his beautiful blue eyes. Blue eyes that were gazing at her full of love.

She leant forward and Morgan placed his hands on her face once again and this time, his lips met hers. She felt herself sink forward into his arms as fireworks exploded in her head and her heart swelled in her chest. She wanted to lose herself forever within his embrace.

When they finally pulled apart, both more than a little breathless, she looked at him and whispered, 'Did you mean it? What you said? About us being together, loving me till the end of time and being prepared to do whatever it takes to give me the chance of having a child?'

'I did. I do. Every single word.'

'Well, before you sign on the dotted line, I have one last thing to tell you. I promised you no secrets.'

'You mean there's more? What else can you possibly have left to tell me, woman?'

'Well, there's the small matter of a millionaire father who lives in a massive villa in Spain...'

FIFTY-FOUR

December

'Daisy, are you ready? Do you need a hand putting your shoes on?'

Perrie walked into the lounge and looked around the empty room. She was sure she'd heard Daisy in here, talking to the cats.

'Daisy, where are you?' she called.

A smothered giggle had her looking over towards the panoramic window and the full-length curtains which draped into pools on the floor. Peeking out from underneath were two thick, bushy tails, swishing in unison over the highly-polished wooden floor.

Perrie walked over quietly and pulled the curtain back to find Daisy sitting cross-legged on the floor, a cat on either side of her and all three of them taking in the magnificent view of the London skyline.

'Hey, monkey-chops, having fun?'

'I was just showing George and Timothy where the

Houses of Parriment are.'

'And were they impressed with your knowledge?'

'George wasn't but Timothy was. He said I was very clever.'

'And he would be right. Now, shall we get your shoes and coat on? We need to go out soon.'

'Are we going on the choo-choob again?'

Perrie had to turn away to prevent Daisy catching her smiling at her words. Seeing London through the eyes of a five-year-old brought whole new meanings to even the most mundane everyday occurrences. She'd given up trying to explain that the underground system was just called the Tube. Daisy thought choo-choob was better and wouldn't be swayed to call it anything else.

'Hey, ladies, are we good to go?'

Morgan walked in and Perrie's heart began its usual Grand National-style racing. She couldn't help it. Every day they were together brought them closer and she loved him more than she'd ever thought it possible to love. The smile he bestowed upon her and Daisy made his face light up and his eyes twinkled under the fringe which now draped itself across his forehead. He'd let his hair grow out a bit and with the slight wave now allowed to be present, the tousled look he was sporting had only served to make his cheek-bones sharper, his chin more chiselled and his blue eyes brighter. He was sex on legs and all hers!

'Daisy was just educating the cats on the view. She's getting her stuff together now, aren't you, sweetie?'

'Yes, Merida.'

They shared a little secret smile before she ran off to her bedroom.

Morgan walked over to look out of the window.

'I just can't get over your father buying you a penthouse apartment in London! Seriously, it's just…'

He looked at her, still speechless even though they'd been living there for three days.

'He didn't really "buy it" though – it was a part exchange in the sale of the Hampstead house which I was never going to live in again. I only accepted this from him because it was more practical for us to use when we come to visit the city. It's closer to the centre and only a few choo-choob stops the other way to get to Aggie's.'

'Choo-choob?'

'Don't! Daisy has me saying it now!' She rolled her eyes as she laughed.

'I'm ready now. Time to go!'

Perrie found herself laughing again at Daisy's comment and carried on doing so as the banter continued in the flurry of getting their coats on and gathering up what they needed for their day out.

As Daisy asked Morgan to explain how the train they were on could be driven without a driver, Perrie thought back over the last four months and how much of it she'd spent laughing. Every day began and ended with a smile and she wanted it to always be that way.

Morgan and Daisy's visit, while Morgan's ankle healed, had turned into an almost permanent situation. "Almost" because they hadn't officially declared they were living together but the town had accepted that they were to the point where the postie now delivered Morgan's mail along with her own to the cottage.

They'd all settled in perfectly together with almost no teething problems. George still tended to sleep in the bottom corner of her bed but Timothy was always to be found curled up with Daisy. Their little escapade had only served to strengthen the bond between them and the cat must have learnt to tell the time for he was always waiting on the bottom step of the stairs when Daisy returned from school.

'You alright, love? You're a bit quiet.'

She turned and smiled at Morgan. Again! So much smiling!

'Yes, I am. Thank you. I'm just thinking of how much you both make me smile.'

'My mission is to never see you cry, my darling, unless it's tears of joy.'

The lump in her throat prevented her from answering and she turned away to look out of the window, not wanting him to see the tears which had filled her eyes. They were tears of happiness – knowing that someone cared so much about how she felt was still taking some getting used to.

'Merida, where are we going today? Daddy won't tell me.'

'Ah, this is a special surprise for you so I'm not telling you either.'

'Hmph! That's not fair!'

Daisy folded her arms and stuck out her bottom lip.

'Tell me, young lady, have we done anything yet that you haven't enjoyed?'

'No, not yet but it was nearly close with those boys last night.'

They'd visited Aggie the previous evening and things had been a bit tense between her nephews and Daisy for a short time until they found out how much space stuff she knew and then suddenly she became "kinda cool" for a girl. Well, she liked to think it was the space stuff and not Aggie threatening them with no sweets for a week for being sexist!

'But they were okay in the end, weren't they?'

'Yeah. I loved Bertie's star lamp thing... can I have one of those?'

'We can look into it. After all, you got some money for Christmas, you could use that.'

'Okay.'

'This is our stop, make sure you have everything, Daisy.'

They alighted and were soon walking up through Greenwich Park – Daisy running ahead and letting off some steam.

'You do know what tomorrow night is, don't you?'

Perrie looked at Morgan.

'Er, yes! New Year's Eve.'

'Good! Well, because I know you're not really big on surprises, I'm just giving you the heads up that I'll be asking a certain question.'

'I see. Thank you for the advance warning.'

'You're welcome. Daisy, don't you dare climb that tree...'

Morgan rushed off to stop his daughter breaking her neck as Perrie stood still, stunned into silence from the bombshell he'd dropped. Okay, sure, he'd been saying for the last couple of months that he planned to ask her to marry him one day but she hadn't thought it would be so soon. It was certainly a surprise she hadn't been expecting and she was trying to fathom out how she felt while her head was spinning and her heart was racing. Was she ready for this?

She pondered over it as she caught up with Morgan and Daisy and they made their way through the door of the building ahead. Perrie looked about her and wondered what was going through Daisy's head at the sight of all the space paraphernalia surrounding her. She waited for the plethora of questions to begin but strangely, the little

313

girl was the quietest she'd been all day.

Morgan went over to swap their tickets for seats and then they walked into the vast auditorium and found where they were sitting.

Daisy sat between them and Morgan looked at Perrie over her head.

'Thank you,' he mouthed. They both knew that what was coming next was going to blow Daisy's mind.

'I love you,' she mouthed back.

'I love you too.'

'I can *see* you two talking above me!'

Daisy's comment was delivered in such a droll manner that Perrie snorted through her nose and she had to dive into her handbag for a tissue. When she looked back up, wiping her face, Daisy was kneeling on her seat and looking at her with a very serious face.

'Are you okay, Daisy?'

'Yes. I just want you to know I have a new name for you.'

'I see. Can I ask what it is?'

'Yes, it's Mummy Merida because you help Daddy to look after me and that's what mummys do.'

Before she could reply, the auditorium went dark and Daisy turned to sit down in her seat.

A few seconds later, the Planetarium show was underway and the roof above them lit up with stars.

'WOW!'

She could see the awe on Daisy's face so leant down to whisper, 'Well, was this a good surprise?'

Without taking her eyes off the celestial vision overhead, Daisy replied, 'Mummy Merida, it's the best. Thank you. I love you.'

And in that moment, Perrie knew what her answer was going to be tomorrow night. With her decision made, she felt a soothing sense of peace and serenity glide through her body.

Babs liked to call Broatiescombe Bay "The Bay of Lost Souls".

Well, her soul was no longer lost.
Her soul had found its way home.

ABOUT THE AUTHOR

Kiltie Jackson spent her childhood years growing up in Scotland. Most of these early years were spent in and around Glasgow although for a short period of time, she wreaked havoc at a boarding school in the Highlands.

By the age of seventeen, she had her own flat which she shared with a couple of cats for a few years while working as a waitress in a cocktail bar (she's sure there's a song in there somewhere!) and serving customers in a fashionable clothing outlet before moving down to London to chalk up a plethora of experience which is now finding its way into her writing.

Once she'd wrung the last bit of fun out of the smoky capital, she moved up to the Midlands and now lives in Staffordshire with one grumpy husband and another six feisty felines.

Her little home is known as Moggy Towers even though, despite having plenty of moggies, there are no towers! The cats kindly allow her and Mr Mogs to share their home as long as the mortgage continues to be paid.

Since the age of three, Kiltie has been an avid reader although it was many years later before she decided to put pen to paper – or fingers to keyboard – to begin giving life to the stories in her head. Her debut novel was released in September 2017 and her fourth book was a US Amazon bestseller in Time Travel Romance.

Kiltie loves to write fiery and feisty female characters and puts the blame for this firmly on the doorsteps of Anne

Shirley from Anne of Green Gables and George Kirrin from The Famous Five.

When asked what her best memories are, Kiltie will tell you:

1. Queuing up overnight outside the Glasgow Apollo to buy her Live-Aid ticket.
2. Being at Live-Aid.
3. Winning an MTV competition to meet Bon Jovi in Sweden.

(Although, if Mr Mogs is in earshot, the latter is changed to her wedding day.)

Her main motto in life used to be "Old enough to know better, young enough not to care!" but that has since been replaced with "Too many stories, not a fast enough typist!"

You can follow Kiltie on the following platforms:

www.kiltiejackson.com

www.facebook.com/kiltiejackson

www.instagram.com/kiltiejackson

www.twitter.com/kiltiejackson

Printed in Great Britain
by Amazon

21003531R00188